The Reverend Lucas Holt—the vicar of St. Margaret's Episcopal Church in downtown Austin. After serving as a prison chaplain for twenty years, he remains friends with several former inmates, much to the aggravation of local church authorities.

Nikky Dorati—The Rev's right-hand man. They met in prison when Dorati was doing hard time for some hard crime. Although he's changed his ways, he's not above using his street smarts and old connections—especially if it helps the Rev catch killers.

Maxine Blackwell—The church secretary. While in prison, the former madame served as the Rev's inmate secretary. When he took over at St. Margaret's, he insisted that she come along as part of her parole.

Lieutenant Susan Granger—An old friend—and sometimes romantic interest—of Reverend Holt. As a member of the Austin Police Department, Susan doesn't like the God Squad getting involved in her business, even when they help her solve the crime.

Don't miss the first two Reverend Lucas Holt Mysteries

The Saints of God Murders

Lucas Holt's parish is plagued by a serial killer who chooses victims to coincide with lyrics of an old church hymn, "The Saints of God." According to the song, the next victim is a priest.

Blessed Are the Merciless

Funeral services are part of the job description for a church pastor, but suddenly Holt's parishioners are dying at any alarming rate. All of the victims are in their thirties and forties, and all have placed their parents in nursing homes.

BESIDE THE STILL WATERS

CHARLES MEYER

BESIDE THE STILL WATERS

PRINTING HISTORY
Stone Angel Books / September 1997

STONE ANGEL BOOKS
P.O. Box 27392
Austin, Texas 78755-2392

ISBN 0-9631149-4-8

Printed in the United States of America
at Morgan Printing in Austin, Texas

For the city I love:
Austin, Texas.

Special thanks to Kim Osmer for telling me about the tunnels; to Rhonda Cloos for reading and suggestions; to Kathy Saideman and my wife Debi for their brutally honest editing; and to Christopher Chenault, M.D., for medical accuracy.

• Prologue •

Susan Granger hated election years.

She pulled her forest green Blazer out of the Good Foods Grocery lot and made a mental note to call the Pace campaign from police headquarters. One more instance of APD playing babysitter. They knew damned well they couldn't stake signs on business property without the consent of the owners. As if Ryan Pace didn't already have his grinning mug plastered on every surface in Austin. You'd think he was running for President instead of Senator. She glanced at a poster on a phone pole. Maybe he was.

She took a swig from the small bottle of bubbly Driskill Springs water she had just bought. Recently discovered under the antebellum Driskill Hotel, the spring from the Edwards Aquifer provided naturally effervescent water and a profitable subsidy to refurbish the place. The label touted the motto: "Have a drink of history." Buying it was a political act, supporting the preservation of the hotel and calling attention to the environmentally sensitive aquifer which was threatened by overbuilding and overpumping. Right now it was as political as the dark haired police lieutenant wanted to get.

The campaigns never knew when to stop. There were always nuisance complaints from ordinary citizens whose rights were infringed upon by overeager supporters; but the ones she really despised were the whining sycophants who called to piss and moan like four-year-olds about what the other camp was doing to them. Like APD didn't have crooks to catch. Other crooks.

She crossed Highway 183 and saw yet another Pace billboard, within spitting distance of the one for his gorgeous opponent, Kristen Wade. At least it was an interesting contest. The ultra-conservative Pace against the liberal Texas House of Representatives Female Legislator of the Session. Leave it to the lege to call it "Female" instead of "Woman." Granger took another drink of history and wondered why they didn't call it the "Darlin'" or "Honey" of the Session, which was what they meant.

The special election for the US Senate seat was made necessary by the sudden unexplained resignation of Bailley Graham. Cop scoop included everything from the absolute fact that she had cancer to the absolute fact that she embezzled funds from her Baptist church. Who knew or cared? She only got elected because Texans love to vote for famous names. Jesse James was state treasurer for years and Buster Brown never lost an election to the House. Most of the people who checked the box by "Bailley Graham" thought it was a famous evangelist.

Granger looked at her watch as she turned onto MOPAC and headed south. A Missouri-Pacific train, for which the divided highway was named, chugged steadily up the median. It's whistle always reminded her of her childhood in Dallas, snug in her bed while her cop pop typed his reports in the kitchen. She took a deep breath and relaxed; she'd handle the Good Foods complaint about the Pace signs tomorrow. Right now she just wanted to be home, groceries put away, ready to eat dinner and criticize the hell out of NYPD Blue.

At the Spicewood Springs exit she clicked on the police radio. Even though she was off duty she monitored calls in her car. You never knew. The election campaign added to the possibility somebody might need her. And the shift was always short handed so it was good to stay in touch. And she was a Lieutenant so she should be monitoring her troops. And then there was the fact that her job was her life.

She took another swig of the cold bubbles. "Well so what?" she argued to the disapproving voices in her head, the ones that told her she should be married with babies by now. She liked her job and there wasn't anyone whose genes she wanted to replicate anyway, or anyone interested in replicating hers. And Lucas Holt didn't count. Not exactly. Though the last year had been interesting. With Kristen Wade mostly out of his life, spending all her time focused on this election, Susan and he had developed something dangerously close to a relationship.

Granger's internal dialogue was interrupted by staccato sounds from the radio. So far the dispatches were all routine, strung together with two second pauses like a stream of consciousness novel.

"EMS on route to pedestrian/car accident at Braker and Lamar. Report of DWI southbound IH 35. Domestic disturbance 2500 block of Exposition Boulevard. B&E Third and Comal."

Thank God for crime, she snickered. Like Quixote's barber, she'd always be employed.

The radio blared: "9-1-1 to Las Ventanas. Report of gunshots."

Susan Granger floored the Blazer and cut across two lanes of traffic, barely making the Far West exit. She clicked on her flashing lights and punched the radio.

"Granger to base."

No response.

Louder. "Granger to base, dammit."

An embarrassed reply. "Base, Lieutenant. Sorry. Thought you were off duty."

"I am, but I'm right near Las Ventanas. What's the call?"

"Gunshots heard by neighbors of 1510 Muheres."

"On the way."

"Computer says it's the home of - "

"I *know* who lives there, Sergeant," she said, blaring her siren through a stop light. She turned it off to silence her approach.

No sense scaring people into the street where they could get killed by stray bullets or drivers like her. The Blazer skidded around the corner of Greystone to Valburn and raced to the gated entrance of Las Ventanas. She swiped a police key card through the security box.

"Hurry the hell up," she yelled at the slow moving gate, then gunned the vehicle through the opening.

Granger slowed past 1510, noting no signs of disturbance. She parked in front of 1514 and slipped out of the car without latching the door. Sticking close to the houses and out of sight of 1510's front window, the Lieutenant unholstered her .44. As neighbors watched her cautiously approached the house, she saw the elaborately carved front door was slightly ajar.

Silently, she climbed the steps and stopped to listen for voices. Hearing none, she kicked the door open and rushed inside.

"Freeze!" she yelled at the man kneeling over the bloody body of Kristen Wade with a gun in his hand.

Lucas Holt looked up and aimed the gun at *her*.

• One •

Nikky Dorati stood at the back of the Four Seasons Grand Ballroom, finishing his second rye. He wasn't fond of political rallies and he wouldn't have come to this one if the Rev hadn't told him to. At least the booze was free.

He listened to the diatribe from the too-handsome-for-his-own-damned-good Ryan Pace. The sucker must have been a Gerber baby. Dorati wished the face was on a milk carton. If there were genes for politicians, Pace had gotten all of them: dark wavy hair with just a few perfectly placed strands of grey, smooth skin with a meaningful wrinkle accentuating his honest deep blue eyes, a resonant radio voice that gripped the entire audience with sincerity. The entire audience except for Nikky, who wanted to puke but ordered another rye instead to inoculate himself from the stench of the garbage strewn from the podium.

"The people of this great nation have become too complacent." The perfectly straight teeth telegraphed a punch line and Dorati heard it coming. "For the Democrats in the crowd that means lazy."

Supportive laughter from the adoring masses, Dorati thought. Go ahead and laugh. That's what he wants you to do. How could someone humorous be dangerous? How could someone funny and good looking be anything but worthy of all their trust?

Nikky winked at the barmaid who handed him his drink. He wondered if she listened to this crap or if she just concentrated on getting the orders straight. Would the handsome Pace-face get her vote, or would she realize he wanted people like her to earn even less than she did now and be happy with no healthcare, no childcare, no minimum wage? Dorati tipped her a sawbuck. She winked back and nodded.

Looking at the podium, Nikky remembered an inmate known as "The Senator," a man so handsome the female guards fought over who got to take him meals in solitary or the infirmary, or who got to escort him to his trial. The man stood six foot two, had romance novel eyes, a face that convinced you his parents were Cindy Crawford and Antonio Banderas, and black grey hair that shouted airline pilot brain surgeon.

Why was it that gorgeous people got away with murder—literally? The Senator had used his handsome face and silver tongue to get inside the hearts and bank accounts of widows across the country, twenty five of whom, after a small change of beneficiary, woke up serially dead. And age was not a problem. The guy pulled thirty year olds as easily as women in their fifties. In the case of the former, he sometimes provided the opportunity for their grief by offing the existing husband.

Dorati squinted and put the inmate's face on the man at the dais. Same deal. This guy made book on the assumption that good looks automatically meant trust and competence and it would take one hell of a lawyer—or a giant mistake—to convince the enthusiastic audience otherwise.

Of course The Senator finally got caught. Hard to argue with a preacher who came back from the dead to point the finger at him in front of a jury. "Should have made the poison stronger," he told Nikky with a smile, knowing he'd do ten of his twenty-to-life and make parole on the backs of the women guards he'd been porking. They had plenty of influence with the parole board (some were on it) and they hoped to see that handsome face in their bedroom on the outside. Though they never would. The Senator was handsome but he wasn't stupid.

Dorati wondered who Ryan Pace porked—other than the crowds. He made a mental note to try to find out. Hopefully Pace would turn out to be handsome *and* stupid, though Nikky would settle for merely careless.

"We live in a world of welfare cheats ripping off the hard working, God fearing, family minded Americans that carry the freeloaders on their backs." Pregnant pause. "Well NO LONGER!"

Dorati sipped the rye as the room filled with applause. Pace knew how to stir them up, make them feel wronged, vengeful, energized to send him to the front to fight their battle and regain their rightful place in society. Nikky grinned and shook his head. He wished Lucas Holt was there to nudge. Hard to believe people were so gullible as to actually believe this shit. Unless you had done twenty years in the pen with little else to do than study human behavior like he and the Rev had. Then it wasn't hard to believe at all. Holt believed it wasn't gullibility, but neediness. Nikky thought it was fear and greed that convinced people to ignore their better instincts and follow people like Ryan Pace.

And Kristen Wade for that matter. She was clearly the better choice in this election but that was like saying herpes was better than AIDS. Or blind was better than deaf. They were both politicians, people who loved power and money and used anybody they could to get both. He sipped the rye to wash the taste of them out of his mouth.

"My opponent, Kristin Wade, would take even more of our gouged tax dollars and spend them on what she calls the 'underserved'—but if you take the "r" out of "underserved"— because they're wasting "r" tax money and panhandling "r" street corners, and sleeping in "r" doorways as we try to do business with "r" customers who are terrorized by them, the "underserved" become the 'undeserved.'"

Dorati grimaced at the louder applause.

"They are the multitudes flagrantly disregarding our borders, then demanding the same rights as those of us born here—more importantly who *work* here, pay taxes here—and who are not being treated fairly because of services leeched off by these undeserved people." Still louder applause. "These are the criminals pouring out of our overcrowded prisons, wasting our tax dollars on frivolous jailhouse lawsuits, then returning to the street unrepentant and unchanged, to mug and maim our families. They are not underserved. They are undeserved."

The crowd was on its feet now, and Dorati looked at his watch, which had stopped. He cursed and knew it was past time to go. He had shot men for lesser lies than Pace was telling. Good thing he left his gun in the glove box, knowing security would be tight, including the metal detector at the door. Even handsome Ryan Pace couldn't escape the inevitable enemies in the crowds of humanity he stirred up.

Dorati turned to leave when commotion up front stopped him. A Pace flunky impeccably dressed in the blue blazer and khaki slacks that defined the neatnik tone of the campaign staff ran up to Fearless Leader and placed a piece of paper in his hand.

Ryan Pace read it and frowned. "I'm afraid I've just been handed some very bad news." Nikky watched him solemnly place the note on the podium and, dripping with sincerity and concern, address the crowd. "As you know, my staff regularly monitor police radio calls to stay in touch with crime issues and the evil element in this city." Pace took a deep breath, obviously for histrionic effect. "I am shocked and saddened to announce to you that a series of such calls have just indicated that my worthy opponent, Kristen Wade, has been fatally shot at her home."

The crowd gasped and Dorati cursed as he elbowed his short frame through the stunned mass mesmerized by Pace's pious voice blaring over the speakers. One small suggestion from the leader and the mass would become a mob.

"But this is not a time for panic," Nikky thankfully heard him yell. "It is a time for prayer. So let us drop to our knees right now before our Lord God and pray that this initial report is not true—pray fervently that Kristin Wade be raised and healed even as we ask it right now, and that her assailant be captured quickly and brought to feel the swift sword of justice from our civil authorities who must act in God's stead."

Nikky Dorati was glad they had all dropped in prayer. It got them the hell out of the way so he could find the exit doors and race down the street to his car.

"Drop the gun, Lucas!" Susan shouted, her own weapon extended and finger on the trigger. She moved toward him.

"Drop yours first!" the Rev demanded. "And don't come any closer." He cocked the hammer.

"Dammit, Lucas! You know I won't shoot you."

"Then drop your gun, Susan, or this Mexican standoff will up the body count here by two."

"Shit!" She knew it was improper procedure, but her whole history with Holt was improper procedure. "Same time."

Holt nodded.

"Uncock."

They gently released the hammers.

"Safety on."

They flipped the safeties.

"To the floor." She watched as Lucas Holt lowered his weapon, and saw the mass of blood on his arm.

"Skid them toward the door."

Both guns clattered across the hardwood floor as Granger hurried to Kristen Wade.

"I didn't do this, Susan."

"Shut up." She pressed the carotid artery, cursed, and grabbed her radio. "Granger to base."

"Base, Lieutenant."

"I need LifeFlight out here STAT. Initial report confirmed. Gunshot victim. Pulse thready, chest wound. Do it NOW."

"On the way. Out."

The Rev took Kristen's hand. "I didn't *do* this, Susan."

"Yeah, I can see from the powder burns on your hand and the blood on your clothes you were an innocent bystander." She reached for her cuffs.

Holt pulled back and stood. "What the hell are you doing?"

"You have a right to remain silent and all that shit. Consider yourself Miranded."

"Just let me explain—"

"You can explain to that old drunk attorney of yours down at the jail. I don't want to hear shit from you." She frowned and stood to face him, her voice quaking with anger. "I don't know what happened here, Lucas, but it looks like you just bought a ticket back to Huntsville and this time it's not as a Chaplain."

"She was shot when I got here," Holt pleaded.

Granger could see the tears in his eyes, and she barely held back her own. She and Holt had become closer this year, even intimate, rekindling the flame from long ago. But his presence here meant he still had feelings for Kristen, though it appeared those feelings had turned homicidal.

"She's not dead yet, damn you," Susan said defensively. Granger had known Kristen Wade years before Lucas had and in fact had introduced the two, to her own regret, she often felt. "Is this what happens to people who care about you, Lucas? To be sprawled on the floor in a pool of blood?"

"Susan—"

"Just put your hands out and let me do this," she ordered.

"I need to bandage my arm." He held up his left hand. "I cut it on the glass in the side door, getting in. Her dog Aspen ran out terrified when I opened the door."

"I ought to let you bleed to death." She nodded in the direction of Kristen. "Like her." She retrieved her weapon. "We'll find the dog."

"Susan," he said, as she slapped a cuff around his right wrist, "let me tell you the truth."

"Save the truth for the toilet." She dragged him to the bathroom and clamped the other cuff to the cold water handle of the wash stand.

"What're you doing?"

"I'm making sure you don't wash those nice incriminating pieces of gunpowder from your hands when you're through, accidentally of course."

A sputtering cough sounded in the living room, followed by a moan.

"Kristen's rousing!" Granger said, looking back over her shoulder, not certain whether to leave her captured prey. "You stay here and stick your arm under the faucet. And if you wash your hands, I'll shoot you for escaping."

"Two stories up?" she heard him say as she ran to the living room.

Granger assured Kristen, in whatever state of coma or unconsciousness was holding her vital signs stable, that EMS was on the way and she'd be in San Jacinto hospital in a matter of minutes. She ran back to the bathroom as the thudding beat of copter blades shook the house. The door was closed and she could hear the sound of running water.

"Hurry it up, Lucas," she yelled at the door. The screech of tires also told her other cops had arrived. "LifeFlight's landing. Cavalry's here. They'll bandage your arm."

The water sound continued and she started to go check again on Kristen, then quickly turned the doorknob. It was locked.

"Damn you, Lucas!" she yelled and crashed open the door.

Handcuffs dangled from the spigot handle.

The window was open.

Holt was gone.

* * *

It was the most popular service of the week. Held at nine o'clock at night in the main sanctuary, which was illumined only by flickering candles, the Order of Compline attracted members of St. Margaret's Episcopal church from across the theological spectrum. That's what Cora Mae Hartwig liked about it as she sat in the reader's chair by the choir, glancing out over the shadowed congregation. As a lay reader, it was her turn in the rotation to open and close the service. The rest of it was chanted by the choir and whoever else in the church knew the music, or thought they did.

Cora Mae had led the opening prayer from the service in the Book of Common Prayer, then nodded to the organist and sat down to wait for the scripture reading. She liked the musty smell of incense and beeswax that was St. Margaret's. With the sanctuary darkened, the chanting of the choir and the scents of wood, wax and perfume transported her to her childhood in the old church.

She had been baptized in the huge hand carved wooden font right by the front door; she had knelt at the polished brass rail to receive the Body and Blood of Christ since before she could speak, and she expected to lie in the transept with a pall upon her casket at the end. St Margaret's was a comforting place traversing her life and the lives of so many others, and it had become more so with the arrival four years ago of former prison chaplain Lucas Holt and his ex-con followers everyone called The God Squad.

They had helped a very reluctant Susan Granger solve a couple of the most baffling cases the Austin Police Department had known, and had been accused of everything from grand theft to murder; but this latest business was different. This time instead of being on the outside looking in, providing help to the ex-cons, Lucas was the one being blamed, needing help. She had heard on the news driving over tonight that Lucas was sought in the shooting—they actually had called it "attempted murder"— of Texas House Member Kristen Wade. Cora Mae shook her head and sighed. He couldn't have done it, she thought. But then he had told her prison was a two way street. Maybe he picked up as much from the inmates as they did from him. Could he?

But why? the old woman wondered as the chanting stopped and she stood to read the psalm appointed for the night.

Before she could begin, she heard a familiar deep voice pass behind her and watched the man she had been thinking about step up into the pulpit.

"The Lord is my Shepherd, I shall not want.

He maketh me to lie down in green pastures,

He leadeth me beside the still waters—"

"Lucas!" Cora Mae said, her eyes open wide. "What are you doing?"

"He restoreth my soul; he leadeth me in the paths of righteousness for his Name's sake."

Cora Mae walked to the pulpit next to him. She put her arm on his. His face was flushed and his hands were bright red, his black shirt and blue pants stained with the same bright color of blood. Kristin Wade's blood.

"Lucas, dear." Cora Mae tried again, softly. "There are people standing up in the congregation now, staring at you." The initial gasps had turned to murmurs that nearly drowned out his words. Sooner or later someone would come to their senses and try to subdue him.

"Yea, though I walk through the valley of the shadow of death, I will fear no evil; for thou art with me; thy rod and thy staff they comfort me."

"Lucas?" She stepped back as he suddenly yelled out.

"The Religious Right is *neither*! They are not *religious*. They do not bind people together, they pull us apart. They do not heal, they destroy. They do not praise, they defame. They do not honor. They defend. They do not help. They blame."

As if in a trance, the priest whose progressive theology Cora Mae had defended, at least up until this moment, sounded like he had suddenly changed denominations and taken up a t.v. pulpit. His eyes were glazed and his voice strident. She wondered if he would collapse, or if this seeming stupor would last long enough for him to escape the inevitable questions looming in those pews, as well as in her own heart.

"And they are not *right*," he continued, almost without breathing. "They are self-righteous. Their unctuous piety cloaks a mean spiritedness that condemns, demeans, casts the first judgmental stone and ignores Jesus' admonition to take the log out of their own eyes before pointing out the speck in the eyes of others. But they must be allowed this license no longer. They must be stopped, met by those voices who have been silent too long. We must show their insidious agenda for what it is, a forceful imposition of their neofacist values upon a society too distracted with material consumption to notice, or possibly to care. Until it is too late."

Cora Mae glimpsed someone talking on a cell phone. In a few seconds, sirens would announce the arrival of APD from down the street. "Lucas," she whispered, "someone called the police." She touched his bloody hand. "Please, dear."

"Thou preparest a table before me in the presence of mine enemies; thou annointest my head with oil; my cup runneth over."

Tires screeched at the front of the church. Whatever had happened, she couldn't let him be taken here. Not now. Not yet. Not until she and the others figured out what he'd really done—and *why*. Cora Mae Hartwig closed the Prayer Book on the pulpit and took the Rev's face in her hands.

"Go, Lucas. Go now."

Holt blinked, as if seeing her for the first time; he kissed her cheek and rushed into the blackness of the unlit sacristy. As the police dashed up the front stairs from the street to the main aisle in the sanctuary, Cora Mae stepped into the pulpit and finished the psalm.

"Surely goodness and mercy shall follow me all the days of my life, and I will dwell in the house of the Lord for ever."

• Two •

Omar Kandu looked like Mr. Clean with a clergy collar and an attitude. He stood, arms folded, outside Kristen Wade's room in the Intensive Care Unit of San Jacinto Hospital. Doctors and nurses slunk by him, ignoring him like a dormant pit bull. If he coughed, they jumped; which was exactly the way he wanted it.

When Maxine Blackwell, the Rev's ex-madame secretary, called and told Omar to get his ass down to Maggie Mae's because the Rev was in trouble, he had been ready to threaten, fight, cajole, or con for Lucas Holt. He owed him that much for things the Rev had done for him at the pen. What he had not been ready to do was strap on a white collar and a black clergy shirt.

"I don't know nothin' 'bout this reverend-stuff," he had told Maxine. He hoped his African, six three, muscled countenance would intimidate her, but knew from experience she had handled much worse than him in her career, and won.

"Wasn't your daddy a storefront preacher in Houston?" Maxine said, up in his face.

"Hell, no! He was a con-man, pickpocket, flim-flam artist, alley cat with the ladies Bible study, and, yeah, he held a Bible in one hand and a rag in the other every Sunday and Wednesday night."

"Like I said, he was a preacher. You believe in God, don't you?"

Omar Kandu smiled. "I've met her more than once."

"And you pray don't you?"

"Prayin's the onliest thing got me out of tight spots."

"Then you're better than most preachers in town." She had handed him the collar. "Put this on and get moving."

So here he was in a baggy black shirt left over from the overweight previous rector of St. Margaret's who had died of a heart attack after bankrupting the parish. Omar guessed the shirt was appropriate since that incident—and the murders that followed—had brought Lucas Holt and The God Squad together in Austin from the Texas Department of Corrections in Huntsville.

That "Saints of God" case and the one that followed it furthered their reputation and deepened the animosity of the cops who resented their successful meddling. The Rev and the Squad got more information with their underworld contacts than the Austin Police Department did from their snitches and fancy computers. So Omar knew APD detectives and Lieutenant Granger would eventually show up at Kristen's bedside and be pissed to see him standing guard outside her room. They would know the God Squad was on the case.

"Can I get you anything, Chaplain?" the busty unit clerk with the glistening corn row braids asked sweetly. Apparently she wasn't afraid of pit bulls, Omar thought. He wondered if she had one at home. On second look he wondered if she *was* one at home.

"No, thank you," he said cordially. No sense pissing off the staff. Better to be nice to them because you might need them for something—like saving Kristen's life. "But if you have an extra chair, I'd appreciate it." Give them something to do for you and they feel connected. In his former life it was the first step of the con.

"I'll see what I can find," she said with a determined smile. Omar knew she'd return with a chair if it meant pulling one out from under a doctor.

Behind him, the door to the room opened and a nurse dressed in blue ICU scrubs came out. She stripped off the latex gloves and shook his hand. "Marion Josey. Sorry about the glove powder."

"Omar Kandu." He slapped the white flakes from his black hands. "How's she doin'?" Omar asked, taking in the appearance of the nurse. Her makeup was perfect, from eye shadow to the matching colors of her lips and nails, but her jet black hair was pulled back in an uneven pony tail and her white Keds were dirty.

"Same." She noted something on the cardex and checked the chart. "Still holding her own."

The woman was a study in contradiction, he thought. Her scrubs were starched and clean, but her breath smelled like smoke. "Doc ain't been by since I been here," he said.

"Nothing for him to do. With all that machinery on her, you can hardly even see Kristen Wade. Though every press photographer in the lobby would love to get a picture. One even got hold of a pair of scrubs like these and tried to get in with a camera. Fortunately, Dominick, the security guard in the hall, nailed her before she got in the unit."

"Picture of her'd go for a lot of money, huh?" Omar said.

"Lot of money." The nurse looked up at him. "You're not thinking of taking one, are you?"

"Of course not," he lied, half wondering if she'd already done it. Omar thought of everything to supplement his income from the bus driving job the Rev helped him get. Even though he'd worked his way to supervisor, the thrill of the con would never leave him. He imagined handing over the negative of Kristen Wade on a ventilator with tubes and machinery running in and out of her bandaged body. The check from the tabloid was six figures. But on his way to the bank the Rev killed him.

Suddenly his attention snapped back to the present at the shrill voice of the unit clerk across the room.

"You can't just walk in here with that gaggle of press behind you! I don't care *who* you are!"

Omar moved in front of the door to Kristen's room as the handsome politician strode toward him. The nurse in scrubs intervened.

"What do you want, and why are all those people here outside visiting hours?"

"I think you know I'm Ryan Pace, young lady. Candidate for the U.S. Senate and running against the patient in that room."

"Well since she's not runnin' very far today you can take your jogging companions with the cameras and *get the hell out of my unit!*"

Omar watched the face he had seen on billboards smile for the cameras, the candidate condescending to the ire of a protective nurse. Drama in real life. 'Senate candidate crosses line to visit downed opponent.' Trying to discount the obvious sympathy vote on her behalf. Making political hay off a helpless Kristen Wade. Shit, he thought, knowing what the Rev would do. Two could play at that game.

"So how can you run for office and not be able to read?" Kandu's deep voice hushed the reporters.

"Who are *you*?" Pace asked, obviously taken aback.

"The new chaplain on the block." Omar struck his Mr. Clean pose and frowned. "You got a problem with that?"

"None at all." Pace took a small step back. "I just came to visit my erstwhile opponent and wish her a speedy recovery." He raised his voice. "Unless, of course, she's unable to re-enter the race."

Kandu knew what this guy was doing in front of the press; giving them ideas to pursue, headline leads to make it look like Kristen was either dying or out of the election. Anything to cast a doubt on her and boost himself. But Omar wasn't finished. It wasn't so much that he liked politicians, but this was the Rev's sometime squeeze, or had been.

"Does that sign on her door say 'Nobody except his asshole self Ryan Pace can visit?'"

Pace stared at him. The press took notes and pictures.

"No, it don't," Omar answered his own question and looked at the unruly crowd. "And does it say 'Nobody except the rude, nosey, inconsiderate, gutless, slimeball press can visit?'"

Pace clearly was not ready for this scene. "But I'm not just *any*body."

Chaplain Kandu ripped the "No Visitors" sign from the door and held it up in the candidate's face, as cameras flashed. "Okay Mr. *Some*body. What part of 'NO' don't you understand?"

Pace had racial epithets written all over his face, and Kandu knew it. They were the ones of a different color he was thinking about Pace, along with wishing the little shit would take just one swing so he could rearrange that pretty face to reflect the bigotry it hid. But Pace wasn't about to make a mistake in front of cameras. He backed down first, with a parting shot for a six o'clock sound bite.

"The part I don't understand is why no information is being released about her condition—and how she got in it. Are the police covering up the pursuit of her assailant because, as everyone in town knows, the Reverend Lucas Holt is an old friend—and more—of the investigating lieutenant?"

Omar moved to deck him but the nurse stepped in. "Patients have a right to privacy." She looked at Pace but spoke to the cameras. "For instance, you wouldn't want the public to know if you, say, had your vasectomy here last year, would you, Mr. Pace? So everybody in town would know you're shootin' blanks?" She didn't wait for an answer. "Or that your HIV test was processed in our lab? How did that come out? Or am I mistaken?"

Suddenly no one cared about Kristen Wade or Lucas Holt. They were clamoring for information about whether the leader of Revive Austin had his sperm tubes clipped and why he had been tested for HIV.

"All of these statements are untrue," he smiled and waved as he turned to leave the unit. "I'll be happy to answer any questions you have downstairs in the lobby." He glanced angrily at Kandu. "In accordance with the visiting rules of San Jacinto hospital."

Kandu looked at Marion Josey. Although he liked what she said, he was somewhat shocked that she said it. Even he knew about confidentiality in hospitals. "How long you been a nurse, lady?" he asked, with a grin of approval.

She gloved and picked up a syringe to go back in the room. "Longer than you been a chaplain, darlin'."

But when the crowd reached the ICU doors, Pace turned back abruptly. "I'll be right out," he motioned them forward, agreeing that they should all clear the unit. "I forgot to leave my card with the nurse."

"He'll try an end run," Josey said to Kandu.

"I don't think so. But just in case, can you jab him with that needle?"

"And waste the morphine?"

Ryan Pace approached them both and whispered so no one else could hear. "I want you to know you will both pay for this outrage."

"I'm peein' my pants," Kandu whispered back, ready to strike.

But Pace was not through. "I hope the bitch lives," he grinned. "It's harder than hell to beat a martyr." He turned and hurried from the ICU.

                              ❋ ❋ ❋

Susan Granger stared at the paperwork on her disheveled desk, and drank her fourth cup of coffee of the hour. She'd been meaning to cut down on caffeine since her last mammogram, where she'd learned about the correlation with breast lumps, but every morning that black liquid mysteriously found its way into the styrofoam cup in her office, just as it had now. Sometimes it interfered with sleep, but that was not what had kept her up last night.

She was up all night with Lucas Holt.

Was he alright? What would happen next? When would the inevitable call come from the new Police Commissioner, summoning her to his office for an explanation? Would he order an Internal Affairs investigation of her conduct at the crime scene? Should she take herself off the case?

She rubbed her eyes and reminded herself to wash her hands next time she got up. She still smelled like Kristen's golden retriever, Aspen. The terrified dog had gotten out of the house and roamed the neighborhood until a kind neighbor took her in and called the police. Susan had decided to kennel her until this was cleared up. Whenever the hell that was.

The phone jolted her from her thoughts and she jerked the coffee, spilling it on the papers.

"Shit," she answered.

"Good morning to you, too, Lieutenant." The strong male voice caused her to sigh and shake her head. Christopher Dillon was the new Police Commissioner and she didn't know him well enough to make a smart-ass comment.

"Sorry Commissioner," she said. "I spilled my coffee on the report."

"Nice timing. I want you to come to my office and make it in person, anyway. I need to know exactly what happened out there—and why."

"On my way." She hung up and tossed a few tissues on the spill, then nudged the soggy mass into the waste basket. Someday she'd have to learn to do that report crap on the computer so she could erase it instead of dumping food on it. Since she always ate at her desk, she had a reputation for sending reports down to central office with various stains. The last one was referred to by her staff as the Potato Salad Crime, the one before as Barbecue. Kristen's shooting would be filed under Coffee.

"Kristen's shooting," she thought as she headed for the elevator. The words echoed in her mind as unreal still. It was one thing to see people as "perps" and "johns" and "stiffs." It was another when those people had names you knew and cared about.

She exited the elevator on the top floor and stopped. She had not been here since the renovation, and was stunned by its opulence. Formerly the mundane, city-sterile cookie-cutter office of the Austin Chief of Police, the area was redone when city and county police activities were combined under one department after the last election. Now she stood before a glass wall housing the waiting area and receptionist, with light oak paneling sectioning off the Commissioner's office and conference room, both of which overlooked downtown Austin.

Before she could open the glass door she saw the Commissioner's door move and watched him plant a kiss on the lips of a bleach blonde only an inch or so shorter than his six foot frame. The way he patted her butt, Susan hoped it was his wife. Or maybe not, she thought as she pushed through the door.

"May I help—?" the receptionist started.

"I've got it, Annie," the man interrupted. "Thanks." He stuck his hand out to Susan. "Lieutenant Susan Granger, meet my wife, Donna."

"Glad to know you," the wife said sweetly.

"You, too, Mrs. Dillon."

"Oh, call me Donna, everyone does."

Susan Granger wondered why they didn't call her Barbie, who was her twin sister, separated at birth. "Certainly."

"See you tonight, honey," the Commissioner waved her off, winking.

"Goodbye, Lieutenant," Donna Dillon breathed more than spoke her words. Granger thought she was either practicing her Marilyn routine or had emphysema. She and the Commissioner both watched until Donna was on the elevator, he in admiration, Granger in shock.

"I call her my 'trophy wife,'" Commissioner Dillon said when he closed the door to his office.

Oh great, Granger thought, we got a cowboy for a police commissioner. "Really? What'd you get her for?" She knew she shouldn't have said that, but what the hell. She was here for a whippin' and might as well earn it.

"That probably sounds crude to you, but I don't mean it thataway." Dillon went behind the huge light oak desk and picked up his mug of coffee. "Java's over there if you want some. My wife makes it for me every morning. Gets it at Anderson's, best place in town she says. Help yourself."

She did and listened as she poured.

"I was on my last rodeo in Lubbock, gettin' too damned old to ride, you know, and there she was in the arena, restin' after winnin' her division in barrel racin' and I knew I had to have her and that was it. I kicked the shit out of the bull, stayed on eighteen seconds and damned near took him home tame. I got the trophy, the buckle, and Donna, all in one night. Drove to El Paso and got married in Mexico the next day."

Happiness is Lubbock in your rear view mirror, Granger thought as she sat down across from him.

"Been happy ever since." His friendly face seemed to have a constant Stan Laurel grin, but the lanky boyishness was a cover and she knew it. You didn't get to his position without knowing where the bodies were buried. And maybe having buried a few.

"I would imagine you're not too happy right now." Susan Granger took the offensive. Maybe it wouldn't sound as bad if *she* stated the case. The best defense was a good offense. Or was it the other way around? Who knew? She hated football. "You've got a candidate for the U.S. Senate in San Jacinto Hospital ICU in extremely critical condition from a gunshot wound inflicted by the most well known priest in Central Texas."

"Well known to associate with criminals and murderers."

"That too." She held her cup in both hands and kept her eyes on him as he leaned forward in his high back chair. "And you have the apprehended perp escaping because the arresting officer—myself—left him unguarded and unobserved for a few minutes in the bathroom. Said arresting officer is also well known to the perp, having known him twenty years ago at UT Austin when she was young and dumber, but not dumber than when she cuffed him to that wash basin and trusted him to stay put."

Christopher Dillon rocked back and looked at her. The way he sat and the way he held his head made it obvious why his officers often referred to him as "Marshall" Dillon, but not to his face. It was, for some reason, the one thing about which he had no sense of humor. Susan hoped he had a sense of humor about last night, but doubted it. She certainly wouldn't. If the shoe were on the other foot, she'd suspend the officer who made such a stupid mistake and ignored procedures because of friendship. As he was about to speak, the intercom buzzed. She hoped it was Chester telling him to hurry down to the Long Branch for a drink with Miss Kitty.

"Governor Doggett on line one."

Dillon picked it up, his eyes still on Granger.

"Morning, Lloyd." There was a long pause. "Yes, that's basically the right story." Another pause. "I know this is an election year and you were largely responsible for the mayor appointing me to this position." He was obviously repeating the conversation to educate her about the depth of the problem here, as if she didn't know. "But I'm looking right now at the person responsible for resolving this crime and I want you to know I have full confidence in Lieutenant Granger to do just that—and quickly." He sipped the coffee while the Governor answered. "Better than that, Lloyd," Dillon said, staring at Granger. "If she doesn't have it solved in a week—I'll resign."

Susan had to stifle a choke. Her heart beat fast and she flushed from head to toe.

"No, I'm not kidding. I mean it and I'm telling the press that today. Someone in public service has to put their butt on the line and take responsibility. If this were Japan, you know, I'd have already resigned in disgrace for losing the prisoner. The buck stops at the top, Lloyd. She'll find Holt, and this new department of city county law enforcement will be well on its way to showing what we can do as one outfit."

Granger wanted to puke, right on his desk, right before she tossed him her badge. Or maybe after.

"Right, Governor. See you later this week." He hung up the phone. "You could make Chief off of this case, Lieutenant."

"Unless of course, you're not around to do the promoting," Granger replied, standing to move before her nerves overtook her. She hated this unexpected demand that upped the ante. "What if I *can't* find him in a week? What if I can't get MOM settled?"

"Hell, Lieutenant, this is Austin. In El Paso he'd be over the border by now. Where can he hide here that you don't know about? And you got the first two letters already. He had *M*ethod and he had *O*pportunity. All you need is *M*otive. And from what I've gathered you can't be far from that."

Susan Granger looked puzzled. Which motive? That they broke up? That Kristen wanted a free affair and Lucas wanted something more? "What are you talking about?"

"According to the media file from downstairs, we have evidence of their arguing publicly over the last two years—once on a Channel 24 interview with Judy Maggio where he walked off the show—about their differing positions on the religious right."

"They were both against the religious right."

"But at different levels. He was vehemently opposed to them. She was willing to cut them political slack to capture some of their more moderate votes."

"Lucas Holt wouldn't shoot her over a thing like that. He couldn't even handle a weapon. The man hates handguns."

"Really?" Dillon tossed a file across the desk to her. "Did you know he outshot the guards at Huntsville every year in pistol competition? That the Warden thinks he shot at least one inmate— killed the sucker with another inmate's zip gun—in a disturbance at the prison? And did you know he purchased a Smith & Wesson nine millimeter at McClain's ten months ago, a few weeks after that on-air argument?"

Susan Granger slowly took her seat and picked up the file from Dillon's desk. The Commissioner poured her another cup of coffee from the hot pot as she glanced through the papers. "You know what's missing from these reports and clippings?" she said.

"What's missing is any mention of your relationship with him—and, quite frankly, that's the wild card that bothers the hell out of me, Lieutenant."

"Let me—"

"No, you let me for a minute, then the floor's yours." Dillon stood, towering over her, and sat on the edge of the desk. "Every officer in this department is wonderin' what I'm wonderin'— whether you *let* Lucas Holt escape from that crime scene because you and he are on-again off-again lovers when he's not hooked up with Kristen Wade or some other object of his obviously specious affections."

Susan Granger looked up at him, wanting desperately to defend herself. She knew she had to remain calm, stick to the facts. Any show of emotion would confirm his thoughts, and she couldn't afford that right now. "Are you through?" she said, with as much restraint as she could muster.

"No, I'm not," the Commissioner said, returning to his chair behind the desk. "I meant what I said to the Governor. I have every confidence you will right the wrong done at the scene—and you will do it in a week." Susan noted that the boyish grin had faded to a straight line. "If I find that you have lied or misled me about anything concerning this case, I will summarily dismiss you dishonorably with no benefits. Is that clear?"

Susan worked to keep control. "What's clear is that you don't have all the facts. What's missing from this file is not my relationship with Lucas Holt, but information that any idiot could have gotten from his parishioners if they wanted it." She sipped the coffee to buy time to breathe. "And that is that over the last year Father Holt's patience with the ideology of the religious right has evaporated into weekly confrontational sermons from the pulpit of St. Margaret's Episcopal Church."

"Which, if the pattern is normal," Dillon added, "resulted in death threats which in turn might lead even a man of the cloth to purchase a Smith & Wesson? Is that what you expect me to believe, Lieutenant?"

Granger shook her head. "That's not where I was going, but it could fit." She wondered why Lucas hadn't told her about the gun, though she had read the hate mail he had received. Actually, he had blown off the threats, seen them as part of doing business, a "professional hazard of preaching the Gospel," and relied on the God Squad for protection, rather than turning the letters and calls over to APD.

"Then where *were* you going?"

Granger leaned forward and gestured. "What if someone from the religious right wanted them both out of the picture? What better way than to set up Lucas Holt and eliminate Kristen Wade at the same time?"

Dillon grinned. "Spoken like a true friend, Lieutenant."

Susan stood and erupted. "Listen, Commissioner. You can fire my ass here and now if you want. But I'm tired of this bullshit innuendo about me and Holt. Here's the story and I'm only going through it once, though frankly it's none of your damned business."

"Lieutenant—" Commissioner Dillon warned.

"Sit down and listen to me." Her brown eyes burned at him, her round face calm and her voice clear and steady. "You had your say, now I'll have mine."

He sat, his hands interlaced at his chin, as she told him of their relationship at the University of Texas, drawn together from opposite sides of every issue. They had gone their separate ways until four years ago when he showed up at the church and she had just made Lieutenant. "We met over a dead body—the first 'Saints of God' case."

Dillon's nod acknowledged he'd heard of it and Granger acknowledged that she and Holt saw each other socially—more off than on lately—and that they were friends until he and his God Squad butted into police business. She leaned back in the chair to communicate with her body the opposite of what was going through her mind. She had to make this convincing, for Lucas, for Dillon, for herself. "Now here's the clincher: I am *not* in love with the man, and he's *not* in love with me. And even if I were I would not impeach the integrity of this job by *letting* a perp escape a crime scene."

"Lieutenant—"

"No, Commissioner." She took a deep breath. "And if you believe I *would* do that, then you need to discharge me before I leave this room." She thought a second and realized she was through, though it felt more like empty. She guessed she would let him talk now.

Dillon lowered his hands from his chin. "Ordinarily the display you have just provided would result in immediate insubordination charges. Under the circumstances, I'll ignore that and thank you for the clarification. I will assume that your relationship, whatever it may be, has no bearing on your investigation of this case, and take your theory under advisement."

"Thank you, Commissioner." She rose to leave.

"But you will find no other theory that fits the facts."

Granger frowned, puzzled, as Christopher Dillon removed a mini-cassette tape from his desk drawer.

"There is no other explanation for the shooting than the one I have given you, Lieutenant, and this proves it."

"What is it?" she said, fingering the tiny object.

"Kristen Wade had an unusual security system in her house. From the time it was triggered either by her or by Lucas Holt, it tape recorded everything that occurred." He looked at her with what she thought was real empathy. "I'm truly sorry, Lieutenant, not only for you but for this community that has so relied on him. But we have the entire ugly scene in living sound right here."

"Can I take this with me?" she said, stunned and feeling like an idiot for defending him.

"It's a copy, sure. I can tell you what happened."

"I think I'd rather hear it myself." She put the tape in her pocket and turned to leave.

"Let me summarize so you'll know what the first sounds are." Dillon walked her across the office. "He breaks in when she won't open the door. They argue—about several things, but mainly about the religious right, as I suggested. It gets louder and louder, then threatening. He pulls a gun and shoots her. You arrive. You talk. He vanishes as your backup rolls up." He opened the door and shook her hand.

Granger patted the tape in her pocket. "I'll keep you posted, Commissioner," she said seriously.

"You'll do a hell of a lot better than that, Lieutenant," the boyish grin replied. "You'll get your ass out in the street and find Holt and resolve this open-and-shut case. And you'll do it in a week."

Susan Granger nodded. "Yes, sir." She opened the outer door to the hallway, hoping she could make it to the street before her lungs burst for want of air.

Christopher Dillon followed her into the hall, out of earshot of the receptionist, as the elevator arrived.

"You're a good cop, Lieutenant," he said as the doors closed. "Don't end up like your father."

Susan Granger held it together until she got behind the wheel of her car. Her uncontrollable sobs of anger and sadness made it difficult to find her way home.

※ ※ ※

Cora Mae Hartwig parked her red Celica GT in the lot behind St. Margaret's Episcopal Church. She glanced up at the unusually overcast March sky and prayed it would rain just a

little more than February so there would be a good crop of
bluebonnets in a couple weeks. Maybe the rain would end the
mugginess that seemed to settle in her joints and made the first
mile of her daily three mile run more painful than usual. She
had just come from that routine lap around the lake and was
ready for something to drink at her meeting on Sixth Street.
Fluid replacement, runners called it; even runners in their
eighties like Cora Mae.

Dressed for Lent in her purple jogging suit and blue running
shoes she pulled on her backpack and headed down Trinity to
Sixth. She thought it appropriate that Maggie Mae's was bounded
on one side by Trinity Street, as if the Holy Spirit had planned an
Episcopal church there. She remembered all the wonderful old
houses that lined those streets when she was a girl. The east-west
streets were named for Texas trees and the north-south streets for
Texas rivers, until the City Council in its wisdom determined
people were too stupid to remember trees and numbered the east-
west streets north from the Colorado River. Now they were all
lined with parking lots or businesses. But when she got to Sixth
she was home again.

Though the store fronts on Pecan had changed, the old buildings were the same, carefully restored and protected by the historical society. She passed the restaurants and bars opening for
the lunch crowd and shooing the homeless and the drunks out of
doorways to forage elsewhere or panhandle on the corners.
Sooner or later they all ended up at the back door of Maggie
Mae's where the Homeless Program invited them in, assisted the
ones who wanted referrals and provided food chits to those passing through.

She passed a "Pace for Senate" poster in a bar window and
blinked at the contradiction. The man who abstained from alcohol and women had his face in a honky tonk where people came
to meet and mate. It was the closest to homelessness he would
get, seeing it through the eyes of the poster.

She rested a moment at the stop light at Neches and wondered if Pace had ever been hungry? Then maybe he wouldn't be so self-righteously demanding the cutoff of funds to feed these people, assuming they could lift themselves by their own bootstraps when they had no shoes.

The light changed and she crossed to the older and less developed end of Sixth, the part inhabited by locals and lost tourists. On the corner, in a turn-of-the-century stone building, stood the last vestige of old Austin street life, where Cowboy culture and Hispanic music mingled easily among thick smoke and cold longnecks. Even as a kid, Cora Mae's father had taken her to THE BUFFALO BARN GRILLE, hoisted her up on the saddle barstools and taught her how to two-step to music by local bands. Lucas Holt joked to her that it was the only building in town older than she was.

Right now, though, as she walked inside and up to the bar, she felt maybe that wasn't true. And she wished Lucas was here to tell her differently.

"Good morning Jill," she smiled at the blonde in the red halter top, wondering how in the world she could bend over in those jeans.

"Mornin' Miss Hartwig," she glanced at the neon ringed clock above the door. "But it's fixin' to be afternoon in a few minutes." She nodded to a table by the empty fireplace. "As you can see by the eating habits of Austin's finest over there."

Cora Mae turned to see two APD officers talking over club sandwiches and iced tea.

"You boys doin' okay over there? Need anything?" Jill tossed her blonde mane. "Anything at all?"

They smiled back and shook their heads as the gorgeous woman whispered to Cora Mae. "Nikky's upstairs waitin' for you. He came in before I opened up this morning so nobody saw him. I know those guys over there and they don't work the Sixth Street detail. They're the current stakeout looking for the Rev or anybody associated with him." She handed the old woman a key. "You pretend you're going to the restroom and the flatfoots over there won't miss you when they leave."

"Could I get something to drink first? I walked down from the church and I just finished my workout before that."

"Taken care of, Miss Hartwig. I made Nikky take iced tea and drinks upstairs with him." She picked up a pitcher. "Now you wait till I'm on the other side of the table, leanin' over to pour their tea refills and then you vanish while they're not starin' at my cleavage."

"You're a dear, dear," Cora Mae said, patting her hand. "And lovely cleavage it is, too."

"Here's the key to the restroom, ma'am," Jill said loud enough to be heard by the two cops. "Just drop it on the bar when you're done."

Cora Mae took the key and walked down a dimly lit corridor past the john doors with dogs painted on them marked "Pointers" and "Sitters." She ducked through the kitchen to a hallway door, knocked twice, waited, knocked twice again, heard the lock click, then entered and climbed the steep flight of narrow stairs. At the top she found Nikky Dorati sitting at a domino table with a whisky bottle and a shot glass in front of him.

"Nicholas!" she smiled. She liked all the God Squad, but had special feelings for Dorati, probably because of his special protection of the Rev. Nikky had taught her the finer points of poker, a few self defense moves in case she got mistaken for an old person, and she had made him walk around Town Lake with her twice a week before breakfast at The Omelettry at Deep Eddy.

"Come on in, Cora Mae."

Nikky sounded as despondent as she felt. "Are those stairs getting longer or am I just getting older?"

"Neither," Dorati protested. "We're both drained 'cause of the situation with the Rev. Which I'm gonna tell you about right now." He pulled back a chair for her and poured her iced tea.

Cora Mae interrupted. "I want to hear about Lucas, Nikky dear, but first how is Kristen?"

Dorati explained she was still on the ventilator.

"She looks okay and the nurse says she's a little better but not near out of the woods yet. That could take days."

Cora Mae tried to discern how much was bullshit and how much was truth. Was Nikky shielding her from the horror of Kristen's impending death? Maybe she was just being morbid.

"The ICU's the best place for her right now in terms of security as well as treatment. If she gets to where they can move her to a regular room she'll be a lot more vulnerable to unwanted visitors. So they're going to try to keep her there the rest of this week, till they see how things go."

She might as well be direct with him. They always were with each other. "Do you mean to tell me she might not make it?"

"Sorry, Cora Mae, but it depends on what happens the next few days. That's all I can tell you right now, other than Omar's on the case watchin' over her like a brood hen with a shotgun, and keeping us all informed."

Cora Mae felt Nikky was holding something back and whatever it was couldn't be good. Funny how people never held back good news. But she also knew he'd tell her when the time was right, as he always did, so she changed the subject to Lucas Holt.

"He's okay," Dorati responded, pouring another rye into the small glass. "I just can't tell even you, Cora Mae, where he is right now. His life is in danger if anyone finds out, anyone at all."

"I understand perfectly, Nikky," the old lady said. "It's like Ben Franklin said—and no, I didn't know him personally— 'Three can keep a secret, if two are dead.' I just want to know that he's safe, I mean secure from being found until we get this cleared up?"

"He's safe. He's secure—where nobody would think to find him." Nikky smiled. "In fact he's a lot better off than those of us walking the streets."

Cora Mae Hartwig had lived in Austin all of her eighty-some years. If there was any place to hide in this town she knew it, either because she played in it as a kid or had recently stashed refugees of one nationality or another there. So, unknowingly, Dorati had just tipped her to the limited possibilities.

"I notice you didn't ask me if he did it?"

"I didn't ask him when he showed up at St. Margaret's at Compline." Cora Mae took a sip of her tea and smiled. "What difference would it make anyway, Nicholas? It doesn't sound like something Lucas would intentionally do, but it could happen. In either case we're still us and he's still him and our Christian commitment demands that we stick up for each other."

"In other words we kick butt if anybody touches the man."

"In the words of the Apostle Paul, yes." Cora Mae smiled. She liked the God Squad version of the Bible they had learned from Holt. She knew Lucas had something for her to do or she wouldn't be sitting here with Nikky. "So where do I fit in?"

"The Rev has got to stay underground for a while. Everybody in town will be lookin' for him, but we can't do what we have to do to straighten this all out if he's behind bars. I got assignments for all the Squad and I had to get to you first."

He knocked back the rye. "Here's the deal. He needs a contact at the church and you're it."

Cora Mae looked puzzled. Something didn't make sense. "What about Maxine? He certainly trusts her after all these years."

"Not a matter of trust. Matter of who's obvious and who isn't. We know that the cops—and whoever else is involved here—will be watching Max like a hawk, probably bug her phone and follow her car. You, on the other hand—"

Cora Mae smiled and patted his hand. "I know, Nikky, dear. I'm a harmless old lady that nobody would suspect as a pipeline to the church. I can come and go unobtrusively and get and deliver messages to Max and the Vestry if he needs it."

"That's generally the idea."

"Sometimes agist stereotypes work in my favor—and I use the heck out of them," she said, her blue eyes twinkling. "You just tell me what to do, Nicholas." She knew Dorati liked her. His own mother, Helen Pelham, had appeared in that nursing home mystery the Squad had helped solve two years ago and now was off working for the FBI. So Dorati adopted Cora Mae as a suitable stand-in.

"For openers, get Max aside and tell her the Rev's okay, and that she should get messages to him through you. You and I will meet here, or I'll leave word for you with Jill, and vice versa. It's better if we only talk face to face though."

Cora Mae finished the tea as Nikky gave her more instructions. As she headed for the stairs, she pulled on her backpack and turned to him. "I know where he is, Nikky."

"I knew I said too much at the beginning. Here's hoping you're the only one old enough to remember," Dorati replied.

"It's a very religious idea, you know. Like the catacombs."

"Yeah," Dorati replied. He poured another rye and relit his cigar. "I just hope he makes it out of the tomb."

* * *

Five minutes after Cora Mae Hartwig left The Buffalo Barn Grille, Lucas Holt answered his cell phone.

"Yo, Rev. Nikky. Everything workin' out okay there?"

"Everything's everything. Great job. All the creature comforts of home, including the creatures. I probably don't want to know where you got all this stuff, right?"

"I borrowed it."

"The porta-john?"

"From a construction site. They had two of them."

Holt smiled at the prison logic. Unfortunately, it made sense to him. Incarceration was a two way street. "What's the latest?"

"Cora Mae's in place. Got a frantic call from the Lieutenant wanting to meet with me this afternoon. Seems her boss wants this wrapped in a week or they're both toast."

"We need to talk and not on the phone."

"Ten tonight? Usual spot?"

"Right." Lucas Holt punched off the phone and settled back in the chair Dorati had "acquired" for the place they had set up—thirty five feet *under* Rio Grande Street.

✳ ✳ ✳

Leaving the party at Green Pastures Restaurant with the excuse of having to go out for a smoke, the person walked out onto the old wooden porch, nodded and chatted politely with other well wishers. The car was parked at the end of an unlighted gravel drive at the far edge of the property of the elegant restaurant known for its huge sheltering live oaks. One of the many unassuming peacocks that skulked the grounds of the Koock Mansion wandered too close and found itself the target of a cigarette flicked in the darkness.

Electronically popping open the car trunk, the figure retrieved a trenchcoat and hurried down Live Oak Street to the corner of South Congress.

The marquee of the small movie theatre flashed garish lights around the words 'Double Feature—Adult Movies' and a bored fat woman with greasy black hair sat in the money booth reading a magazine. Like a vulture, the person in the trenchcoat thought. Waiting for the roadkill to come to her, pay her money to watch people debase themselves, demeaning both the actor and the watcher, while she sat absently collecting the filthy profits. She would be surprised to learn that vultures choked on roadkill.

On the corner by the theatre two hookers in hot pants and thigh high boots wore cheap fur jackets against the March cold. The figure ignored them, though imagined taking one home, imagined all the things it would be pleasant to do to her. With her. Of course that kind of risk could not be taken. Not now. Not when the goal was so close within reach. But why not alter the plan just a bit to include these two unanticipated whore additions? There would be no harm, so to speak, inviting them to the party.

Donning dark glasses, the person motioned to the bosomy redhead to come to the shadowed corner. She offered her services right there, but the patron deferred pleasure now, told her to come into the theatre in fifteen minutes, and to bring her friend. A crisp fifty dollar bill was tucked into her halter with the promise of nine more if the ladies sat in the rear row of seats, one on each side. Protection was, of course, not a problem.

And of course she agreed. It was almost too easy, adding two more at the last minute. With a glance at a Rolex, the patron hurriedly bought a ticket from the vulture and entered the garishly painted movie house. It took a second to adjust to the darkness, then gradually the disgusting display of immorality on the screen became clear. Three big breasted young women performed sex acts on two men as well as on each other.

The figure took a seat in an empty row in the middle of the crowded theatre. Though NO SMOKING signs were everywhere, the place reeked of smoke and alcohol, and the sticky cement floor was repulsive. Looking around, wondering who the hell these people were in the daylight, the patron felt both pity and disgust for these souls of the damned, and happy to be so unlike them.

The gyrations on the screen continued against an inane dialogue of excuses to remove clothing and fondle body parts. A small square packet was removed from the trenchcoat pocket. In the darkness, hands fumbling in the seat, the patron appeared to be doing nothing out of the ordinary. The metal leads easily pushed into the white cache and the tiny switch on the battery was clicked on. The sticky floor anchored the square under the seat so it could not slide out of position.

The figure stood and walked down the side aisle to an EXIT door near the screen as the two women entered the theatre and took seats in the last row.

Once outside, it was simple to circle around the back of the building to Live Oak Street and return to Green Pastures. Another cigarette reinforced the excuse to be outside, but also removed the vile taste of filth.

The coat and glasses were rolled up together in a bundle to be burned later and a sweaty finger pressed the electronic button on the key chain. As the trunk popped open, the theatre down the street exploded in a huge ball of fire.

Guests from the party would come running from the mansion and witness their friend smoking a cigarette by the car. Joining them to look for victims, they would race to the scene and use the cell phone to call for help, be taped by the media in their formal evening attire dragging charred bodies from what the press would appropriately name the "inferno."

Hell, the figure thought, they couldn't smell any worse than they did on the corner. Especially the dead vulture.

• Three •

Travis Layton parked his battered Ford pickup in the lot behind St. Margaret's Episcopal Church. The dark blue truck had seen better days and so had he. He had acquired it as full payment for defending a Mexican national in a murder case. A twelve year old girl was viciously raped and strangled, then left to die in a field off South IH 35. She apparently regained consciousness enough to crawl through the undergrowth to the edge of the highway before drowning from the blood in her battered lungs. In a dragnet the police arrested Eduardo Renteria in a bar two miles from the site. The Mexican accounted for the blood on his clothes by insisting he had seen her in his truck headlights and had stopped to help her, then realized he would be blamed and left the scene.

In a long and racially divisive trial, Layton offended every power group in Austin, some at his own peril, in an attempt to prove the man's innocence. When the jury deadlocked, the judge sought to save face and avoid riots by offering Layton a plea for his client: involuntary manslaughter with extradition to serve his time in a Mexican prison. Layton wanted to finish the trial, but Renteria quickly took the plea and vanished the next day, accompanied by three Federales and one Texas Ranger. The keys to the pickup were left with a note to Layton thanking him for "trying to spare me" and begging him to accept the truck as payment for his legal services.

It was months before Travis learned Renteria had been ransomed out of prison by his politically well connected family, who probably had also paid the Austin judge to cooperate with the extradition arrangement. It was about the same time that Layton tried to rotate the truck's tires and found the spare flat and loose on the rim. As he lowered it off the back of the truck bed he saw a white patch inside, and pulled out a pair of blood encrusted panties.

So Travis continued to drive the old pickup as a reminder not to get self righteous over anything because you couldn't trust anybody anyway, and as another reason to drink Jack Daniels, which he had done before the trial in slightly lesser quantities.

The only person Layton ever told about the tire, ever trusted to keep the confidence and to understand what it meant, was Lucas Holt. And now the priest was on the run for what looked like the murder of his girlfriend, Kristen Wade.

Travis opened the briefcase on the seat and took a drink from the silver flask inside. The Black Jack burned his throat, then warmed his body in the cold March dusk. He didn't see how Lucas could have done it, though. As chaplain at Huntsville prison, Holt had walked the last mile with dozens of condemned men who he knew deserved the plunge of the needle, and still he was against the death penalty as barbaric and unforgiving. But he had also told Layton that he understood the *urge* to kill, the same urge that made him feel like pressing the plunger on the syringe or flipping the switch for the chair himself.

In fact, it was Lucas who had insisted on locating the parents of Eduardo Renteria, retired in luxury in the mountains of Southwest Mexico. Then, ostensibly on a long weekend retreat, Lucas, in his clerical collar, had delivered the dead girl's panties to those parents. Later, after attempted explanations and the tearful pleading of Eduardo on the floor before his disgraced father, Holt had been immediately escorted off the property and flown back to Austin on their personal jet, so as not to witness what followed. The next morning the church received a copy of Eduardo's terse obituary, and Holt could report to Layton, and eventually the girl's family, that it was finished.

No, Travis thought as he left the truck and headed for the back door of the church. Lucas couldn't have done it—and not just because at one time he loved Kristen Wade, but because it made no damned sense. Holt was nothing if not logical.

"Hey, you old ambulance chaser," Maxine Blackwell said as he entered the hallway. "Where the hell have you been?"

"Chasing ambulances, obviously." He winked at the church secretary and found her open necked blouse more warming than the Black Jack.

"Do I have to get in an ambulance to see you?"

"Hell, Max, I took you out a year ago and I haven't recovered from the bill yet. Besides, you only go out with me when I change my shirt. Ain't been two years yet." He walked to her desk and she faced him. He could smell the sweet mixture of perfume and smoke that was Maxine, and he smiled.

"I know that smile, Travis. Years of observation." She hooked her arms around his neck. "Anytime you're ready to change this old stinky shirt," she said, running her fingers inside between the buttons, "you let me know. I'll even help you off with it."

Layton started to move his lips to hers.

She pushed him away. "But right now we gotta do something about the Rev," she said with sudden sobriety.

Layton took a deep breath and reached for the flask in his pocket. "You heard anything?"

"Nothing." Maxine slipped back around to her own chair and pointed to the stack of papers. "And the phone calls keep piling up, not to mention the normal, daily stuff that needs to get done." She looked up at him seriously. "You and Cora Mae are Senior and Junior Warden for the place. What're you gonna do?"

"I'm afraid it's not what *we're* going to do but what the Bishop's going to do." He motioned toward Holt's office. "You got the speakerphone rigged up?"

"Phone's ready, coffee's fresh, Upper Crust cookies are on a plate waiting for you and the rest of the Vestry." She looked at a list. "Luis Arredondo's kid is sick so he can't come and Toni Lord had a meeting with the Austin Black Realtors Association so she may be late or not here at all. They both said for you to call them no matter how late you finished."

Travis opened the door to the Rev's office. "That means it's Cora Mae Hartwig, Case Atkinson and me."

"The good, the bad and the ugly," Maxine mumbled under her breath.

"I heard that," Layton replied with a frown, "and Case Atkinson isn't ugly."

"I was referring to *you*." She winked at him. "You're not attracted to Case, are you?"

"Maxine!"

"Sorry," the red haired ex-madame stood and handed him a pad and pencil. "I got nothing against gays, you know. Most days I like 'em better than straights, 'specially Case. And I certainly employed my share of lesbians over the years at the South Congress house. But I don't know about him and his s.o. adopting a baby."

"I'm helpin' them with the papers," Travis said, admiring the effect of the cleavage and the Jack. "It's a good thing they're both successful architects. Getting a kid from China is expensive."

"Call me old fashioned, Travis, but this is probably the only issue I'd tend to believe Ryan Pace about. It's not enough to make me vote for the bastard, you understand, but he does make a point about the unnaturalness of a kid growing up in a two daddy family—or mommie."

"Better than not growing up at all, isn't it?" Layton poured himself a cup of coffee. He had to get straight if he was talking to Bishop Casas. "Or growing up in a family where the parents fight, or beat each other, or they have to share a bed with rats?" He checked the dial tone on the phone. "Listen, Max. I'm old fashioned too in a lot of ways. But the more I learn about this stuff, the more I think you got to trust the kid's genes. Even if the baby grows up with two same sex parents, his genes will take over around age twelve anyway and tell him what his sexual inclination is—regardless of what he sees at home, which becomes one more interesting variation on a theme."

"I hope you're right." She took hold of his bolo tie. "Maybe we could discuss this after the Vestry meeting, say at *dinner*?"

"I certainly hope I heard someone say the word 'dinner' because I'm starving," said a familiar voice down the hall.

"Hi, Cora Mae," Max said. "Best I could do on short notice was cookies."

"That will do fine, dear," the old woman replied, removing her backpack and jogging jacket. "Just a little something to tide me over till I get home and pop something in the nuke." She pecked Travis on the cheek as she passed him on her way into the office. "What did we ever do without them, Travis?"

"I'm not as old as you are, Cora Mae," he replied. "I don't remember wood stoves."

"Nobody's as old as I am, Travis." Cora Mae poured coffee for herself and Max and returned to the outer office. "I remember when we invented fire." She sipped the black liquid. "Of course, the coffee was better back then."

The phone rang and Travis looked at his watch. "That's probably the bishop, Max. Put him on speaker in the office and send Case in if he gets here." He closed the door and punched the speaker button.

"Hello?" A deep voice came through the small box. "This is Emilio Casas."

"Evenin' Bishop," Layton said. "It's just me and Cora Mae Hartwig, so far. You'll remember we're Senior and Junior Warden, respectively. Case Atkinson, another Vestry member, is expected to be here shortly."

"Thank you, Travis. I remember you both from confirmations at St. Margaret's, and I know how you both love the church."

Travis looked at Cora Mae. While neither held quite the animosity that Lucas Holt had for the man, they both rolled their eyes at the unctuous pretention evident in the bishop's manner. It was no secret that Casas had transferred the Rev here from the prison hoping he would fail and be bounced out of the diocese, that the bishop disagreed with Holt's theology on everything from the purpose of the church to the meaning of the resurrection and prayed daily for Lucas to do or say something that could get him defrocked. From the cheery sound of the bishop's voice, those prayers had been answered.

"I know also that Father Holt has engaged in conduct unbecoming a priest and has absented himself from his assigned duties at that great church."

"Which conduct are you talking about, Bishop Casas?" Cora Mae interjected. "Would that be the HIV education classes for our preschoolers or the conference on assisted suicide for our families with terminal illness?"

A slight chuckle echoed over the speaker. Case Atkinson opened the door and Layton motioned him into a chair.

"No, dear lady, I may have my little theological disagreements with Father Holt, but murdering a State Legislator in cold blood after having gratuitous intercourse with her certainly is not the role model I desire for priests in the Diocese of Austin."

"Do we know that's what happened?" the architect asked, announcing himself to the prelate in the box.

"Not unless Bishop Casas was there watching," Travis Layton said, splashing contents of the flask into his coffee. "Far as we know, she ain't dead yet, Bishop, so it ain't murder. Then there's the little matter of being innocent until proven guilty, except in the French courts of Louisiana. And finally, I don't know that they had sex, but if they did, I can guaran-damn-tee you it wasn't gratuitous."

The bishop cleared his throat and continued. "I appreciate your defense of the priest you have come to know and love, but as the spiritual leader of this diocese I must take whatever actions seem appropriate to continue the ministry of St. Margaret's in a manner consistent with the Gospel of Jesus Christ."

"I'm sure we can do that ourselves, Bishop," Cora Mae said. "I've already talked with the other Vestry members about taking over certain functions until Lucas returns. There is Biblical precedent for this, I believe. The disciples—and we—were forced to take over the running of things till Jesus gets back. Some people think that's the point of his leaving."

"That's right, Bishop," Case Atkinson sat forward on his chair. "We've started organizing to manage the various outreach programs we have—home visits to the elderly and hospitalized, the homeless shelter, the Next-to-New thrift store, the needle and condom distribution program, our youth activities, even Sunday services can be covered."

"Yes, I'm sure they can. But Father Holt's absence provides us with an opportunity to revisit the effectiveness and *advisability* of such programs, given the current political climate and its repercussions for the financial support of such charities as the church. There are those, you know, who would like to delete the tax deduction for donations, and we must be sensitive to their interests as well."

"Let me guess, Bishop," Travis Layton said, trying to lighten the terse tone of the conversation. "You're going to put Ryan Pace in charge of St. Margaret's?"

Cora Mae and Case smirked, but the voice from the box became more rigid.

"Mr. Pace is an excellent candidate, Travis. He is a former Episcopalian who was chased from our sanctuary by the dangerously liberal pronouncements of the national church which he, like many others, find unconscionable. I can personally say that he is a fine Christian gentleman who only wants to restore truly moral values to a culture—and a city, I might add—that consistently takes the moral low road. Austin not only provides insurance for the fornicating sexual partners of unmarried city employees—as if they were *spouses*, for God's sake—but turns a deaf ear to those who would remove smut from the school libraries."

Travis Layton put aside his coffee and drank directly from the flask. Cora Mae reached over and took a drink herself, passing it to Case, who nodded his thanks. She imagined early disciples taking communion from a common flask.

The Bishop's tone became less strident, more in control. "I personally know Mr. Pace and would support him any day over that misguided woman who currently holds the seat in the State Legislature."

"Actually, Bishop," Cora Mae interrupted, "she's currently holding a bed in the San Jacinto Hospital ICU, barely clinging to life."

"That is true, Miss Hartwig. And I apologize for what must seem like my insensitivity to her. I assure you she is in my prayers daily, as are you all. But because your priest put her in that ICU, I am assigning an interim priest from the seminary faculty to take over the liturgical and the *management* functions of St. Margaret's until such time as a replacement can be found for the man who abandoned his flock."

"Now, wait a minute, Bishop," Travis Layton stood up.

"I am very sorry about this, Travis. But I'm sure you can understand my position. I have to protect both the spiritual integrity and the physical property of the church, and I must tell you that many people higher up than I think that both have been in jeopardy ever since I made the mistake of assigning Lucas Holt there."

"Actually," Case Atkinson said, "it was the priest before him—the guy you liked—who embezzled the parish. Father Holt bailed us out."

"Exactly my point, Mr. Atkinson." Casas remained cool and direct, clearly doing his best to sound sympathetic and win them to his side. "Must I remind you that bail out was with the blood money from a murderer's insurance policy?" He paused and took a deep breath. "So until this matter is resolved I think you can see that my only ecclesiastical course is to ban Father Holt from functioning as a priest in this diocese."

Travis Layton motioned to the other two to be calm. It was time to play attorney. "Of course we understand that, Bishop." Placating him now might prevent more extreme measures like dismissing the Vestry.

"And I have asked the Dean of the Episcopal Theological Seminary of Texas, The Very Reverend J. Everett Bergen, to bring over to you the woman who will temporarily replace him."

"Woman?" Cora Mae said and looked at Case. At least this was promising.

"The Rev. Rhondalyn Doss is professor of history and liturgics, someone who has a sense of the mission and the accurate theology of the church. Ev Bergen will introduce her to the staff tomorrow and I expect the Vestry in particular to exercise cooperation in whatever she finds it necessary to do. She will report directly to me, though she will retain a reduced teaching load at the seminary."

"And when Father Holt turns up and is found not guilty of your accusations, Bishop?" Cora Mae Hartwig spoke directly into the box, her voice firm and unquavering.

"*If* that occurs, Miss Hartwig, and *my* sources assure me that will not happen, but if it does we still need to evaluate the effectiveness of his ministry in that setting. I find it extremely difficult to believe that Lucas Holt will rise from his self imposed exile totally expunged from this nasty business, in which case, of course, I shall be forced to take action to defrock him permanently."

"I suppose there is no alternative here, Bishop?" Case asked.

"Travis knows well that we could argue this out in a canonical court."

"But by the time that was constituted, Lucas Holt would be retired," Travis added, frowning at Case.

"Any further questions before I ring off?"

"God bless you, Emil," Cora Mae said. "You'll need it before this is over."

"Is that a threat, Miss Hartwig?"

"No," she replied, pouring herself another coffee with the help of Layton's flask. "It's a certainty."

The line buzzed and Case Atkinson hit the off button. "Frock you very much," he said.

Cora Mae smiled. "At least it's a woman. How conservative can she be?"

"If Emil Casas likes her, she'll make Margaret Thatcher look radical." Travis Layton moved to the chair at Lucas Holt's desk. "We've got to find out what the hell happened and get him back here, soon. This place needs him close by. And he needs us as much as we need him."

"Regardless of what the bishop says," Case Atkinson added.

The old woman looked out the window at the neon and noise of Sixth Street.

"He may be closer than we think, Travis," she said. "Much closer."

* * *

Thirty five feet below Austin's infamous Sixth Street, Lucas Holt paced across a cut limestone bridge. Above him, "Pecan Street" was just cranking up for business. College students began their night of drinking. Musicians and singers of all kinds turned up the volume and hoped to be heard by an agent or an audience anxious to purchase their latest release at the bar. Sexual alliances of every gender mix began with carefully orchestrated rituals in bars and clubs. Street smells of perfume, fried food, and burnt sugar wafted through the milling crowd.

But beneath their feet, Lucas Holt heard nothing but the occasional drip of water from the walls of the cavern to the small stream below. The only smell was the damp sulphur stink from the layers of rock holding up the streets and skyscrapers of Austin. His night was cranking up, too.

Illuminated by battery operated lamps he and Nikky Dorati had installed, the bridge Holt walked over spanned what was called Little Shoal Creek over one hundred twenty five years ago. He had discovered it by mistake, reading an old history of St. Margaret's church that Cora Mae Hartwig had loaned him.

When the church was constructed in the 1840's with money won from poker games in a bar at the corner of Sixth and Congress, it enacted a strange requirement for its clergy. Neither the rector nor senior warden could weigh "more than one hundred fifty pounds and must be of trim build." Knowing the church had been a sanctuary for everyone from poker cheats to runaway slaves to persecuted Mexicans, the Rev began looking for a hollow wall with a secret exit. Finally, after two years of nosing around, Holt was checking a roof leak when he found a boarded up door at the opposite end of the belfry. The door opened to a very narrow stairway about a foot across which descended in the north wall down behind the altar to the basement, sub-basement, down beyond the Treasury room to a four foot hollowed out tunnel that led, eventually, to where he was now. A fat man would never have found it. What had begun as a secret exit for sanctuary in the 1840's had been hooked up to the 1870's tunnels for the modern purposes of that time—and now this one.

He went to the ice chest and opened a bottle of beer from a local micro—Pecan Street Lager. Obviously Dorati had thought the local brand appropriate, since Holt was going to be living *under* Pecan Street. Speaking of Dorati, where the hell was he?

Holt looked at his watch, then heard footsteps echo in the tunnel leading to the limestone bridge. Retrieving the 9mm Smith & Wesson from under the pillow on the Army cot, Lucas pressed a remote light switch, plunging the area into thick darkness. It was nearly impossible for anyone *but* Dorati to be in the tunnels; few if any Austinites knew of their existence. Even the helpful assistants at the refurbished old library that served as the Austin History Center had no idea what he was describing. In fact, he had had to rummage through the basement of the State Engineering Library to find an obscure copy of the original blueprints for the tunnel in which he now stood with a loaded weapon.

An approaching flashlight in the distance looked like the beam from a locomotive. Holt crouched under the bridge and waited. He hated this. The gun in his hand felt like a cannon compared to the ones he had shot at the pen. It was too heavy, too big, too powerful, and as he knew from yesterday, too dangerous. Why didn't Dorati identify himself? If it *was* Dorati. This was stupid. He couldn't wait any longer.

"Yo, Nikky!" Holt yelled into the darkness.

"Bang. You're dead." A voice whispered behind him as he jumped in terror.

"Dammit Nikky! Don't *do* that!" Holt shivered. "How'd you get behind me, anyway?"

"Years of practice. And don't take chances," Dorati said, clicking on the light and helping the Rev up to the stone pavement. "You don't know who knows about this place besides us. You got to always assume the worst and if it turns out to be me, great."

"I'm just on edge." Holt picked up his beer and got one for Dorati. "Besides, nobody knows about this place. It's the best forgotten secret in the history of the state. The copy of the plans I saw was there because it had to be filed—but even it was *mis*-filed. It's as if they built this whole drainage system for flood control and then literally buried it."

"Maybe it was the City Council's Boondoggle Du Jour," Dorati laughed, pulling over two plastic chairs. "These bridges were more than flood control, Rev. All four of them down here are hand carved limestone, and the tunnels run all the way from

Sixth Street up to Twenty Second. If it was me, I'd say somebody was runnin' booze or guns when Little Shoal Creek wasn't flooding through here."

Holt tossed the gun on the cot. "My point is that you and I aren't likely to run into anyone but each other, so quit scaring the shit out of me." He took a drink of the lager. "And fill me in on what's happening up there."

Dorati told him what he knew. Kristin was in the hospital with Omar holding off all external assaults. Susan Granger was getting reamed by the new Commissioner of Police and was under the gun to find Lucas in one week. And they had talked with Cora Mae Hartwig, who had just called Nikky to say the Bishop had banned Lucas from functioning as a priest and was assigning somebody to take over St. Margaret's in his absence.

Lucas took a deep breath. He hated being down here, out of the action. "And Pace?"

"Nada," Dorati replied. "Same ol' same ol'. He keeps hammering away at all the shit he knows will scare people the most. Though with Kristen out of the campaign picture, he may be turnin' up the heat a little."

Holt stood up. "I need to see her, Nikky."

Dorati leaned back in the chair. "Rev, you know APD's got San Jacinto hospital locked, man. They friskin' the cockroaches goin' in and outta that place." He shook his head. "It's too soon."

"Tonight, my man," Holt said, tossing the empty bottle into a bag. "I want you to pick me up at Twenty-Second Street—I can get that far in the tunnels—and get me into the ICU."

Nikky shook his head. "That should be no problem since, being invisible, you can also walk through walls."

Holt ignored him. "And I want you to call the Squad to meet tomorrow night. But not at the Buffalo this time." He thought a second. "At Mother's. You call the owner, Charles Hayes, and tell him to lock up and leave the key in the usual place. We'll run a tab and pay him later."

"And the reason you're not sitting down here letting things blow over a few days before you take these risks would be what?" Dorati said, knowing the Rev's mind was made up.

"Look, Nikky," Holt said, furrowing his brow. "Susan's got a week to wrap this up or she's out of a job. We don't know if Kristen can last that long. And there's somebody messing with St. Margaret's that's got no business being there."

"The stand-in priest or Bishop Casas?"

"Both of them." He snapped the gun into the waist holster Dorati had loaned him. "Now let's go."

An hour later Nikky used a passkey to open the Food Service door at the San Jacinto Hospital loading dock.

"Where's the APD guard back here?" the Rev asked.

"Having coffee with the Director of Security who I know from doin' time together a couple of dimes ago." Dorati opened a freezer in the kitchen and took out a brown bag. "Pull these on over your clothes," he said, handing the contents to the Rev. "You've got thirty minutes before the guy has to call in a status report. Five minutes to get to ICU and five to get back here gives you twenty minutes with her."

"Thanks," Holt said. He quickly donned blue surgical scrubs, shoe covers, hat and mask and walked through the basement corridor to the staff elevator. A nurse with an i.v. pole spoke to him.

"Which floor, Dr. Sandbach?"

Holt glanced at her name tag and said "How'd you recognize me, June?"

The nurse smiled. "Well if it didn't say it on your scrubs right there, I'd know those eyes anywhere, surg mask or no surg mask." The elevator stopped at the second floor. "But you must be a walking advertisement for that new hair grow stuff just came out." She winked at him. "You used to be bald as a bat on top."

Holt quickly exited. "Yeah, thanks for noticing. See you later." He hoped he didn't run into anyone else who knew Doctor, what was the name, Sandbach? And he would take the stairs back down. For now, he cut through a back corridor that had an unmarked nondescript door looking like many others. Only hospital employees and clergy whose high profile parishioners had to go to ICU knew that this door led to Bed 16. It was a way for VIP patients like show people and politicos to get past reporters, or spouses, with relative privacy. And it allowed their doctors to visit without being assaulted by family and onlookers.

Holt inserted the master key Nikky had copied from the security director and entered the bathroom of the ICU suite. He recognized the blue silk bath robe hanging on a hook. He had seen her in it, and out of it, so often that maybe he took it and her for granted. Suddenly he missed her next to him. But why? He had spent this last year getting closer with Susan after he and Kristen decided her political career would always take first priority over him. And the time with Susan had been basically good, though lately they seemed to have gotten on each other's nerves more, needed more distance from each other. Was that part of a normal relationship that waxes and wanes, or was it the unravelling of their entanglement, again? He turned the corner into the room.

She looked like an angel, he thought, as he stood and gazed at her. Her auburn hair spread across the pure white pillow, shining even in the harsh hospital light. Her soft face looked like she was sleeping, save for the steady pumping of the ventilator tube ungraciously taped to her mouth, making her full lips pouty and puffy. He counted six blue boxes monitoring the flow of various drugs and fluids through small plastic tubes that vanished under the white sheets.

He had seen it all hundreds of times, from the makeshift prison infirmary at Huntsville to parishioners here in this very high tech room. But it was different when it was one of your own, when the person attached to the tubes and machinery was someone attached to you, so that it was a part of you those needles stuck into. He wanted to help.

Lucas looked at his watch, then back at Kristen. In the remaining fifteen minutes there *was* one thing he could do. He had seen it done dozens of times, been in the room as the respiratory tech flipped the switches and pushed the buttons, knew the exact sequence because he had memorized it for such an occasion as this, so he would know how to disable the alarm and the backup system and turn off the ventilator. It would end her pain and their suffering. It would complete what he had begun when he pulled the trigger at her house yesterday.

He moved beside her and bent to kiss her, then stopped. He did not want to startle her, to have her open her eyes if that were possible, to see him turning off the machine.

Holt straightened up, turned to the ventilator, and pressed the button that silenced the alarm.

⁕ ⁕ ⁕

"Don't get caught, man," Jimmy Brickhouse said to the curly haired, dark featured Frankie Colovas as he let him out of the car in front of One American Center at Sixth and Congress. "The Rev's got a lot ridin' on you gettin' these bugs placed."

"Hey, Brick," Frankie replied, patting his pocked where the tiny devices were, "this is 'Doors' you're talkin' to, man. I ain't lettin' nobody down." He disappeared down into the freight entrance at the rear of the building everyone referred to as "Woolworth's" because that was what the twenty stories of stacked brown boxes had replaced. Austin singer Nanci Griffith had immortalized the old store with her "Dancin' at the Five and Dime" and Austinites who remembered it wished they could still stop in for a real cherry Coke and twirl on the stools. Instead the building housed nearly as many lawyers as pigeons. It was a toss up as to which was responsible for more shit.

Frankie Colovas twisted the small wire in the stairwell door lock and entered without a sound. He smiled at his own memory of the Woolworth's store—breaking into the back door at this very location as a kid. My God! he remembered as he hurried up the fire stairs. It was even with Jimmy Brickhouse! He rested a minute at the tenth floor landing and recalled how he and Brick had each downed about four "Black Cows" from the soda fountain before the APD flatfoot spotted them. The only good part of the bust was puking all over the back seat of the old squad car.

When he reached the nineteenth floor, Doors carefully opened the fire door to the silent corridor. He walked down the vacant hallway to the office marked "Ryan Pace for Senate." The campaign maintained a highly visible storefront on the street level of the old Scarbrough building, hoping to connect that old Austin name with what they proclaimed to be old Austin family values. But the brains of the Pace organization operated from this expensive office overlooking the capitol city of the state that they soon hoped to control in Congress.

"Goin' in," Doors whispered to the tiny stick mike Brickhouse had insisted he wear inside the lining of his jacket. If there was no door "Doors" could not open, there was no bit of communications technology Brickhouse couldn't operate, once he "acquired" it.

Colovas flicked on the desk light and reached into his pocket for the bugs. "So we both don't forget," he whispered, "I'm sticking one under the stapler." He peeled the adhesive off the small pellet-like device. "And one behind the picture of Pace shaking hands with Nixon." He paused. "It just seems right, somehow. Like what goes around comes—" Doors froze in his tracks. "Shit," he said to Brickhouse. "Somebody coming down the hall." He turned off the desk light and felt his way to a door, hunched down and closed it behind him. "In a closet," he whispered. "Get me out of here, Brick."

He leaned back against some rolled up papers and wondered what they were. Stuffing a towel from the mop cart against the bottom of the door to block out light and sound, he pulled out the pen light he always carried with him. They looked like maps, but not of cities. The circles of lines seemed to connect similar areas or something. He turned the light off when he heard the office door open.

"See," a deep voice said. "I told you wasn't nothin' up here. Pace is gettin' paranoid the closer we get to the kill date for Dead Ed."

"He said he saw a light as he drove by a few minutes ago. And a little more paranoia on your part wouldn't hurt," the other voice replied, "with as much as he's got ridin' on this—like his whole future includin' the White House." Doors thought he sounded a little too cautiously for his liking. This one wouldn't go away so easily. He hoped Brickhouse was on his way up with the Marines.

"How could he tell from that far down? He could've been off by a floor or two, lookin' up from the street. Come on, let's go. We got other fish to kill—if you get my meanin'."

"Your puns suck, Pete."

Colovas heard the other man walk by the closet door, pause, then walk away.

"And I'm not so sure we don't have company here."

Frankie heard an automatic click a round into a chamber. "Guns," he whispered almost silently.

"Why are you sayin' that?"

"Put your hand on the desk lamp, Pete the Punner, and see if that warms your brain any."

Another bullet clicked into place. Two sets of footsteps approached the closet door where a sweating Frankie Colovas crouched behind the mop cart and the strange maps. If they fired through the door, he was dead. He waited, his heart pounding, as the knob slowly turned. Then, with all his strength, he slammed the door open into the face of one man and leapt on top of the other, knocking the exploding gun from his hand.

Colovas pounded his fists into the man on the floor, stunning him long enough to reach for the loose gun a few feet away. A shot from behind knocked it across the room.

"Next one goes up your ass," the deep voice said. "Now get off him and stand up—slow, real slow."

Doors turned around to see the bloodied face of a squatty man with huge biceps and broken glasses.

"You alive, Pete?" the man said to the groaning form on the floor, who stood up and swung at Colovas, knocking him back against the wall.

"Who da hell are you, buttface?" the large man with blonde hair said. "And why'd you break in here?"

Frankie wiped his own bloody lip on his sleeve. Had to think fast. Give Brick time to get here. If he was coming. If he was hearing all this right now. "Heard you kept money here. Lots of it."

"Yeah, and what else did you hear," the deep voiced man stepped closer, "in that closet?"

"Can't hear shit in there," Colovas squinted with anticipation of being pistol whipped. "You try it. Closet shuts tight. Only knew you were there when you turned the knob."

The man with the broken glasses stuck the gun into Frankie's face. "I can't kill you yet, you Mexican son of a bitch, because Pace has to approve first and besides, your body'd be too hard to flush down the toilet."

"Greek," Colovas said, stalling. Hurry the hell up, Brickhouse.

"What?" the other man said.

"I'm Greek, not Hispanic."

The gun smashed against his face. "I don't give a shit if you're full blooded Cherokee. I'm gonna teach you a lesson about stealing and then I'm taking what's left of you to Pace to see if you need swimming lessons in Town Lake, unconscious of course." The man nodded to Pete. "Put his hands on the desk there."

"I think you should shut up, is what I think. I think you said too much about Pace already," the blonde man said as he grabbed Frankie and held one arm in a hammer lock while forcing the other, left hand, onto the top of the mahogany desk.

"They should have taught you this in school, sonny," the squatty, muscled man said, adjusting his broken glasses to stay on his blood splotched face. He held the gun by the barrel and smashed the butt down on Frankie's hand.

"No!" Colovas screamed as the crunch of broken bones sent a shock of pain through his entire body.

The man nodded to Pete to put the other hand down. But as the blonde haired man lifted Frankie's right arm, Colovas suddenly looped it around the man's neck and slammed his face down on the desk, breaking his nose.

The other man crashed his pistol butt into Frankie's neck and sent him sprawling to the floor.

"You're right," the blonde man yelled. "We ain't waitin' for Pace!" He aimed the 9mm at Colovas. "I'm wastin' this asshole here and now." He squeezed the trigger as the office door burst open.

"APD! DROP IT OR DIE!" Susan Granger said, her gun held in both hands and aimed at the blonde man's head. Two uniforms swept in behind her, their automatic weapons ready to fire.

The two men cursed and dropped their guns.

Frankie Colovas raised himself on his good elbow. "How?"

"Break in reported about ten minutes ago. Somebody called 911." She knelt by him as the officers cuffed and Miranded the two men. "You I'm personally taking to the ER myself."

"He broke in here, you idiots," the deep voice said. "We were protecting the property of Ryan Pace."

"What about it, Frankie?" Granger said. "You on business for a mutual acquaintance of ours?"

"Hell no, Lieutenant. I was lookin' for my dentist's office." He couldn't believe Brick had actually called 9-1-1. Brilliant. What were cops for, anyway? "I got an appointment tomorrow and wanted to make sure I knew where it was. I guess I got the wrong door."

Susan Granger shook her head. "Lame, Frankie, but I'm sure Travis Layton will make it sound like the Gospel." She helped him up. "I'm not cuffing you because of that hand, but I'm not making the same mistake twice. If you bolt I'll shoot you." She motioned to the uniforms. "Book 'em and hold 'em till Pace's attorney bails 'em. I'll be at San Jacinto Hospital with this one."

Ten minutes later Frankie Colovas relived another old Woolworth's memory. He puked all over the back seat of the squad car.

* * *

With the alarm silenced, Lucas Holt had ten seconds to turn off the back up battery and then the main switch for the ventilator before the alarm cycled back on. He had watched it done many times as his parishioners breathed their last. As he flipped the switch for the battery, he heard commotion in the ICU just outside the door to Bed 16.

A male voice bellowed. "If this man doesn't let me by right now, Lieutenant Granger, arrest him for obstructing police business."

"With pleasure, Commissioner," the familiar voice responded.

"Let them through, Chaplain," a younger woman said close to the curtained window, as Holt quickly moved to the bathroom and shut the door. In the darkness he could not find the lock.

The door to the unit opened and he heard footsteps softly enter.

"Don't just stand there looking like imbeciles," the young voice who must have been the nurse admonished. "You wanted to come in and gawk at her. So don't stand ten feet away from her; get up in her face and get a good close look, 'cause unless she dies it's gonna be your last one, and I don't care *who* you are. Just be careful what you say and talk like she can hear you because comatose people *can* hear."

"What are all those machines doing?" Susan Granger asked.

"Either monitoring or pumping medication and fluids into her," the nurse answered, obviously puttering around the boxes, checking their numbers. "I have to adjust the flow of the morphine from time to time to make sure she stays out of pain."

"And what about—?" Commissioner Christopher Dillon was interrupted by a shrill, piercing noise.

"What the hell?" Omar's voice yelled and the Rev knew the "chaplain" was ready to take someone out.

The noise stopped.

"Just the ventilator alarm," the nurse explained. "It was switched off."

"What!?" the Commissioner exclaimed. "Who had access to her?"

"Don't get your panties in a wad, mister," the nurse said nonchalantly. "Happens all the time. The respiratory techs come in to suction her and forget to switch it back on. That's why it's set to remind us."

Holt wanted to lean back against the wall but was afraid to move. There were too many implements in there and he might knock something over. In the darkness he saw the outline of a metal bedpan. He picked it up in case he needed a weapon. Most of all he wanted them all to leave. He knew he was taking a risk coming here, but this was not the time to get caught. Not yet, he thought as sweat dripped down his back.

"Here, Lieutenant," the nurse said. "Make yourself useful. Go in the bathroom there and wet this wash cloth. You can wipe the sweat from the fever off her face."

Every muscle in Holt's body tightened.

"I'm closer to it, Lieutenant," Omar said. "I'll get it."

Lucas breathed a sigh of relief.

"Let me do something," the Commissioner's footsteps got closer.

"Jeez!" the annoyed nurse said. "I'll do it myself."

Holt tried to be invisible as the door opened and the nurse flipped on the light. For some reason she looked vaguely familiar.

"You got to put yourself in the position of the patient in this situation." She glanced at what must have been a strange sight of a man holding a menacing bedpan, then walked right past him and turned on the faucet, raising her voice. "Think what it's like to be sweaty and uncomfortable and not be able to do anything about it." She wrung out the washcloth, took the bedpan from Lucas' upraised hand, blew him a kiss and closed the door.

Holt was immobile. He thought he'd never breathe again.

"Wipe off her face and then you'll have to leave," the nurse said. "Bedpan time."

"What's her condition?" Christopher Dillon asked. "There's blood on the sheet there."

"Seeps through the bandages no matter what we do. Her condition's guarded. Very guarded."

"Thanks for letting me—" Susan's voice cracked, and Lucas wanted to go to her. How the hell could he have feelings for both women? What if he had to choose right this second?

"You'll have to leave now," he heard Omar say, apparently opening the ICU room door.

"You need to nail that preacher, Lieutenant," the Commissioner's strong voice said, "and *soon*. There was no call for this, no matter what went on between them."

"We'll find him, Commissioner. Austin's not that big, yet."

"After seeing this, I'm changing my order," Dillon said. "I'm putting out an APB to bring the bastard in *dead or alive*."

"Is there a reward on that?" the nurse's voice said.

"State legislature put up fifty thousand this morning," the Commissioner answered. "Why? You know where he is?"

Holt tensed again. Get them the hell out the door.

"Sure I do," the nurse said as Holt heard her calibrate the humming blue boxes surrounding Kristen Wade. "He's in the bathroom."

Lucas heard Susan unsnap the holster of her gun and approach the bathroom door. She slowly turned the handle. His heart beat through his chest like a kettle drum. Maybe the choice would be made for him.

"What're you doing, Lieutenant?" Commissioner Dillon's impatient voice filled the room. "She's kidding. Come on! We have a meeting with Pace to get to."

Susan let go of the slightly open door and holstered her gun. "Right," she mumbled to Omar. "Thanks for letting us see her."

"Like I said, this is it. She's my patient and unless the doctor writes an order for you to come in here because he thinks it's good for Miss Wade's health, I'll have Chaplain Kandu and Dominick from Security toss you out in a second. Now if you'll excuse me I have to get this bedpan positioned."

Holt heard them leave the room as the nurse kept talking.

"If you can hear me, Miss Wade, I know this thing's uncomfortable. But I'll leave you alone on it for ten minutes and then I'll come back in. If anybody tries to bother you, just give them shit."

Lucas heard her walk to the door of the room and pull it closed. He seemed unable to catch his own breath, and had to take air deep into his lungs several times to regain his balance. It was too close, too soon.

He glanced at his watch. Dorati would expect him in ten minutes sharp, exactly when the nurse would return. He had to do the sequence *now*.

Holt moved to the ventilator and again silenced the alarm. Quickly he flipped the switch for the battery back-up. Then, looking at the angelic Kristen Wade, Lucas Holt turned the final knob to OFF.

The pumping stopped and the room was suddenly silent.

Lucas lifted off the green plastic mask covering her nose and mouth and withdrew the round hard breathing tube from between her clenched teeth. He bent over and kissed her dry lips.

Kristen Wade opened her eyes and threw her arms around him, pulling him into bed on top of her.

"Geez, Prince Charming, I thought you'd never get here. Get me off this bed pan. I need a drink."

• Four •

"I need to take this surplice home and wash it," Cora Mae Hartwig said in the St. Margaret's sacristy. She took the long white garment from the closet and showed it to Maxine Blackwell, who sat on the couch sipping coffee. "There are wine dribbles here and here. That means Dick Jones wore it last night at the five o'clock communion service. He's the lay chalice bearer who always fills the cup too full and then wonders why it sloshes over."

"Either that or he took a last minute leak with the alb on and didn't zip his fly." Max smiled at the old lady, who laughed appreciatively.

"I'm sure that's it," Cora Mae said, folding the alb. "The old fart hasn't kept it zipped in seventy two years, why would he start now?"

Max choked on her coffee. "Girl! How you talk!" she laughed. "Is there anybody in this parish you don't know the poop on?"

"When you've been around Austin as long as I have, dear, you've been pooped on by almost everyone. Their scent, so to speak, is recognizable."

Maxine stood to look out the window.

Cora Mae tidied up the room. "They can wear his robes, but they'll never fill his shoes." Though the congregation had done a good job of covering things in his absence. Lay readers and chalice bearers distributed reserve sacrament and led services. Cora Mae got the sick and shut in calls from Max so she could see them or get some one to do so. Most programs still ran nearly full tilt, at least for now. "I think the momentum keeps us going. I just hope we don't have to do it for a long time."

"We won't." Max nodded out the window.

"Oh, goodness!" Cora Mae rushed to her side to look down at the parking lot behind the church. "Is Lucas back?"

"Not hardly." Max pointed with her coffee cup. "The black dude is the Dean of the seminary, right?"

Cora Mae straightened her glasses. "J. Everett Bergen himself. The 'J' stands for Jawanda."

Max looked at her like she was kidding.

"It was the Sixties, dear. Lots of people changed their names to suit the times."

"Handsome sucker," Max said as they watched the husky, medium height man get out of the white two-door sedan. He wore a grey wool suit with his black clergy shirt and white clerical collar. "I've always had a thing for bald men. Something about rubbing over that tight round surface really turns me on." She looked at the old lady blushing beside her. "Oh, sorry, Cora Mae."

"Don't be," she said. "I was thinking the same thing," she giggled. "I had dinner with him when he first came to town two years ago and couldn't hardly keep my hands off that smooth brown head of his." Cora Mae frowned. "I wonder why that is?"

Max looked over at her and grinned. "Think about it, honey."

"I will, dear," the old woman said, still puzzled. "And that must be the Reverend Doss getting out of the car now. Funny, I don't remember her from all the times I've been at the seminary for meetings and things."

"Nice haircut, if you're Prince Valiant."

"That's a page boy and it looks very nice on her, Maxine. I always wanted straight black hair like that, that fell into place when you just shook it. My hair was always naturally curly and I could never do a thing with it. Still can't, like a white Brillo pad."

"And I always wanted curly hair instead of this straight red stuff it takes an hour to hot curl every morning. Guess you always want the opposite of what you've got."

Cora Mae turned and draped the folded alb over her arm. "We'd better get downstairs and greet them."

"So we can get the poop before anyone else does?" Max winked.

"Of course, dear. Did you think I was just being courteous? As Nikky would say, we've got to get a bead on this chick to see if she'll screw up everything Lucas has done." She hurried out of the Sacristy and down the stairs with Max at her heels. "You know old Casas wouldn't have appointed her interim unless she was the exact opposite of what we want."

The man and woman came through the back door from the lot. In five minutes they were seated in the Rector's office with coffee all around.

"Welcome to St. Margaret's, Ms. Doss," Cora Mae said. "I'm sorry I'm the only Vestryperson to greet you, but Travis Layton must've been delayed at the courthouse. He's helping out one of our parishioners."

"Trying to keep him from going back to prison. Which is where I met Father Holt," Max smiled as Cora Mae glared at her.

"Please," the dark haired woman replied. "Call me Rhon. Everyone has since I was born. I think my Daddy wanted a boy and since I was the only child my mother would have—she developed an ovarian infection right after I was born that sterilized her -they gave me both their names, Ron and Lynn."

"And where was that, Rhon?" Cora Mae asked. She thought the woman either had great genes or her own makeup consultant. For a person who had to be in her early fifties, she looked thirty-eight. Unless you looked real close at the crow's feet at the eyes, you'd be fooled by the trim body and tailored a-line skirt. She wondered what else that cool, crisp exterior covered.

"Scarsdale, actually," Doss replied, glancing over at the Dean. "Ev and I grew up at opposite ends of the spectrum."

"Harlem," Dean Bergen said. "PS 121. School of Hard Knocks. While I was gettin' my butt beat at 125th and Lex, she was practicing her ballet at Miss Janet's."

"Sorta like Cora Mae and me," Max chimed in. "'Course she was born during the war." She smiled at Cora Mae. "Was that the French and Indian, or the Civil?"

"No dear," Cora Mae replied straightfaced. "It was the Big One. You know, the one with King George?"

Rhondalynn Doss did not laugh with the other three. "You know," she said calmly but directly, "I really do not appreciate jokes about old people or any other minority group. I find them discounting and demeaning."

Cora Mae set her coffee cup on the table beside her. It was not the first time in her octogenarian life that she had been in a tense social situation. She was probably the only one there who wasn't uneasy about the new priest's comment. "I'm sorry if we offended you, dear," she said, "but you need to know a few things about St. Margaret's." Cora Mae looked straight into her light blue eyes. Who was this woman? Why had Casas chosen her? What did Bergen think of her? Would she turn out to be as anal retentive—the phrase Cora Mae learned in her psych class at UT—as her neat as a pin appearance conveyed?

"You are here as a guest of this congregation, no matter what the Bishop said," Cora Mae Hartwig began, her voice steady and strong. "And we'd like to work *with* you rather than against you, since we have to get along with each other for a while. As someone who is also straightforward with her feelings, I appreciate you telling me your prejudices right off the bat, but I would encourage you to lighten up a bit until you get the lay of the land, so to speak."

"I only meant—"

"I know what you meant, dear. You'll learn that we're nice people who are without a Rector in circumstances that have us all a little on edge. We have come to love and trust Lucas Holt, to confide our deepest selves to him, to rely on him to help us make sense of things. And now something has happened—to him and to us—that makes no sense. We will love each other through this, just as we have loved each other through other disruptive crises in our parish life together. And some of us will do it with a sense of humor about ourselves." Cora Mae smiled, indicating both that she was finished, and that she had forgiven the woman for jumping the gun. "Besides, I *am* old, in case you haven't noticed."

Doss smiled at her. "I *had* noticed, actually."

"But I'm *not* a minority," Cora Mae continued. "There are more people over age sixty five than under twenty. And my age group is the fastest growing one." She smiled back. "So you needn't defend me or treat me as an age group, Rhondalynn. That too is demeaning."

"Well, I see we're getting off to a great start," Dean Bergen smiled and shook his shiny head. "But at least you're consistent, Rhon." He turned to Cora Mae and Max. "She does the same stuff at seminary faculty meetings."

"I feel really bad about this start, you all," Doss said, standing to walk as she talked. "I'm nervous as a cat coming into St. Margaret's under these circumstances, trying to fill a hole left by the damned-near legendary Lucas Holt, knowing I can't do it. I think I just wanted to say 'I'm not *him*' right from the start."

"We figured that out before you got here, Rhon," Max said. "Nobody *wants* you to be him—" she stopped. "Boy, I got stuck there for a second. I almost called you 'Father Doss.' What do I do about that?"

The woman answered. "Some people call me Mother."

Max laughed. "At the pen, 'mother' was half a word."

"Then Rhon will do or, even though it's grammatically incorrect, 'Reverend,' which, by the way, is an adjective, not a noun."

Cora Mae had watched the exchange with interest. There was still something in the woman's stiffness, an uncomfortableness with herself or a fear that the others might find out something she did not want to reveal, that went beyond being the new kid on the block. Cora Mae would remember to report to Lucas her perceptions of this interim who seemed so much his opposite, assuming he or Nikky surfaced at the Buffalo any time soon.

Cora Mae stood and shook her hand. "Then welcome to St. Margaret's, Rhon. I'll leave you in the capable hands of Maxine to show you around the premises and fill you in on the schedule and programs and such. I have to go meet 'Dez—Ricardo Valdez is our Sexton—to help distribute our daily supply of condoms and needles."

Rhondalynn Doss opened her mouth to speak, then stopped. "I was about to voice my opinion on that program, Miss Hartwig, but I will take your advice and, for the time being, just listen."

"A good move for a change," the dean said. "I gotta be going too. I'll walk you out, Miss Hartwig."

Cora Mae took his arm, though she wanted to rub his head. "Why don't you go with me, Everett? We can get better acquainted, and you can buy lunch."

The Dean nodded. "You going to east Austin?"

"Speaking of prejudices," Max replied.

"No, dear, we're going to the Drag at the university to hand the things out to students and street people. God knows they need them."

"Not if they exercised any self control," Doss said, shaking her head. "I'm sorry, I have to agree with Bishop Casas on this one. All you're doing is encouraging immoral, not to mention illegal behavior by *giving* those people the implements of their sin!"

"Like they'll stop having sex and doing drugs if we *don't* give them condoms and needles?" Max replied with a smirk.

"Yes! That's exactly right. It's just like Ryan Pace says in his t.v. commercial. If they don't have them, they'll think twice about the behavior—or they'll all die off from overdoses and diseases associated with their choice of lifestyle and then society will be rid of them. The wages of sin is death, after all."

Cora Mae looked at Maxine. She didn't know whether to laugh or cry. Her blood pressure was rising to stroke level. Bishop Casas had really done it this time. He had a window of opportunity to tear apart everything Lucas Holt and the congregation had built up, to swing the considerable resources of St. Margaret's in the direction of his own theological preference—the religious right. And there were plenty of people who would rally behind that cry.

"I never understood that," Max said to Doss before Cora Mae exploded.

"Which part are you talking about?"

"Why does it say *is* death? Why isn't it *are* death? The wages of sin *are* death?"

"You two can figure that out and let us know," Everett Bergen said, as a red faced Cora Mae let him drag her out of the office. "We're going for a ride."

Once outside they waited for Valdez and the church van.

"Calm down, now," Bergen said. "Hopefully it's only for a little while."

"Like the plague was only a little while. Like Hiroshima was only a little while." The old woman sighed. "I usually can take differences of opinion, Everett, but I'm afraid I've been around too long—and around Lucas Holt too long—to tolerate intolerance, stupidity, and just plain meanness. That woman obviously has no children, or no feeling for children, especially the homeless ones on the Drag who are into drugs and sex for a million different reasons and who die before they get a chance to figure out why and get out of the cycle. Where the hell does she think Jesus would be in all that mess? In frigging *Scarsdale*?"

J. Everett Bergen opened his eyes wide. "Cora Mae, I don't believe I've heard you curse before."

"I apologize, but not much." She shook her head. "We need to get this thing straightened out quick, get Lucas back here before the Sunday Fundys move in and take over."

"Fundys?"

"Sorry. That's what Lucas calls the Fundamentalists, those who think God personally dictated the Bible in King James English, and self righteously defend their particular version of it. They, like her, give conservatives a bad name. Lucas always said it didn't matter whether you were conservative or liberal—the point was to 'do justice, love mercy and walk humbly with God.'"

"I'm sorry I had to bring her over here," Bergen said. "Just tell the Vestry to watch her. She's clearly the Bishop's puppet. And by the way she's not a New Yorker, like I am."

Bergen smiled and Cora Mae took a deep breath. There was something about being around this man that made a person relax, made you want to kick your shoes off and talk over a beer with him. Now if she could just keep her hands off his dome. "She's not?" she said, focusing herself. "She said she was from Scarsdale."

"Her parents are Texans, from Brenham. Dad worked for an oil company in the boom days and got transferred to New York. They are *so* Texan that they brought dirt to sprinkle on the labor room floor so she'd be born on Texas soil. Her first food was Blue Bell ice cream flown in from Brenham."

Cora Mae shook her head. "How is she at the seminary?"

"Good academician and a pain in the ass, just like here. She's part of the reason I got picked for the job when Dean McDougal got elected bishop of Idaho. He'd tried for ten years to liberalize the place, bring in more balanced theological points of view. But the trend of the times is against it, and the money's with the right. So I'm going to give it a shot and see what happens." He grinned at her. "And I agree with you, you have to have a sense of humor about it."

Cora Mae looked at her watch and wondered where Valdez was. She was suddenly hungry and wanted to have lunch with the

Dean to strategize how to handle the interim meddling of the newly acquired Rhondalynn Doss. What she couldn't discuss was yesterday's conversation with Nikky Dorati.

"Do you think he did it?" Bergen asked her.

"Who?"

"Lucas, of course. Do you think it's all true about him and Kristen?"

Cora Mae glanced down the driveway and was relieved to see Ricardo Valdez about to turn the corner. "I don't know what to think, Everett. I'm old enough to know that sometimes caca just pasa's."

Bergen stared at her, clueless.

"Shit just happens," she said, interpreting the Spanish for him. "Get used to it or you'll never live as long as I have. It's important not to be too judgmental about it till you get all the facts, and even then you ought to give it a second look. All I know so far is Kristen is in ICU at San Jacinto Hospital and APD is crawling all over everybody looking for Lucas because he was last seen holding the gun that shot her. Whether those two things are at all related in any way—well it remains to be seen, doesn't it, Everett?"

"The majority of people at the seminary think he did it, me included," Dean Bergen said.

"That's why it's fortunate we don't convict people by popular vote, isn't it? Your seminarians and faculty seem to get most of their exercise jumping to conclusions, theological as well as legal ones." She pointed to her face. "Trust these wrinkles, Ev. They say to keep your pants on till the fat lady sings."

Bergen laughed. "You wouldn't believe he did it if he personally confessed on the five o'clock news."

"I'll believe he did it when he tells me personally. Until then, you're as much a suspect as he is," she scolded. "Especially since you're from New York where people think nothing of shooting each other over a stalled car."

"Aside from the fact that Texans are the ones carrying concealed weapons, and that I have the distinction of being the only New Yorker who has never shot anyone, I was having dinner with the Bishop when Kristin Wade was shot." He squinted his eyes at her. "But where were *you*?"

Cora Mae smiled at him. "I was home." She liked his quick responses and felt comfortable playing with him. No wonder the trustees of the seminary chose him to lead them into the next millennium. The man had his bald head on straight, could handle conflict, and, like Lucas Holt, had a sense of humor that put otherwise difficult events back in their proper perspective. "I was home, alone, reading a book, with no alibi. So we're both suspects—which means we probably should have lunch when we're through 'flipping rubbers' as Ricardo calls it." She motioned to the alley. "And here he is."

When Ricardo Valdez stopped the van, Cora Mae got in and made introductions. She watched as J. Everett Bergen pushed aside a box of condoms on the seat and lowered his shiny brown head to thrust it into the passenger side. Then she started laughing.

"Did somebody say something funny?" Valdez asked.

"No," she said, continuing to giggle. "Let's get going." She couldn't wait to tell Max that she got it.

* * *

When they got outside the courtroom, Travis Layton shook hands with Frankie Colovas. "Let me tell you something, son," he said, pulling the dark mustached man into a secluded corner. "The reason you got bail on the b and e charge back there wasn't because I'm such a damned good lawyer."

"You looked pretty good to me, Mr. Layton. The Rev says you're the best and I believe it."

"Listen to me." Layton lowered his voice and smiled briefly at people across the corridor. "You bailed because His Honor owes me a few and this paid off a personal chit for him. That's the definition of justice in these parts. But if he sees you for anything between now and the hearing my chits won't mean shit and your ass will go back to Huntsville to finish your nickel."

"I got the picture, Mr. Layton," Colovas said seriously.

"I don't think you do, Frankie," the old attorney said. "My guess is that you were in Pace's campaign headquarters at the specific request of Lucas Holt."

"Actually, my dentist—"

"So when you see or talk to our illustrious Rector, tell him he shouldn't put people in jeopardy who stand to lose as big as you do." Layton pulled Colovas nose to nose. "Tell him if he wants something done to contact me. He's going to need me anyway when he gets caught."

"The Rev won't get caught, Mr. Layton. He's way too smart for that."

"Right." Travis knew there was some truth to that. If anybody could disappear in Austin, Texas it would be Lucas Holt with the God Squad protecting his backside. But Frankie's little caper happened in the campaign office of a senatorial candidate—and that would allow the feds to stick their noses into the deal. If they got interested, Lucas would have not only every APD officer scouring the city for him, but the FBI too. "And when you talk to Dorati, tell him I said to quit playing Watergate and tell me what he wants so I can get it with a court order. We need to start now to build Lucas' case—or he's going to find out what Huntsville looks like from *your* point of view."

"Okay, Mr. Layton. If I run into him somewhere I'll tell him." Colovas turned to leave. "Thanks again. And you run me a tab, too. I pay my bills, Mr. Layton, every last one of 'em. So you let me know how much I owe you for your services and I'll pay it out or work it off, one."

Travis Layton shook his head. He needed to go to the office for a slug of Black Jack. "Let me walk out with you, Frankie. There are a few things around my house I need tended to, if you'd be willing to do that to pay your bill, and assuming you can work in that cast."

"No problem at all, Mr. Layton," Colovas said as they walked out of the tall, white limestone building to Guadalupe Street. "And I could fix your place so it was burglar-proof, almost, if you wanted."

The March sun was living up to the tourist propaganda, sending the temperature to seventy, gliding through the cloudless blue sky. Travis Layton looked up and squinted his eyes. It was enough to make a man stop drinking and walk around the lake. Well, walk around the lake anyway. He was about to ask Frankie if he wanted to grab some lunch when a white stretch limo stopped at the curb in front of them.

"Uh-oh," Frankie muttered. "It's Ryan Pace."

"Let me handle this, son," Layton said, stepping in front of him.

"I can take care of myself, Mr. Layton." Frankie edged ahead.

"That's what I'm afraid of," Travis said to himself as Pace stepped from the limo wearing reflective sunglasses. His dark suit looked as unwrinkled as his youthful face. Though his campaign ad claimed literally "Humble" beginnings in an oilfield family from that town outside Houston, it neglected to mention his granddaddy owned the well. The man was used to luxury, to buying what he wanted, from women to elections. And now a lot of people exactly like him wanted to propel him into the Senate to defend their interests. Travis knew, or thought he knew, that the man's born-again alignment with the religious right was just one more political force to buy to assure he got there.

Not that he didn't walk the talk, Layton thought as he watched Pace shake hands with an apprehensive Frankie Colovas. In the mid-eighties boom days of Austin, the name Ryan Pace had been synonymous with parties, big parties, helicopters landing on the ranch parties. The twentysomething rich kid was awash in a sea of expensive drugs, fast women and big money. Or was it big drugs, expensive women and fast money? Or big women? In any case, when the kid hit thirty and his parents were killed in a private plane crash, he went to church, sobered up, got celibate, and tithed.

That's why Travis Layton never trusted him. Too much of a switch. Looked great politically and played so well in the media that the conservative swing of the nation just might swell the boy into the Senate—and higher. But the old lawyer surmised from years of courthouse politics that somewhere hidden under that self righteous exterior, somewhere beneath the silk shirts and leather Bible, between the silk sheets and leather upholstery there was a bottle, a woman and a bet. The slight bulge under his left arm indicated one more item for that list.

"You're looking well as usual, Mr. Layton." Pace thrust his hand out and Travis shook it. A firm grip, muscular. Certain. Not unlike his own at that age, or Lucas Holt's.

"You're as full of shit as I am, son," Layton replied with a smile. "What business do have with my client?"

Pace held up his hands. "Truce business," he said, turning back to Frankie. "I'd like to offer Mr. Colovas a job."

"As what," Layton said, "a hood ornament?"

Pace shook his head. "Water over the dam, Mr. Layton. I'm dropping all charges against you, Mr. Colovas, and inviting you to join my campaign staff as my companion for security."

Frankie looked at Travis, puzzled as to what to believe or to say. Layton said: "Hear him out before you deck him."

Pace continued. "I don't know what you were doing in my campaign office the other night and I don't care. There's nothing incriminating in there and I would personally escort you to take whatever you wanted in broad daylight and give it to Mr. Layton, Reverend Holt, or whoever else it is that thinks they need it to defeat me. The bugs were removed, by the way." He took off his sunglasses and showed his honest blue eyes. "I'm not stupid, you two. I know talent when I see it and I want it close to me. Frankie, you're responsible for the firing of two of my top security men, both of whose faces you rearranged last night."

He pointed to Colovas' casted left hand. "I read the E.R. report that said your hand had two broken bones and required that fiberglass cast for six weeks. I'm sorry that happened, but it did provide the opportunity to meet you and to see if you want to take the job."

"As security guard?" Colovas asked, incredulous.

"Better to employ your enemies than to love them, huh?" Layton said.

"It's only about a week until the special election. There are some really crazy people out there that hate the principles I stand for and the groups that back me. You don't have to agree with my philosophy to believe I have a right to express it—and to believe that the people of this state have a right to choose the kind of person they want to represent them. Even Kristen Wade would agree with that."

"Kristin Wade is a friend of ours," Layton said.

"It's not personal. It's politics. I want her to recover as much as you do, believe me. And I want Lucas Holt, who I also know is a friend of yours, to be skewered in a courtroom for shooting her."

"If he did," Travis interjected. He wasn't sure why Pace was doing this, but distrusted even the man's most altruistic motives. There was no such thing as altruism, anyway. If Pace wanted Colovas it was to keep an eye on him, and to try to get to Kristen or Lucas through him if he could, for whatever reason.

"*If* he did," Pace repeated with a smirk. "But who else could it have been? Have the police come up with other suspects?" The candidate did not wait for an answer. "Anyway, Frankie, do you want the job? Pays two thousand a week for fifteen hour days until the election. If I win, we renegotiate your salary upward. If I lose, you're out of a job. You're a convicted felon so you can't carry a gun and I don't want you to. It's part of my right as a Texan to carry my own. All I want you to do is run point for me. You're my first line of protection, just as those other two were. The PJ under my arm is the second."

Travis wondered what the police had determined about the gun that was used at Kristen Wade's house. He'd ask Susan Granger when he saw her and hope it was a Smith and Wesson 4PJ. Right now he had to help Colovas make a decision.

"Take it," Layton nodded. They could sort out the details later.

"Are you nuts? Of course I'll take it!" Frankie smiled at his new employer. "When do I start?"

"Now," Pace replied, pointing to the open door. "First you go shopping for some better clothes with my chauffeur." He opened his wallet and handed Colovas ten crisp fifty dollar bills. "I have six speech stops starting at noon and ending with a fund raiser at Esther's Follies tonight so you've got an hour to meet me at the office. I believe you know where it is."

Travis shook Frankie's good hand and patted him on the back. "I'll call your parole officer and tell her the charges are dropped and you've got a temporary job."

"Temporary?" Pace said.

"Yeah," Layton replied, tipping his Stetson. "Even from an ICU bed, Kristen Wade will win the election."

The grin returned. "Depends," Pace replied, stepping into the car.

As they drove off, Layton finished the sentence for Pace: Depends—on whether she lives or dies.

The First Street Carillon bonged out a tune that could have been a hymn, a hit or the national anthem as Travis walked down Guadalupe Street. He had no ear for music, which is why he liked the Episcopal Church where he considered the hymns irrelevant interruptions to the liturgy. Notes fell on his ears like horseshoes on cobblestones, one clop indistinguishable from the next. Like the events of the last two days, bonging on his ears one after the next. Kristen shot. Lucas hiding. Frankie busted, then hired by his victim. The rumor all over the courthouse that Lieutenant Granger and her boss Commissioner Dillon would be history in a week if Holt wasn't found and charged with Wade's—what? Shooting? Murder?

Where was the tune here? he thought as he turned on Congress toward the welcoming smells of Las Zapatas. Though he couldn't yet hear it, there must be something that logically tied all this up in a song, even if it was a dirge for St. Margaret's. He waved at Rosie behind the counter and took his usual seat. She knew what he'd order. And when the hot black coffee appeared in the chipped ceramic mug in front of him it's sweet steam smelled of Jack Daniel's.

What the hell got into Lucas? he wondered as he raised the thick white mug to his lips. He set his Stetson on the booth seat and shook his head. Damned fool should tend to church business. Baptize babies. Preach about sin. Hold the hands of sick folks in the hospital instead of putting them there. Shit. He liked Holt. Felt for him like a son. Would beat his butt like a father when he found him. If he found him.

"Excuse me, Travis?" a voice in front of him said. Layton looked up to see Case Atkinson holding a newspaper. "I know you come here a lot and hoped I'd find you. Mind if I sit?"

The old attorney did mind, but for once didn't say so. Nothing against Case, but he had planned to eat alone and think. Instead, he nodded and shook the man's hand. Travis hated stereotypes more than most people, but Atkinson's mushy handshake, like squeezing a wet sponge, fit with his thin frame, moustache, short haircut, wire rim glasses, and crisp attire to scream GAY at whomever he met. But Layton's own Stetson, boots, two day beard, belt buckle and tobacco breath screamed OLD DRUNK COWBOY. So what the hell?

"Take a load off your feet, son. A light load." He knew the successful architect from years at St. Margaret's where Case had assisted with renovations and been elected to the Vestry. He was highly respected in Austin, the liberal mecca of the state where it was joked that everyone was either a writer, a singer or a healer.

Case was an artist of sorts; he designed architectural plans so unique that they appeared in international journals. "I just recommended you to someone in Westlake the other day."

Atkinson thanked him and waved off the coffee pot. "I'd like an herbal tea, por favor?"

Layton interrupted. "Son, this here's a Mes'can restaurant. You can get reg'lar tea, coffee or beer."

"I'll have whatever coffee he's having," Case Atkinson told the waitress.

Travis winked at her and she smiled as she poured.

He took a sip of coffee and leaned over the table. "Did you ever think you'd be having lunch with an openly gay person in a Mexican restaurant on Congress Avenue?"

Layton leaned the other half of the way. "Did you ever think you'd be having lunch with an old drunk redneck attorney in a Mexican restaurant on Congress Avenue?" he responded. "Hell, son, that's why we're Episcopalians, at least Maggie Mae's brand. One church, one cup, one liturgy, and all kinds of screwed up individuals at the communion rail next to each other." He patted Atkinson's hand. "Just don't kiss me on the lips, son, or I'll have to kill ya."

Case laughed. "You're not my type, Travis."

"Thank God for small favors," Layton said as the sizzling cast iron platter of fajitas arrived. "Help yourself, son. I can't never eat 'em all myself." He handed the tortillas across the table. "Now what did you come to see me about? You're not in some kind of legal trouble are you? That adoption going okay?"

"Adoption's going fine, Travis, thanks for asking. And thanks for all your help with it. Lot of people against it, you know, wondering how a gay couple can adopt a Chinese baby; wondering how the kid will get mothered."

"They don't know Max's girls will provide more mothering than you or I ever got from ours." Layton could take both sides of any argument, and even though he thought the arrangement a bit odd from his conservative background, he'd defend Case's legal right to adopt any day. "So what's up? You look bummed."

"Didn't you see today's Austin American-Statesman?"

Layton shook his head and took a bite of the rolled, stuffed tortilla.

Case held up the front page headline: "TAPE SAYS HOLT SHOT STATE SENATOR." "Somehow the security tape from Kristin Wade's house got leaked to the press."

Travis Layton wiped his guacamole stained hands and spread the paper out on the table. The verbatim—set off in a box in the center of the page—portrayed a fight over their relationship as well as political issues, leading up to name calling, pushing and finally, shooting.

"I'm worried about him, Travis. I can't believe he did it. But maybe, I don't know. All those years at Huntsville? Hanging out with ex-cons? That's what people are saying anyway. Even people at church. As the Vestry, we need to do something. Help him out. Prove he's innocent. Or, after this newspaper, get him to turn himself in." Atkinson looked at the table as he ate. "You—don't know where he is, do you?"

Travis sipped the coffee, holding the mug with both hands. With forty years of courtrooms, criminals and cuckolds in his background, he could smell a set up before the buzzards arrived. "Who's askin', Case? You or somebody else?"

Case lowered the tortilla and looked up sheepishly. "Sorry, Travis. I should have known better." He leaned forward. "I'm just embarrassed, is all. I'm caught in something I can't even discuss with you, but I *have* to talk to Lucas about it. It may possibly affect the adoption going through. I'm sorry I misled you. I *am* concerned about him. I want him to be cleared of this. But, dammit, Travis, he's still my priest and he's gotten me through some damned difficult things and I *need* him now."

Layton finished the coffee and put down the mug, watching the man wipe tears away. "I don't know where he is but I think I can get a message to him." Something still didn't add up in his gut, and it wasn't just coffee, Jack, and fajitas. The architect clearly needed to see Lucas, but Layton guessed there was more to it than that. It sounded like Case was being used to find Holt. "What do you want to tell him?"

Atkinson straightened up. "I have to *meet* with him. See him face to face. Tell him—what's happening, and get his advice."

Hunch confirmed, though he'd push a bit further. "There's an interim priest at the church. She's sworn to confidence also. Why not talk to her?"

"No—"

"Or another priest at another church? Or Cora Mae for that matter? You know her pretty well and she's a fount of wisdom for everybody." He looked at Case. "Or Max, for God's sake. She's got stories in her head that would blow the Capitol off its pink granite foundation." He knew Atkinson wouldn't buy any of them. It had to be Lucas or the deal, whatever it was, was off. And it must be a hell of a deal to turn in Holt. Hopefully more than thirty pieces of silver.

"No, Travis! You don't understand! You can't! Only Father Holt can!" He stood from the booth and tossed a five on the table. Layton handed it back.

"Food's on me, son," he said, grasping the spongy hand. "I'll do what I can. But you also have to feel free to come to me no matter what the trouble is. I'm your lawyer, in addition to your friend."

Case smiled and shook his head. "As my lawyer you can set up a meeting with my priest."

Layton watched him leave the restaurant as Rosie brought another cup of his special coffee.

He picked up the paper and looked at the headline. Who had leaked the tape to the press? Besides the police, of course, who had an interest in knowing the whereabouts of Lucas Holt? Reporters could have. Maybe the Feds, if they were even here yet, though he hoped they weren't. They always bungled things so someone got hurt, or killed. What about a Pace supporter? Was there some political leverage in leading the charge against Lucas? Or could Pace's interest somehow involve what happened to Kristen? What about someone on the Vestry or in the congregation?

And how had Case Atkinson become vulnerable to threat? Was it a former partner, or a former life? Maybe Bishop Emilio Casas had used his considerable clout to dig up something to make the architect lead authorities to Holt?

"You want a go-box, Señor Layton?" the waitress asked.

"Por favor," he said absently as he read the Statesman story in detail. A quarter of an hour later he had finished both the paper and the coffee and stood outside listening to the Carillon. Two or three of the bongs were beginning to make sense. When he got to the office his first call would be to Nikky Dorati.

Case Atkinson wasn't the only one who needed to see Lucas Holt.

✳ ✳ ✳

Liberty Lunch was one of Austin's oldest music venues. While other clubs had come and gone, succumbed to fads, bad management, the economy, or the law, The Lunch miraculously maintained its small brick building on First Street with the patio out back. Music ranged from punk to cowboy and tonight's group, The Therapy Sisters, entertained the late crowd with songs of angst and humor. It was just what the customer at the bar needed—the location, not the music—as another beer arrived and the neon clock above the mirrored bottles swung its big hand to nine.

At 10:45 a.m., during a set break, the tab was paid. It was risky being out this late, being seen and noticed as always around town. It was hard to be anonymous, given the circles in which the person regularly moved. Actually, great effort had been spent to be seen at this club, to take the edge off the image, to be positioned with the common people—to be positioned one block from the building now being entered.

It was no trouble getting a key to the city-owned building, given who the person was. People trusted there must be good reason for borrowing it and quickly returning it, after making a duplicate at Sear's.

Walking into the City Council Chambers the beam from the flashlight fell on the seven member dais with the members' nameplates in front of their pecking order chairs. The mayor had the highest backed one, supposedly because she was the tallest. A gorgeous six-two blonde in the Ann Richards mold, the council leader and her pack were often referred to as Snow White and the Six Dwarfs. But tonight they would receive different labels, labels that accurately reflected their spineless stands on issues that were leading this city and this country to moral ruin.

Knowing the building was regularly patrolled by APD, the intruder quickly did the work. Red and yellow paint was sprayed garishly on the curtain behind the chairs, with painted arrows to the nameplate and chair of each designated epithet. The press would have a field day deciphering the meaning of each label, some obvious, some uncovering secrets that would hopefully ruin the council member:

BABY KILLER—she had cast the deciding vote to license a city abortion clinic—and had had one herself in Mexico

WITCH—she led the drive against mandatory prayer in schools

PEDOPHILE—he backed a law protecting porno bookstores under freedom of speech, and had an effeminate look

DEMON WORSHIPPER—as mayor pro tem he had denied a permit for a Christian march on massage parlors

SODOMITE—a flaming fag, he consistently voted for gay rights issues

BEASTIALITY—her proposal protected bats and worms against developers

666—the former drunk liberal mayor symbolized all that was wrong with this City of Sin.

The intruder stood back and admired the work. It was perfect, and it would have the desired effect, especially when the press was notified anonymously before the police arrived.

A cruiser flashed its beam in the front window off First and the person ducked behind a row of seats, waited two minutes, then left the Council Chambers and found the car in the lot of Liberty Lunch. Pulling off one latex glove over a spray can the figure tossed it into the club's dumpster and heard a drunken moan from inside the large metal garbage container. Appropriate, the face grinned in the darkness, and yet another surprise addition to the plans, as if this mission was being truly led, affirmed by higher powers supporting the goal.

The remaining gloved hand appeared over the opening and sprayed until the can was empty, saturating the inside of the dumpster and its coughing inhabitant with a fine mist. A lighter ignited a scrap of paper which was then tossed in.

Driving quickly away, the massive flames in the rear view mirror brought a smile of satisfaction. The well deserved, cleansing fire of Hell. And no amount of water could put it out.

※ ※ ※

Lieutenant Granger screeched her green Blazer to a halt at the perimeter. She had fallen asleep in her chair at home when she was summoned by Commissioner Dillon to join him at the scene. At first she thought she was dreaming, that the ringing phone was the alarm and his voice was Bob Edwards on NPR with the news of the day. It was the news of the day alright, she thought as she stepped carefully around the hoses from the five trucks showering lake water down on buildings and cars. By radio she had learned from cops on the scene that the fire, apparently set in the dumpster behind Liberty Lunch, had spread into the nearby parking lot, filtering sparks on adjacent buildings. Though four cars parked next to it were totalled, there was no damage to The Lunch itself, and the Austin Fire Department was making sure none of the flat roofed structures nearby were next.

By the time she found Dillon one of the trucks was already rolling hoses, packing to leave. He was talking to a t.v. reporter in front of a brightly lit camera. She got close enough to hear over the noise of the pumpers and could have sworn he was answering a question about police having found a charred human skull among the ashes. Then he suddenly just looked at the reporter and left her standing as he walked away.

He spoke to Granger with great control. "Damned liberal press don't want to hear anything about the truth here."

She asked what happened and he pointed to the dumpster.

"This is what happens when things get out of control. It's in reaction to all the damned liberal excesses of this city, and of the country in general."

Susan Granger kept her distance. The dumpster wasn't the only thing on fire here tonight. Clearly, "Marshall" Dillon was on a roll and there was no contradicting him, countering his stone cold deadly anger, injecting a jolt of reason to calm him. It was not a pretty sight.

"Sex, drugs, guns and gangs in school. Kids terrified to go and not to go." His tone was almost a lament. "All parents want is for them to be safe and educated and we can't count on either." He motioned for Granger to follow him, and his voice quavered.

"Look at this." He pointed to the skull. "That's a damned *kid*, for God's sake. Some asshole torched what he thought was a wino in a dumpster and it was a homeless *kid*. Damn it! How does this happen, Lieutenant? How does a kid get homeless?" He looked at her, seeming genuinely puzzled. "Donna and I can't have any kids and here's one nobody wanted got friggin' torched by some right wing idiot reacting to some left wing idiot." Granger stood back as he picked up a bottle and smashed it against a building.

"Dammit to hell, this shit's got to stop somewhere and I'm de-claring it's right *now*."

She knelt and looked at the skull. It was either an adolescent or a very small adult. She would deal with her own emotions later. Right now she was dealing with those of her superior officer, who was decidedly in pain and angry in a way she had never imag-ined, but not out of earshot of the press. She had to get him out of sight, find out what triggered this display.

"How do you know it was a right winger?" she asked, as he turned to see her kneeling.

"How do I *know*?" His eyes widened and he yanked her to her feet. "Come the hell here and I'll show you." He let her go and marched across the street, past yellow crime scene markers, into the now brightly lit Council Chambers. "Look at that shit and tell me what you think their message was. Torching the dumpster was the exclamation mark."

Susan stared at the violent messages sprayed across the coun-cil dais. "First the movie theatre, now this." What would be next? It reminded her of her fear in the years with Lucas at UT when draft boards were bombed, demonstrators beaten, public figures assassinated; painful memories of her Dad taking responsibility for a lapse in security that permitted the Ruby shooting in Dallas. Though she was sure he was set up, she still felt insecure about somehow repeating the mistake that had cost him his reputation on the Dallas Police Department. How had things gotten so out of control again? Would she repeat the past?

"But you know, Lieutenant, sometimes I think you can't en-tirely blame them," Dillon said pensively as they stepped into a room behind the chambers. "Kids in unsafe schools are just the tip of the iceberg. Welfare cheats demanding more money for more illegitimate babies, porno shops pandering to teenagers and damned Hollywood glamorizing drugs, sex and violence." He shook his head and pointed to the Chamber. "It's no wonder people are going nuts and doing shit like this. They must feel like they have to take back this country."

Susan Granger knew this was no time for reason, but she also couldn't be silent. She had as much a right to free speech as he did. Although, she admitted to herself, there was a part of her that agreed with him, or thought she did until she heard it in his suppressed tone of voice. But if she said anything now she would sound like Lucas Holt. She wrote off Dillon's wrath to the shock of finding the remains of a kid in a dumpster—a kid he could never have—and decided to respond more neutrally. "The difficult thing is how to police it and still uphold the constitution and the bill of rights."

"I've got buddies in militias that would like to say to hell with them both!" the Commissioner said almost to himself. "They think we need to suspend them till we get things back together, that we're down to the forces of light and the forces of darkness here. The darkness has won for a long time and we need to see the light get its due finally. Hell, I don't know. Maybe they've got the right idea about how this country is decaying."

Though he sounded more bewildered than vindictive now, Granger looked at him with surprise. Did Governor Doggett know about this side of the man when he appointed him? "Bad idea, Commissioner. Even well meaning people who tried that ended up doing more harm than the ones they were trying to oust."

"That's why there's militias out there, Lieutenant. They took care of these problems in West Texas years ago when I was chief out there. Oh, I had my share of problems with them, but, you know, I have to admit they did some damned good. Porn dealers looked down the barrel of militia guns and left town. And there weren't any abortions there either. Sent them back across the border where they belong. Kept them off the welfare rolls, too. Drug dealers thought twice before coming into militia neighborhoods, because they knew they'd end up in the Rio Grande eatin' rocks."

Susan took careful notes in her head as Dillon seemed suddenly aware that he'd overstepped his bounds, implied things that, had the Governor heard them in an interview or background report, would have kept the police chief in El Paso. But the genie was out of the bottle. While he could argue against both the right and the left, Dillon's sentiments seemed clear. She would be even more careful around him, watch his appointments to leadership posts, and watch her own behavior around the man who she now believed would take the law into his own hands if he had to to prevent the kind of atrocity he had found tonight.

"I'm sorry, Lieutenant. I'm just blowing off steam here. I appreciate you listening and not giving me shit. But this does make me mad—and I guess I'm still trying, after all these years on the job, to figure out exactly where I do stand."

Granger retorted that things weren't all as black and white as the right painted them—or the left for that matter, that those who thought they had a monopoly on the truth were, by definition, erring.

Dillon's smoulder flared. "You sound like that damned Reverend Holt now. Which reminds me, why haven't you found the bastard yet? You must know all his hangouts, considerin'."

Susan held her temper, though she wanted to spray paint his own body, and muttered something about consenting adults.

"I didn't say it was illegal, Lieutenant. I said it was immoral. But then why buy the cow when you can milk her for free? Hell, I never had sex with Donna before I married her, just like God intended it. You know you don't go down to the bakery and eat a piece of cake before you decide to buy it. I bought the cake and turned out I love it. But not Holt. Seems to me he's got a good thing goin' here."

Granger resisted the urge to shoot the man's balls off. "People aren't commodities, cows and cakes, Commissioner. Relationships are different, more complex." She didn't expect him to understand, and he didn't.

"It's those 'complexities', Lieutenant, that drive people to do shit like this." He nodded at the chamber and the dumpster. "What people want are the right answers to how to behave, and they're not that damned hard to figure out." He kicked a chair against the wall. "I want daily updates on what you're doing to find Holt. And I want the other part of your full attention on finding the nut who's sending us smoke signals. I get the feeling he's building up to something bigger than this and we'd better find out what it is before he surprises the hell out of us." He led the way out of the room. "I got to go get some coffee and face a press conference at nine this morning. After a call to Governor Doggett. So get on it, Lieutenant. Sleep isn't in either of our job descriptions until we catch the two anarchists—Holt and this guy."

Susan Granger watched his car drive off as medics put the body remains in a short zipper bag to haul to the morgue. The last fire truck left. One blue and white cruiser still sat in the middle of the street, its occupants securing the crime scene for the night, setting up cones to block traffic until morning when the whole crew would cover the place with a microscope. Austin City Council should hold its session somewhere else tomorrow, but they probably wouldn't. They would see the epithets as commendations. And it would make for great election press.

The Lieutenant recognized Officer Campbell and went to him. "You battin' clean up tonight?" she said.

"Yeah. No problem. It's almost midnight. Somebody should ask that kid's parents if they know where their children are?"

Granger agreed. "By the way," she asked, "who called in the fire to 911?"

"Didn't get called to 911, Lieutenant," Campbell said. "The Commissioner called it in on the radio himself. Said to send all available cars to Liberty Lunch. I guess he was in the area."

Susan Granger smirked. At eleven p.m.? she thought. When he should be home in bed with Blonde Donna Barbie in their pink

Barbie bedroom? Why the hell would he have just happened to be in the area? She turned to leave, then stopped. "You remember who called in the theatre explosion?"

Campbell thought a second and laughed. "That was the Commissioner too. He was down at Green Pastures at the Pace reception and heard the noise. Hell of a sense of timing, huh?"

"Right." Susan Granger thanked him and walked slowly to her car. At times like this, when too much had happened, too much was at stake, and she was feeling overwhelmed with events and possibilities, being alone was more than she could take.

She started the engine and sat for a second, waiting for the heater to warm and comfort her. But it was not enough. She would find Lucas Holt tonight.

• Five •

The system of lights they had set up worked off batteries and motion sensors that turned the spots on for one minute intervals. Holt triggered them as he rode the small electric cart through the carved limestone tunnel running north/south beneath Rio Grande and San Antonio Streets. The fifteen foot width provided plenty of room to maneuver the cart, even turn it around. And the height of nearly twenty feet had accommodated the small truck they had needed to bring in their equipment. The hundred year old walls were amazingly dry and critter free, though he had seen enough snakes and scorpions to shake out his sleeping bag every night and check his boots before stepping into them each morning.

It had taken them three weeks working at full tilt to ready the tunnels, set the lights, stock the food and living area, and establish the security that would lead to the Rev's disappearance after the "shooting" of Kristen Wade. Later tonight they would meet to take the next steps, he thought as he turned the corner under Sixth, but first he would make an appearance at Esther's Pool.

He stopped the cart and pulled the bricks out of the sub basement wall deep below the building housing Austin's best known comedy venue. Esther's Follies started off in a storefront, moved to an old theatre and now, with a sizeable arts grant from St. Margaret's, had their very own "Esther's Pool" on the corner of Sixth and Trinity. The Follies made fun of everyone and everything but specialized in local politics and businesses, with skits, magic shows, bawdy cabaret songs and raucous monologues. Lucas knew they would skewer him, Kristin Wade and Ryan Pace at tonight's regular shows at seven and nine, but especially at this later midnight show—a fund raiser for the Pace campaign.

He placed a piece of plywood over the hole and used a flashlight to find his way to the door and up the stairwell to the back stage entrance. As he walked in, the strawberry blonde owner looked at her watch.

"On time to the minute, Rev," she said, kissing him hard on the lips. "God, that was good. Can I have another one?"

"Life is short, darlin'," Holt replied. "Go for it."

She did, then wiped the greasy red smudge from his face. Lucas liked the sixtysomething Madelyn Martin, a former stripper who saved her money to put her kid through college and had enough left over to put together her troupe.

"We're just about ready for you. Chi Chi LaBomba is out there bouncing her melons and interviewing Ryan Pace."

"I can't believe his straight laced campaign would ask you to do a fundraiser."

The thickly made-up woman frowned. "They sort of tricked us, actually. Called up our booking agent and said the event was for a conservative group and could we tone it down for them? We do that all the time for kids parties so it was no problem. When I found out it was Ryan Pace I told them to change all the jokes back and insult everything they stand for, like why religious righters don't make love standing up—"

"They're afraid God will think they're dancing?"

Madelyn Martin smiled and winked. "And that's just the tip of the boobie, Boobie. By the time we're finished they'll either be so shell-shocked and offended that they'll all walk out—or they will have learned that the main reason they're doomed to fail is precisely because they have *no* sense of humor about themselves." She took his hand and led him to the stage wing. "Hell, I even agree with some of their stands on things in my old age, but their candidate gives new meaning to your phrase 'terminal seriosity.' I just can't be apolitical around him."

Holt watched from the shadows as Chi Chi LaBomba, barely restrained in a skin tight red dress, spoke with a slinky Spanish accent and rubbed up against a rigid Ryan Pace like a cat against a post.

"I am Chi Chi LaBomba and *theeeeese* are my *breassssts*."

Pace must be dying out there, Holt thought, briefly feeling sorry for the man. But his political agenda was a little to the right of Attila the Hun and the tactics of his organization, though he disavowed any knowledge of them and called them actions of the "fringe," had escalated over the last six months. What started out as an exceptional organizational effort to coordinate all the religious right groups across the state of Texas became a top heavy machine intent on controlling school boards, city councils and now congressional and senate elections.

"I hope your fire insurance is paid up, Mady," Holt whispered. "You know what's been happening to people who piss them off."

"Got a great sprinkler and besides, we could use a new building. I hope he does torch it." She grinned and the red lipstick seemed to cover her entire face. "I just hope I catch him doing it. These things on my chest aren't my only concealed weapons."

Holt wondered if she knew the real risk she was taking. As the right felt their numbers swell and their confidence grow, Lucas—and Susan—had become concerned about the increasing acts of what could only be called terrorism. Cars with liberal cause bumper stickers were spray painted or vandalized with sugar in the gas tank and broken windows. Gay bars and gathering areas were damaged with smoke bombs. An abortion clinic doctor was wounded in a drive-by shooting. Any time Kristen spoke out against these offenses she was accused of being the anti-family values candidate. Now with the movie theatre explosion rumblings of even greater disruption and violence might be in the offing—like the one that had sent Holt underground. In the meantime, Chi Chi LaBomba would nibble the candidate's ear to the uneasy giggles of his supporters in the audience.

"I told her to grab his crotch if she thought she could get away with it, but I can see from here she's pushing the bit as it is." Madelyn Martin pulled Lucas behind a curtain. "You're up next, honey. If you get into trouble I'll bail you out." She kissed him one more time and shuddered. "Thanks for the rush. Now here's what you do."

Two minutes later Lucas Holt heard Chi Chi end her act as the whole room went dark. The Amazing Krisman was announced and a man in a florescent black suit and top hat strutted onto the stage and made his cane magically float through the air. Holt made his move as a large sarcophagus-like box was wheeled out onto the stage and the lights came up.

The magician stood the box on end, opened the door, and turned it all around so the audience could see it was empty. He motioned for the house lights to go off as he lowered a flimsy white cloth screen around the dimly lit box and tapped on it several times with his cane. The piano changed to a hymn the audience would recognize immediately as "Up From the Grave He Rose." It increased in crescendo as the screen slowly lifted. Holt's heart pounded as he waited for the magician to open the door. He hoped the well placed bouncers in front of the stage could hold their ground, and that the defenders of the right to bear arms weren't bearing any tonight.

Suddenly the door was pulled open and Lucas Holt stepped out to the communal gasp of the audience. At first their incredulity led them to believe it was an actor and not the real thing.

"I want to thank you for inviting me here this evening to personally tell you that I did *not* shoot Kristen Wade." Holt looked at the candidate in the front row. "But you already know that, don't you, Mr. Pace?"

"Get him!" Pace yelled to the man beside him, who Lucas saw was Frankie Colovas. But "Doors" didn't move. When he did, halfheartedly, one of the stage goons held him back.

Reporters' cameras rolled and people rushed the stage but the bouncers held the line as Holt re-entered the box. The music came up and Holt heard The Amazing Krisman beat the hell out of the box with his wand. Thirty seconds later, Lucas was in the sub-basement putting the bricks back in place, blocking the hole to the tunnel as sirens blared above.

He rode the cart through the series of floodlights, wondering what the headline would be tomorrow. His appearance had served several functions. It had shown he could appear and disappear at will, further frustrating APD and making them redouble their efforts. Hopefully their searching for him would keep the enemy, whoever it was, on their toes as well. Secondly, his words had cast a nasty Kristen Wade stain on the teflon reputation of Ryan Pace late in the campaign. What did he really know about her shooting? Why did Lucas Holt disavow the event and cast suspicion on Pace? If there was gunsmoke, shouldn't there be a fire around here somewhere? Pace would have to answer the media questions carefully. If he looked at all like he was equivocating, the fickle voting citizens of Texas would assume the worst and that could only help Kristen in the polls. He just hoped Pace wasn't too hard on Frankie Colovas for not jumping him.

Lucas parked the cart a hundred yards from the underground entrance to Esther's, directly beneath the Buffalo Barn Grille. He climbed the steep stairs up to the street and zipped up his jacket against the midnight cold. Donning a gimme cap and sunglasses, he cautiously looked out the Buffalo's side door on Red River, where a black Beemer waited with the engine running.

"God, it's good to be above ground," Holt said when he got in the back seat. "I feel like a damned mole down there."

"With those glasses you look like one," Nikky Dorati replied, shaking his hand.

"Maybe you need a can of pencils and a cane," said the driver, "so you can compete with the crazy flower salesman out there."

"Thanks, Brickhouse," the Rev said, slapping him on the shoulder. "Nice to see you, too. You know where we're going, right?"

Jimmy Brickhouse nodded. "I'm droppin' y'all at Mother's after we make a pickup off of Far West."

"Let's do it," Holt said, settling into the back seat. "And try not to flag down any cops along the way."

At nearly two a.m. Lucas Holt watched Brickhouse drive Dorati's Beemer to the darkly wooded dead end of Forty-third street and park under a huge live oak tree. Having discharged his three passengers, Brick was either to wait for a call from inside Mother's restaurant or, if he saw trouble, to come to their rescue. Two large styrofoam cups of high test coffee were to keep him awake, assuming he drank them.

Charles had left the key in its usual place under the plant pot next to the outside cooler, and, once inside, Holt told Nikky and Cora Mae to get what they wanted and meet him in the more secluded garden room at the back. He waited a minute by the door to make sure they hadn't been followed, then joined the other two at a rear table under an art deco fixture with a dim light.

"Shiner Bock three ways, Rev," Dorati said, opening the squatty bottles of beer.

"And two baskets of chips and salsa, Lucas dear," Cora Mae said with a little shiver. "I'm just glad to see you're holding up so well."

Holt switched on the heating fixture above them. March in Austin meant night temps in the thirties and, even in enclosed areas like this one, glow heaters helped. "Thanks for coming out this late, Cora Mae. Nikky just gets rolling at this hour but for the rest of us, our bodies are wondering why we're not in z-land." He patted her hand. "But I wanted you in on this. We have to have someone inside St. Margaret's and neither Max nor Travis can afford the heat. Max stands to blow her parole if she does anything illegal, and we need Travis Layton to have plausible deniability in case he has to defend us if the whole thing goes south."

"'Illegal'?" Cora Mae repeated.

"Well not exactly. It's sort of—".

"Shhhhh." Dorati lowered his voice. "Did you hear that? It sounded like the click of a car door."

Lucas tossed him the cell phone. "Ten bucks says Brickhouse is napping."

The phone rang five times before being answered by a sleepy voice.

Dorati whispered: "Remind me to kill you if we make it out of here."

"What?"

"Do you see anybody snooping around the building?"

"Wait a minute," Brickhouse replied. Dorati could hear the sound of a coffee lid opening. "Oh shit. Two at the back door. Damn. One's got a gun. I'm sorry, man. Want me to play cavalry?"

"Not yet."

"But Nikky—"

"What?"

"Even in the shadows I can see their car."

"So?"

"So," Brickhouse whispered. "It's APD."

Dorati repeated 'APD' to the other two at the table, and Lucas took the phone.

"Brickhouse? Wake the hell up and listen carefully." If this bust happened they were all going down for a long time.

"I'm awake. I'm awake."

"I'm leaving the phone on so you'll know when to be John Wayne."

"Wesley Snipes, man."

Holt groaned and put the phone on the wooden railroad tie behind him.

"You packin', Rev?" Dorati asked.

Lucas nodded as Cora Mae clanked her purse on the table. "Me too," she said, pulling out a small pistol. "I didn't want to feel left out."

"I haven't seen a Colt .25 since I was a kid," Dorati smirked. "You know how to shoot that thing?"

Cora Mae flipped open the cylinder, spun it and jerked it closed.

"Right," Nikky shook his head. "Hold it in your lap, under the table, like ours." He added, "Aimed at the door."

They heard the back door open and close, footsteps slowly walk across the front of the restaurant, then stop before entering the garden.

Nikky spoke out loud. "Somebody needs to teach you how to close a car door, Lieutenant."

"You couldn't have heard that, Dorati." Susan Granger's voice sounded from around the corner.

"Like an earthquake."

"Put your guns away. I'm coming in."

Three hammers clicked shut before Susan Granger slowly turned the corner into the garden area.

"Where's your partner?" Holt asked, looking behind her.

"I'm right here." Kristen Wade, in jeans and a baggy sweatshirt, followed Susan to the table. "Had to stop at the cooler for two more beers." She kissed Lucas on the lips and sat beside him.

Dorati spoke into the cell phone. "You awake now? I'll call in an hour for you to come to the back door. Wait till the blue and white's gone, though. And stay awake, man." He looked at Holt. "We don't want a repeat of Jesus in the Garden." He clicked it off.

"Are you all right, Cora Mae?" Lucas said to the woman staring at the Senate candidate. "You can close your mouth now."

"Oh, dear me, Lucas. I'm sorry." She took a long drink of Shiner. "Obviously I'm odd person out here. The last I heard you were at death's door, Kristen; and you, Susan, were on an all out manhunt for Lucas for shooting her and would lose your job if you didn't catch him. But we all seem to be sitting here drinking beer and eating chips like Peaceable Kingdom." She looked at her watch. "Either I'm dreaming or Jesus returned when I wasn't looking."

Lucas laughed. "None of the above. But we do need to bring you up to speed." He poured more beer into the small glass and drank it. "I'll start." He leaned over the table and began with what she already knew.

He reminded her that, in the last year, the religious right had become virulent in Texas, more specifically in Austin, even at St. Margaret's. In response, his sermons had become equally more confrontive, condemning the self righteousness, the unwillingness to compromise, the unabating insidiousness of their positions against people who were in any way "different" from them: the poor, the homeless, the pregnant, gays, people they considered "liberals" politically, socially, or theologically.

"And you know that they support the embodiment of those views, Ryan Pace. But what you don't know about are these," Holt said, handing her two pieces of paper. "They're samples of what I've gotten over the last year. Weekly in the last six months."

Cora Mae glanced over the pages. "My God, Lucas! These are death threats."

"So are these," Kristen said, pulling from her pocket two letters with her own name and address cut and pasted on them.

"And these," Susan added more pages, "are threats against an unnamed public target to be assassinated the week of the special election."

"The Rev's had two attempts on his life that the God Squad narrowly stopped," Dorati said.

"I only knew about one," Granger glared at him.

"Well there were two. The other guy got nasty."

"What'd you do with him, Dorati?"

"He went back where he came from," Nikky glanced at Holt for help.

Granger pushed. "Do you mean like to Mexico or to dust?"

"I mean he won't bother Kristen or the Rev again."

Lucas tried to divert. "The second attempt was actually the worse of the two. And, just for the record, Susan, Nikky didn't snuff him. He just made sure the guy won't hurt anybody again. Ever." Partly because he'd spend the rest of his life begging on a skateboard. It was a harsh punishment, but as they said at the prison, 'Payback's a bitch.'

"We would have caught the perps if you had let us in on it," Susan said with an edge in her voice.

"Bull-shit, Lieutenant," Dorati slapped back. The Rev would be *dead* if we let you in on it."

"Water over the dam, guys," Holt held out his arms to separate them. There wasn't much time and arguing only wasted it. They had to pool information to plan the next move.

"After that last close call," Kristen continued, "Lucas, Nikky and I decided it was better if Lucas and I were out of sight for a while."

"I get it," Cora Mae said. "It would protect you both from harm and give you the time and the cover to find the people making the threats." She looked at Susan. "And you went along with this?"

"Not willingly, Cora Mae." She glared at Holt. "They know I think the whole thing sucks big time, that I could give them both police protection until the election is over. In fact, I knew nothing until the day before it was planned to happen and then dragged kicking and screaming into it."

Lucas drank his Shiner and described for Cora Mae the conversation with her. It had been more like a shouting match. She complained that it was unnecessary, risky, that she could lose her job and Kristen her credibility. They were going on the assumption that Ryan Pace—or his organization—was behind the threats.

"That seems obvious, dear, but, to echo Susan's point of view—what evidence did you have?"

Holt explained that Pace, in his wilder and woolier days before being born again, was rumored to have occasional contacts with extremists looking for money for their causes, in exchange for supplying him with drugs and women. If he had kept his little black book right next to his newly acquired Bible, he could easily arrange for accidents or even hits.

"I finally had to agree that we were in territory over my head—but so were they," Susan said. "And as much as I hate it, and will *never* do this again, I decided to go along with the program so I'd at least know what the hell they were up to."

"And, admit it, Susan," Holt replied, remembering what it had taken to convince her, "together we can do things that neither of us could get away with alone."

"We haven't gotten away with it yet, Lucas." Granger sat back in her chair and Holt could see the questioning look in her face; questioning her involvement in this operation, and questioning what he was feeling about the obviously amorous Kristen seated next to him. "And quite frankly I'm less interested in your hides than in finding out who the target of the assassination is."

"Dead Ed," Nikky said to Cora Mae, pouring her glass. "That's our other evidence on Pace. We just wanted Doors to plant a couple of bugs in their campaign office but he overheard them using the code name 'Dead Ed' like it was some big hit about to happen—and he saw something like elevation maps of Austin."

Lucas glanced at Susan, knowing they were both thinking of the Grassy Knoll. Who would be the target this time? And would they get away?

"But I still don't get *why*, and why *now*?" Cora Mae's voice was puzzled.

"Part of the why is to flaunt their power in my face," Susan said. "These groups aren't afraid of the police. We assume they're connecting, however tentatively, with the state militia groups you've heard about, which could be a terrifying alliance. So we've got the FBI watching over the few politicians in town since the Legislature isn't in session this year, and APD undercover is watching people like the Governor, City Council, the Mayor, corporate leaders and names like Liz Carpenter, Ladybird, Willie, Michener, Bobby Ray, Kate Cronkite, and Michael Dell. They've all beefed up their personal security as well as put extra guards on their buildings."

"But it's more than flaunting power, Cora Mae," Holt said. "A major assassination would doubly prove their point. They'd argue that it was more evidence of society being out of control, blame the laxness of liberals against crime and criminals and un-leash a backlash of conservative votes for Pace and his legisla-tion. That's what they hope to accomplish with all the things they've done leading up to the theatre bombing."

"Even if the right is *responsible* for the assassination?" Cora Mae said. "I'd think that would push people in the opposite direction."

"That's 'cause you're you, Cora Mae," Holt responded.

"I reluctantly have to agree with Lucas," Granger added. "Whether the left, right, middle, or end commits a major crime doesn't really matter. What matters is *that* it was allowed—repeat that word—*allowed* to occur in our society. So people react with fear, constrictions to freedom, controls, and a desire to prevent change of any kind."

"That's why we have to short circuit this," Kristen said. "Of course I want to win the election, too. But that's got to be a by-product of smoking out the assassin—which I hope is Ryan Pace." She took a drink of beer. "Because if it's not, we don't have a clue."

"There have been some other developments." Susan filled them in on the City Council defacement and the kid in the dumpster.

Lucas looked at her and sighed deeply. It was one thing to mess with adults, but a homeless kid, mistake or not, crossed the line for both of them. "We need to find this mofo, Nikky," he said, nudging Dorati's elbow.

"We will, Rev."

Holt directed Cora Mae to have the church offer a reward and plan a memorial service for the anonymous child. If Rhondalynn Doss didn't like it, the lay readers could do it themselves.

The Lieutenant also recounted in detail the reaction of Commissioner Christopher Dillon—and the fact that he had called in both incidents.

"That's incredible," Lucas Holt said. "About the Commissioner, I mean. Maybe he should be on our hit parade."

"No pun intended, of course," Dorati said, crunching a chip. "Looks like they're working their way up from porno movies and hookers to City Council members," Dorati observed.

"Not a major leap up in the evolutionary scale," Kristen added, wondering why anyone thought it was *up*?

Lucas agreed and turned to Cora Mae. "Can you see that, depending on the target, killing a famous person engenders outrage that ultimately supports their cause—and reinforces individual fear as well. If it can happen to someone famous—it can happen to anyone."

"Even you," Cora Mae said, taking his hand.

Holt winked at her. "I love you, too."

"Timing is everything here," Kristen said. "The attack has to be in the next two days to propel Pace and his ideology into the Senate."

Lucas checked time. The longer they were together the more dangerous it was for them all. Cora Mae was up to speed, though it would take a day for the emotional implications of everything to sink in. They had to press on. "Okay, what have we got now?"

"Just a minute, Lucas, dear," Cora Mae stopped him and addressed Susan Granger. "I know I'm a little dense, but it just occurred to me that Commissioner Dillon must not be at all aware of this?" She motioned around the table. "Of what we're all doing and why?"

"Hell, *I* didn't know about it till two days ago, Cora Mae," Granger defended. "All he knows about is the assassination threat," she said, "because I've shown him the letters. When Lucas dragged me into this I had to think about whether I could trust Dillon with the information. Given his behavior tonight, it's a damned good thing I kept my mouth shut."

Cora Mae asked about the God Squad.

Dorati put down his beer glass. "'Chaplain' Omar Kandu knows of course, and Brickhouse does now. Then to protect Max from knowing, we had to go through Jill at the Buffalo to get two of her friends from a local parlor to pose as 'special' nurses for Kristen from the time LifeFlight picked her up."

Holt didn't tell them that the doctor who admitted Kristen agreed to go along with the program, including the helicopter ride and all the phony charting, when voluptuous Jill agreed not to call his wife and ask her about the tatoo on his butt.

"The one nurse scared the shit out of me last night when Susan and the Commissioner walked in and I hid in the bathroom," Lucas confessed. "Why'd she tell where I was?"

"To make it obvious you *weren't*, of course," Susan said.

"That's a lot of people," Cora Mae said, "don't you think?"

Lucas knew she was right, but explained it was for a short time—and getting shorter. They only had three days till the election and something would happen before then. They had to find out what it was.

"We're watching for any influx of weapons or explosives," Susan said.

"Us too," Dorati added, glancing at her. "So far nothing has come near the city. And no visiting firemen either."

"That means no hit-persons," Lucas explained to Cora Mae.

Cora Mae said she'd been around Nicholas long enough to *know* what he meant.

Holt smiled at her and listened to Nikky tell him about the phone call from Travis insisting on a meeting and conveying the urgent request from Case Atkinson. It was hard to listen with Kristen's hand rubbing his thigh under the table. Even though her wounds were bogus, this whole hospital thing had stirred up his feelings for her again.

Though they had come to a mutual agreement to split a year ago, they had seen each other periodically to check in when she wasn't in legislative session or running to keep her seat in the Texas House—which was almost never. The check-in's were over breakfast or dinner, catching up with each other's lives while he spent more time—including the occasional overnight—with Susan Granger. When the threats began a year ago, the three spent more time together as the current scheme took shape. In that time, Lucas started to remember what he missed about Kristen, legislature or no legislature. Her willingness to take risks, her playfulness and lightness contrasted intensely with the more staid, rigid conservatism—physically and emotionally—of Susan, who would never be grabbing his leg under the table like this. Maybe the cracks in the relationship recently were more than the stresses of what they were doing. Maybe they were signs of a need for distance for them both.

"So what do I tell Travis?" Lucas heard Dorati say.

Holt took a second to return. "Tell him no," he finally answered. "He's better for us on the outside, ignorant of all this." Lucas nodded at Cora Mae. "You and I will set up something with Case. He's right. I'm still his priest."

"You got anything on what Frankie Colovas heard in that closet, Lieutenant?" Dorati asked, passing her the chips.

"Nada," Granger answered. "You?"

"Double nada," Dorati said. "Does the phrase 'Dead Ed' mean

anything to you, Cora Mae?"

"I've been thinking about that since you first said it. You know in Austin it could mean lots of things." The old woman paused a second. "Deep Eddy swimming pool? The Deep Eddy section of the Colorado? Slaughtering a talking horse at the Elgin Racetrack? A politician or famous person in Austin named Ed? A British person describing a follower of the Grateful Dead?"

"This woman belongs on Jeopardy," Kristen said, moving her hand back to the table.

Susan replied that they'd keep working on it. "It's the best lead we've got."

"It's the *only* lead we've got," Lucas said, "and we have to find out what the hell it means. It may be the key to the assassination."

Kristen said, "In the meantime, Susan, who else do we check? You said the BCI report on Ryan Pace told us he was a saint after age thirty when he cleaned up his act."

Holt finished the beer. "Why don't you see if there's anything to the busts in his wilder days." He stopped. There was a better way to do this without calling attention to herself or to Pace, especially if she was right and he did have supporters in the APD Headquarters, other than the Commissioner, of course. "No, listen. If I can get Brickhouse into the building, can you get him access to the police computer or show me where the lines are in the basement?"

"They're in a locked room in the sub-basement," Susan said.

"Great. We'll do that. Pace might have been able to whitewash his BCI files, but if Brickhouse can do his magic maybe we can fly by Internet to forgotten police records in Pace's hometown of Humble, Texas."

"But how will you get into the police station with everyone looking for you?" Cora Mae asked. "There's something you left out."

Nikky answered. "He left out the part where we busted our humps connecting that old tunnel system with access points around town. He can get into St. Margaret's, the Buffalo, and several businesses downtown from Sixth to Rio Grande. He can even get into the University of Texas Ransom Art Center, which gives him access to the entire system of phone tunnels under UT."

"Don't get any ideas, Dorati," Susan said. "Art theft carries enough time to make you an old man."

Dorati shook his head.

"Why hasn't anyone gotten into them before this?" Cora Mae asked. "I remember as a young kid playing in them. But our parents told us they were dangerous. They could flood any time there was a major storm with two to three inches of rain. Runoff would be diverted into the tunnels and could actually fill them and drown us."

"That's still true," Holt said. "Though so much has been done in flood control for the various creeks around town since then that the tunnels are hardly ever used. They've mostly been forgotten relics of Austin's past, though there seems to be a new colony of Mexican fruit bats who have discovered them."

"They're moving uptown from the Congress Avenue Bridge," Granger said. "But you're right, Cora Mae. The tunnels still could be dangerous if we get a really bad downpour."

They jumped as the cell phone rang. Dorati answered and hung up. "Brick said to bring him a beer when we leave."

Lucas wondered what they hadn't covered, and was glad both of Kristen's hands were back on the table so he could think. "What else?"

Granger spoke. "I wouldn't have given this much thought until tonight, and maybe it's my own jealousy, but I think old 'Matt' Dillon went a little over the top in telling the Governor we'd both quit if I didn't capture you."

"Meaning what?" Cora Mae asked.

Lucas answered. "Meaning she thinks he may be trying too hard to look like he wants the case solved. Of course, it could also be because he's new and he really *is* committed to it." But

Holt knew it was a win-win for Dillon either way. If he apprehended Holt, as well as the perpetrators of the theatre and dumpster debacles he'd look good as a cop. He might even imply Holt had something to do with the other crimes. But if they eluded him further, he could rattle his .45 in front of the media about looking for them while secretly pleased about the actions. He turned to Dorati. "Call Valdez when we leave and tell him Cora Mae's sending him to a church Sexton conference in El Paso for the day and to get his butt to the airport by six this morning. Let's see if Dillon's on the Who's Who of that city."

"While we're all being crazy here—" Cora Mae began.

"Go ahead, Cora," Kristen urged. "You're no nuttier than the rest of us." Lucas felt her hand return with a squeeze.

"I hate to be paranoid about this, but that interim priest Bishop Casas inflicted on us from the seminary seems to be Pace's clone. I can't help wondering if she's there to help—or to snoop."

"You up for a trip home, Nikky?" Holt said, knowing Nikky hadn't been back to New York for years. The 'Mafia Midget' had a reputation that had followed him to his work in Texas, until a Ranger thought Huntsville would make a better residence for a couple of decades. "Think you could find some like-minded citizens in, where was it, Cora Mae?"

"Scarsdale."

"Scarsdale?" Holt poured some of Kristen's beer into his glass and smiled at her. "And while you're up there—"

"I'm way ahead of you, Rev. Already thought of him."

"What are you two talking about?" Kristen asked.

"The Very Reverend J. Everett Bergen," Holt responded. "Dean of the seminary and avowed liberal with a reputation of thirty years and every left wing award known to man on his wall - which might cover more than the wallpaper, don't you think?"

"We have absolutely no reason to suspect the man, Lucas!" Susan Granger protested.

"I know it." Holt backed off. "I was just getting crazy with Cora Mae here. Forget it, Nikky. I just thought that, since he was there he might find something interesting."

"You can go fishing, Lucas, but I ran BCI on him when he first hit town—standard procedure for me since I like to know who's running the streets of Austin—and he's the genuine article. A liberal who really is one."

"I'll bet even old Rhondalynn looks good on paper, though," Kristen reminded them.

"Somewhere in here there's a liar and a fanatic," Holt said. "And we've got to find the right one before Saturday."

"The *right* one," Kristen repeated. "Good." She removed her hand and kissed him on the cheek. "Later."

Lucas kissed her in return. "You okay for a few more days in Intensive Care?"

"Long as Omar's there I feel fine. And Marion is a hoot even if she won't help me kill that bottle of Scotch in the bedside table. Other than stir crazy, I'll do okay. Come visit if you can."

There was no doubt in his mind what she was suggesting and right now, after days and nights under Austin it sounded pretty good to him too. Still, he remembered their arguments over time and commitment. Her career was always first. Being Senator from Texas was more important than being together. The only reason he could get to her was because she was trapped in that ICU room, away from a phone.

"Night, Susan," he pecked her cheek and squeezed her hand. He would have to get his feelings about her straightened out once again. Things had seemed clear with Kristen out of the picture, but now he wasn't so sure. He felt bad about receiving, and returning, Kristen's affection in front of her, knowing it hurt her feelings. He tried to be reassuring, but wasn't sure if he was reassuring Susan or himself. "Talk to you later."

She answered unenthusiastically, as Holt instructed her and Kristen to leave first, then called Brickhouse to drive up five minutes after the APD cruiser was gone. They agreed to meet in forty eight hours at the tunnel.

When Holt and Dorati dropped Cora Mae off at her condominium, Lucas offered to walk her inside.

"That's not necessary, Lucas, dear." She patted her purse. "My little Colt and I will do fine." She nodded and turned away, then came back to the car. "It seems to me we've got a lot of possibles but no probables, Lucas. To tell you the truth, I can't see any of those people serious enough to want to assassinate someone, can you?"

Dorati leaned over the back seat. "You think I'm a nice guy, Cora Mae?"

"Of course I do, Nicholas."

"I rest my case."

The old woman ignored him. "But what if we've left someone out, overlooked someone less obvious who is the really evil person behind all the threats and violence?"

Holt got out of the car and hugged her. "Then we have to hope that God—or the God Squad—leads us to them in spite of ourselves." He pulled back from her. "But who else could it be?"

The question stayed with him as he watched her enter the condo and flash the porch light. Who indeed? he wondered as Brickhouse drove him back to the entrance underground.

✳ ✳ ✳

Maxine Blackwell was pissed. She sulked at her desk outside Lucas Holt's office while the Wicked Witch of the West occupied his chair inside, with the door thankfully closed. Her Holy Hineyness—or was it Her Hiney Holiness—Rhondalynn Doss had managed to rub her the wrong way three times already this morning and it was only nine o'clock. The bitch obviously didn't know who she was messing with. One more time and she was going down.

First Rhude Rhon made a comment about Ricardo Valdez not being around to make coffee and clean up the beer cans from the parking lot. Like it was beneath her starched white little collar to make a pot of coffee or pick up trash. Hell, being from *Scahs*dale, *dahl*ing, she probably thought coffee came hot in silver pots and didn't know how to make it. So Max made it.

Then there was the smiling crack about 'that sweet little old lady' sending Valdez off to El Paso at the last minute, spending church money on somebody they should be watching day and night anyway, given his record and the fact that he was 'a Mexican, you know.' No, bitch, it had escaped my attention, like my red *hair* probably escaped yours, Max thought to herself.

The third strike was rearranging the Sunday service coming up. She commented that the Rev's 'sense of proper liturgy was right down there in the sewer with his choice of friends to hang out with.' So she had picked hymns that were unsingable even by Episcopal standards and inserted them into a piously proper but practically convoluted service that would bring new meaning to "holy mysteries." Actually that was no problem. Max would run off enough copies of that service to convince Rhotten Rhon that her wishes were obeyed. Then she would run off another complete service with hymns she had checked with choir director Burt Lister, and make sure everyone else got that one. The Rev always said there was value in being passive aggressive. It kept Max from decking her.

She had felt like she was back in prison, unable to make a move without getting in trouble, until Cora Mae Hartwig—the 'little old lady'—showed up this morning to reassure her that Rhon couldn't fire either her or Valdez without the approval of herself or Travis Layton. That was when she got the idea to mess with the program.

Cora Mae had been in the office with Rhon with the door closed for nearly half an hour now and Max had intermittently turned on the intercom to make sure Cora Mae was okay. Not that she couldn't take care of herself, really. It was just that Max was looking for an excuse to put Communion-Breath in her place.

Normally the intercom light would come on when she pushed the button, but the first time she sensed trouble from the woman, Max had removed the bulbs from both phone sets. She had to be careful though. If her phone rang they would hear it on the speaker and know what was going on. So Max punched it on and off in quick snippets, just enough to know Cora Mae was fine.

Where the hell was Lucas Holt anyway? And why hadn't he contacted her? She was his private secretary and confidante at the pen and she was worried about him. And why had Jill down at the Buffalo been so busy lately? Something reeked in addition to Rhondalynn's attitude, and Max would press Cora Mae as soon as she emerged from the office, preferably with Doss' scalp on her belt. She was part *Indian*, you know.

Max printed several copies of the Rhotten Rhon version of the service, placed them neatly in her box and saved the other one on floppy to take to the printer later. She had just dropped the disk in her purse when the door to the office opened and Cora Mae emerged. Unfortunately Rhon's coiffure was still atop her pointy head.

"I'm glad we had this little talk, Rhondalynn," Cora Mae said, winking at Max. "There's always a little transition period of getting used to each other."

"Hopefully it'll only be for a few months," Doss said, glaring at Max. "Assuming things work out the way you want them to with your friend, Father Holt."

Keep that shit up and it'll be a few *hours*, Max thought, smiling. She heard the back door open and turned to see J. Everett Bergen walk down the hall. That bald head of his made her smile as she greeted him, and she hoped he could talk some sense into this chick. Where was Travis Layton when you needed his bottle under the front seat of that old pick up truck?

"Nice to see you, Father Bergen," Cora Mae said in her sweetest tone.

Max wanted to know what the old woman really thought of him. Cora Mae was sharp. Not much got past her. Especially the part where Bergen smooched Tight Ass Dossie right on her ruby reds. Max wondered if he'd put those babies on other parts of her anatomy as well. As they talked briefly, he also touched her hand, her arm, her shoulder. He was either checking our her tenderness for barbecue or he was touching familiar territory. On the other hand, so to speak, Bergen was a touchy feely person. He had hugged and glommed on Cora Mae when he came in. Hell, he even squeezed Max's arm when he greeted her. Too bad, though. It made a great fantasy.

"I'll bring you in some fresh coffee, if you'd like to meet now," she said to get Cora Mae alone and gossip. "You know you have a busy schedule today, Ms. Doss."

Rhondalynn looked at Max like she had suggested Bergen take her right there on the carpet. "Why, that would be very nice of you, Maxine." Kill 'em with kindness, Max thought, just like Lucas said. And like Dorati said, if that didn't work, just kill 'em. She liked to keep her options open.

"I'll try not to keep you too long," Bergen said to Doss as he closed the door behind them.

Cora Mae was about to speak but Max held a finger up to her lips and pressed the intercom button. Rhon was speaking.

"—come over for dinner tonight? We have a lot to talk about."

Cora Mae shook her head back and forth and frowned until Max pressed the button off.

"You can't do that, Max!"

"Sure I can. Got to stick up for the Rev around here, Cora Mae. Got to find out as much as I can."

"No. I mean you can't do it because the phone might ring and then you'd be caught and she'd have a reason to fire you. You've got to watch it with her. She'd like to have you and Valdez and Burt Lister and probably Travis and me out of here so she could run her own show."

Max started to protest when the phone rang. Cora Mae widened her eyes to say I told you so, as Maxine put Bishop Emilio Casas through to Rhondalynn's line without warning, then flipped on the intercom.

"I thought I told you not to interrupt—oh, hello Bishop."

Maxine stifled a laugh and Cora Mae pressed the off button.

"I have to go now, Maxine," Cora Mae said in a hurry. Maybe the coffee had gone right through her. "But let's get together tomorrow night for dinner and compare notes. I know there's a lot you're wondering about and I may be able to fill you in by then."

The woman disappeared and a disappointed Max spent the next hour doing desk work and consciously not pressing the intercom button. Other than a few outbursts of laughter, the voices had been quiet on the other side of the door. Finally she got up and knocked, then opened the door abruptly. The two were sitting on the couch side by side, coffee cups in hand, proper as shit. Damn.

"Excuse me for barging in like this but I just noticed the time and I wondered if you wanted me to take the condom-needle van for Valdez today, since he's out of town?"

"Not at all," Everett Bergen stood and said, turning to the woman priest. "I believe the Reverend Doss and I can handle condom duty today, can we not?"

"After that conversation with the Bishop, I can handle anything," Doss said. Max worried what the hell that meant, and kicked herself for not turning on the intercom. There hadn't been one phone call the whole time to give her away, either. Now she had to be content to watch them walk out the door to the back lot together. Bergen was his usual feely self, and Doss was smiling more than she had all morning. But maybe Max was reading stuff into those gestures. Yeah, and maybe the Pope was a Buddhist.

She went across the hall to a window overlooking the lot to watch that bald head get into the van. She imagined being in there with him and remembered a sign that said: "If this van's a-rockin', don't come a-knockin'." But the thought of Doss and Bergen getting it on was repulsive and had nothing to do with race or politics. It had to do with common sense. Deans didn't screw faculty members, other than figuratively.

Maxine Blackwell smiled. Though that would be embarrassing to Bishop Casas if he knew about it. She thought of the conversation on the phone and wished she'd listened in.

The secretary was about to turn from the window when a familiar form in a jogging suit caught her attention. Cora Mae Hartwig left the church through a basement door and headed for her car. And it looked like she had a cassette tape in her hand.

* * *

Ricardo Valdez had slept through the entire nonstop flight on Southwest Airlines from Austin to El Paso, including the mild turbulence of a storm system building around San Angelo. He had been surprised to see the Rev in the car when Brick came to drive him to the airport, and he was glad Holt was okay. The Rev's instructions were explicit, the main one being "don't get hurt," and be sure to be on the return flight tonight.

It had taken him exactly ten minutes after getting out of the cab in the old town area near the bridge to make a contact. Maybe it was the tatoos on his bulging muscles that labelled him more than an accidental tourist, or maybe once you were in the game you never lost the look. Though it worried him a little, Valdez wondered how the hell he ever did this stuff with these people, unless he was just high all the time and had no sense of the risks he took. Maybe his apprehension now had to do with getting older and less happy about dying anytime soon. He hoped he hadn't lost the edge he'd need to carry this off.

Although he had first been approached by two men about drugs, he declined and instead pressed them about militia activity, saying he'd like to sign up, make a good soldier and be able to pass back and forth over the border because he was Hispanic. The men told him to wait in a local bar and he'd be contacted. Now he was walking on the International Bridge over the Rio Grande, flanked by a Mexican who looked like he hadn't eaten in a week, and an anglo who looked like a tank with a crew cut.

When they reached the other side, the two nudged Valdez through dirt side streets to the back door of a restaurant where, brandishing a gun and a knife, they encouraged him to go inside with his hands raised over his head. Valdez complied, not because he couldn't take them both—he was, after all, the kickboxing champion of the southwestern prison association—but because he wanted information.

"Sit in the chair. We will have to cuff your hands," the dehydrated Mexican said.

Valdez resisted any jokes about a 'dry Martinez.' "I don't think so," he said. "I came to help out. If you don't have work for me, or if your militia is a bunch of prejudiced bastards against Hispanics, then I'll just go back where I came from and find somebody who needs my talents." He kept his eye on the big white boy, who he expected to make a move first, though the Mexican bore watching, too.

"Sit down," the tank threatened.

"I do not wish to fight you," Valdez said. He'd always wanted to say that, having seen it on Kung Foo for years. If they'd seen the program they'd know to back off now while they could still move; they'd know that no one would be stupid enough to say that line unless they could back it up with a good ass kicking.

The Mexican said he didn't want to fight either, but that Valdez asked too many questions, like an undercover cop trying to find out about these, what had he called them, militias? The white hulk took one step too close and Valdez jumped. With one foot he dislodged the gun, the other he aimed at the man's chest, just below his throat. The tank crashed against the wall, coughing and gasping for air.

"Next time I close it for him," Valdez said to the Mexican.

"Very impressive, Señor. Indeed any militia would be happy to have you serving in it." He lit a cigarette and glanced at the man on the ground, catching his breath. "Can I see your wallet?"

Valdez held out his driver's license.

"Ricardo Valdez?" The Mexican looked at the white man.

"*THE* Ricardo Valdez?" the tank gargled out in raspy words. "Twenty banks in twenty days? In Texas?"

Valdez indicated it had been twenty-one but the savings and loan didn't count since it was going out of business anyway. He helped the tank to his feet as the Mexican ordered a bottle of tequila from the kitchen. "How'd you get out, man?" he asked.

Ricardo explained that they mainly wanted restitution, plus a little punishment, and he bartered the former for the latter. He had immediately put the money in stocks at a time when the market boomed. In the twenty days he doubled his money, looked like a good guy by giving the original amounts back to the banks and reinvested the rest to have when he got out. Unfortunately, the market took a bearish turn and he was still working his way back up. Now about those militias.

"Loco Americanos," said the Mexican, "con mucho cajones."

"They regularly march people over here to vanish, and they do," said the American tank, still rubbing his chest so Valdez could feel sorry for him, which he didn't.

"But we got a lot more to tell you than that," the Mexican said, pouring another round of drinks.

Six hours later three drunks arrived in a cab at the El Paso International Airport. Two of them poured enough coffee down the third to make him appear sober enough to be allowed on the plane. Fortunately Southwest Airlines had open seating and Ricardo Valdez had only to remember to walk down the ramp without stumbling and take the first seat with nobody in it. Unfortunately the first seat he spotted was against the bulkhead, by the window, in one of the "foursomes," and he collapsed into it.

There was one brief, terrorizing moment of panic when he realized there was a blurry black outline of a person in the seat opposite him and he thought he had mistakenly boarded a train with the Grim Reaper. That thought was quickly dispelled, however, when the plane took off at a steep bank to avoid the Franklin mountains and Valdez, having neglected to fasten his seat belt, rose and flew in slow motion into the body of that person who, much to his relief and further horror, was a nun. A startled, screaming nun.

Once strapped firmly in his seat with the help of his seatmates and the flight attendant, Valdez realized he could not look outside because the lights below were moving backwards at 520mph, which only enhanced his inebriated feeling of whirling into a deep pit at the same speed.

He realized he was in a difficult spot. He couldn't look out the window. He couldn't close his eyes for fear of the whirlies. And he couldn't look forward at the Grim Nun. He wondered how he had let those two talk him in to drinking so much. He seemed to remember thinking he was getting a lot of really helpful information about militias in El Paso for the Rev, with names attached. Names he knew. Maybe he should try to write them down before he went to sleep and forgot them.

Valdez fumbled in his pocket for a pen he had lifted from the desk in the Mexican restaurant. He tried to focus on objects nearby to find a piece of scrap paper and ended up picking a small white bag from the rack beside him. He had written one name on it when the garbled voice of the captain announced that the storm system at San Angelo had stalled and intensified over the day. There might be a little chop.

All Valdez heard was "storm," "intense," and "chop." By the time he filled in the remaining ideas the plane had somehow flown into a blender and the lights outside were flashing zig zags.

He opened the plain white bag with the name scribbled on the outside and used it for its intended purpose. The Grim Nun held his head. Two bags and forty-five minutes later the plane mercifully landed in Austin.

The nun dutifully and sternly escorted a wavering Valdez from the airplane, like an errant child in a Catholic school, and deposited him in a chair in front of the man to whom he handed the barf bag which he had refused to surrender to the stewardess.

"A souvenir from Mexico for *me*?" Nikky Dorati said, opening the bag.

"Actually, yes," the woman in black said, and walked away.

Valdez shook his head slowly and pointed to the outside of the bag, as Dorati held it at arm's length.

The name on the bag was Dillon.

Donna Dillon.

✳ ✳ ✳

It had been hard to find an empty booth in the dim section of the gentlemen's club in South Austin. Like the one who had just paid the entrance fee at the door, many patrons—both men and women—required special anonymity given their high profile in Austin society. The midnight show had just started and three big breasted women straddled and humped chrome poles in high heels and little else. After a few teasing minutes of suggestive facial motions and moaning sounds, three sequined tops simultaneously popped off to yells of delight from all but one of the highly liquoured crowd. That one sat back in the darkened booth and waited, ordered a strawberry marguerita and a glass of water.

Two drinks and twenty minutes later the g-strings had also vanished and all three women, oiled in sweat, writhed around each other at the center pole, stroking, licking, touching. The customer in the back stared at the marguerita, felt repulsed, disgusted, especially about that lascivious stirring just below the navel. Righteous indignation about what had to be done consumed the person, who looked up with pleasure, as if looking at a roach about to be squashed.

When the women strutted off the stage, the "floor" show began. A dozen other topless women flooded the tables, worked their way through the groping hands, performed to the flashing red, pink and blue lights and pulsing music or lap danced for bills tucked into their stringy thongs. The patron in the back booth saw them coming, took out a small bottle with a dropper and, holding the water glass with a napkin to avoid prints, squeezed out one drop.

Five crisp fifty dollar bills were rolled like cigarettes, then held in the middle and dipped, one end at a time into the water glass, enough to wet them slightly. Five women, one by one, danced over to the table as the patron, whose carefully chosen clothes assured not just anonymity but androgyny, held the bills up, pretending to lick them. The women each in turn took the rolled bill and licked it on all sides, sucked on it suggestively, and slid it down their g-strings.

The customer sat back, checked the time and ordered a second strawberry marguerita as the floor women disappeared and the second stage show began. Before they got to the center pole, the patron was gone, driving up South Congress, dodging cops watching for crooks and drunks.

The driver would sleep in tomorrow, or was it today already, then arise and listen to the radio for the news story on the five women.

The election was two days away.

So was the judgement.

Like the five lascivious dancers, they would all die by water.

• Six •

Susan Granger came out of the brown fortress-like APD headquarters and took a deep breath of crisp March air. The cloudy sky was unusually grey, she thought, remembering the storm forecast she'd heard on her way to work. She felt like she'd held her breath all morning and the cold made her shudder, wish she were a little girl again snuggling in her daddy's warm leather police jacket. The Commissioner's comment about him was cruel and she would not forgive him for it.

She pulled up the collar of her own cop jacket around her neck and decided to walk the four blocks up Eighth to St. Margaret's, where she had the unpleasant duty of investigating the latest heinous crime in what now looked like a series. Maybe her head—and her butt—would be back in position by then. Given the reaming she had just gotten from Christopher Dillon, Susan was certain that in a former life he was a proctologist. The jovial good old boy who had promised Governor Doggett his badge if Holt was not caught had lost his sense of humor; possibly because the deadline was now the day after tomorrow, possibly because he thought she was dragging her heels. Which, of course, she was.

But possibly it was something else. It was after that phone call, she thought as she reconstructed the meeting and crossed Red River Street. He had been relatively rational until then, questioning her lack of results, hinting that her feelings for Holt obstructed the investigation, thinly veiling his threat to have her removed from the case right now. Then his charming wife had called with her panties in a wad about something. Susan knew Donna Dillon was upset because she could overhear the high pitched tone as the Commissioner held the phone away from his ear. She thought she heard the words "too close," "Mexico," and "drunk."

"Anything I can help with, Commissioner?" she had asked. He replied that arresting their inebriated gardener was maybe in the league of something she could handle, and things escalated from there, culminating in yet another comment about following in the footsteps of her bumbling father. With a final outburst of red eyed, West Texas cowboy expletives, she had been dismissed from his office—and he didn't want to see her face again until Holt was standing beside her in handcuffs.

She crossed Trinity and headed up the hill to the church, kicking herself for ever agreeing to participate in this sting with Lucas and Dorati and Kristen. What had she been thinking? It was crazy. It was so far outside the law that she had lost count of the number of statutes they'd broken.

The ironic thing was that it was Kristen's idea, thinking if she and Holt got out of sight the people threatening the two of them would feel cocky and make mistakes that could lead to their arrest. Granger had agreed because she felt pressured. They convinced her the operation would only be for two weeks leading up to the election and be over. It would get them both out of harm's way and give the police a freer hand. It would allow her to know what the hell the God Squad was doing for a change. And she could keep an eye on Lucas and Kristen.

What was it about that woman that pulled him away? She understood the why now, just not the why. The why now was because, even after a year of deepening relationship, great sex, and fewer arguments about their considerable political differences, Susan still felt somehow out of synch, scared of committing to something deeper. It was, amazingly, she and not Lucas who was reticent, holding back, and she was sure she communicated that to him in subtle ways, ways that caused him to maintain his distance and be distracted by the ever willing, fun, free and gorgeous Kristen Wade.

Maybe this operation was good for her after all, personally if not professionally. Maybe the proximity to a contender would make her come to terms with whatever this distancing meant, overcome it and let Lucas know where she was and what she wanted. But she'd have to do it soon.

Professionally, the damned thing had better work or she'd be busted back to cadet—if they even let her remain a cop. If Dillon was upset about what she *hadn't* done, wait till he found out what she *had* done.

As she approached the parking lot, she imagined she was casually dropping by St. Margaret's to have coffee and shoot the shit with Lucas, talk about the impending election, about how he was handling the clashes between the liberal and conservative forces in the congregation, the liberal and conservative forces within the two of them.

She walked in the back door of the church feeling a little sorry for Dillon, even though he was out of line. Clearly he was already under pressure from his superiors to address the problem of increasing violence from the right. But this latest attack, which she had been dispatched to investigate at St. Margaret's, had added irate calls from everyone from gay advocacy groups to Planned Parenthood, and calls of congratulations from other groups that thought—hoped—the police had something to do with the episode.

"Mornin' Lieutenant," Max said, handing her a mug of steaming coffee. "I saw you comin' through the lot. Cora Mae and Her Piousness are waiting for you with bated breath."

Granger thanked her and said she was more worried about the "baited" condoms.

"Yeah. Somebody's got a pretty warped sense of humor out there," Max said. "Speaking of warped, how's the search for the Rev?" It was obvious to Susan that she grinned to mask her concern. "I'm pretty worried about him. And nobody'll tell me nothin'. I don't appreciate being protected from I-don't-know-what, but I'd settle for knowing he was okay."

Granger felt for her. In some ways, Maxine loved him better than she and Kristen. Holt had told her that, at the prison, Max had thought otherwise. Eventually they discovered that their interest in each other had to remain platonic, so her love really was unconditional. The only thing she wanted in return was for him to be "okay."

"We've got to assume he's okay, Max," Granger said, touching her hand. "We've got to trust him on this for a while longer. He's probably working it out," she smiled, "like he always does."

"That's what I'm afraid of. Every time he 'works something out' he damned near gets himself killed." She shook her head. "I hope the God Squad's watching him. I wish I knew where he is."

"I know he's not in that office, where he needs to be," Granger said. She knocked and opened the door, startling Cora Mae Hartwig who sat across the desk from Rhondalynn Doss. "I appreciate your seeing me on such short notice," she said to them.

"It's a terrible thing, Susan dear," Cora Mae began. "Who could imagine lacing condoms and syringes with e-coli?"

"Apparently someone who wanted your program to stop," Granger replied, tossing a folded paper on the desk. "Because that's what this court order does."

Doss picked up the paper. "Can you give us an update, Lieutenant?" she said, stern faced. "We just know what we saw in the Statesman today, that as of midnight last night, thirty five people had shown up at the two hospitals."

Granger sat next to Cora Mae and sipped coffee as she explained that the number was now forty three. Symptoms of condom users—only those with sores already on their genitals—ranged from mild inflammation to internal sepsis that left victims in intensive care, clinging to life. Twelve drug users were found dead with the contaminated syringes by their sides, having injected the bacteria directly into their bloodstream.

The Reverend Doss folded her arms over her chest and tightened her lips. "The Bishop believed that program was an embarrassment to the Diocese of Austin," she said quietly, "and to the right thinking people of this church. We will comply with the court order and cease the program immediately."

Cora Mae glanced knowingly at Susan. "If you were so much against it, Rhondalynn, why did you and Dean Bergen so eagerly volunteer to take the van out yesterday when Ricardo Valdez was out of town?"

"Felt we had to, since we had just gotten a huge donation of condoms and needles from—" she frowned at Granger "—from your boss, as a matter of fact. We didn't see how we could shut it down right after that, like a slap in the face to the police commissioner."

Susan was stunned. What the hell was going on here? Commissioner Christopher Dillon had contributed boxes of *condoms* and, of all things, *syringes* to St. Margaret's distribution project. "Are you sure about that?" she asked.

The door opened and Max walked in with a paper in one hand and coffee pot in the other. "Thought y'all might need both of these." She filled cups and handed the paper to Cora Mae, who knew Max hadn't replaced the intercom light yet.

"That woman is uncanny," Doss said. "She probably races in with a kleenex before Holt sneezes, and blows his nose for him." She mumbled something more under her breath.

"No, dear," Cora Mae said. "You're wrong to say that's not the part of him she's used to blowing."

Susan laughed as Rhondalynn's red face contrasted with the white collar and black shirt. "I didn't know you could hear that well," Doss said, laughing at herself.

"Better than you can see, dear." She winked at Granger and read the paper from Max. "And look who gave the supplies that were handed out yesterday." She handed the page to Susan. "It wasn't Commissioner Dillon."

Granger saw the masthead of the coalition of business and community organizations, Revive Austin. The letter indicated support for the program at St. Margaret's to reduce disease and prevent theft. She scanned the list of board members down the left hand side of the page.

"But the officer who dropped them off was in a squad car and said the Commissioner had asked him to bring them by on his rounds," Doss said, puzzled at the confusion.

Granger handed the paper to her. "Looks like he was doing a little favor for the third name on the board list."

The third name on the list was Donna Dillon.

"His wife?" Doss asked. "The wife of the Police Commissioner for Austin-Travis County sent us condoms and syringes laced with a deadly virus?" She frowned. "I don't think so."

Susan sat back in the chair and tried to be rational with them. They didn't know that Donna Dillon had done anything. And they couldn't prove a connection between Revive Austin and the package. Anyone could have tampered with the items at any time before delivery, including the cop who brought them over—or the man who called in the theatre bombing and the dumpster fire.

"We are impounding the van for a couple days," Susan said. "We'll bring it back as soon as the lab's done with it."

"I'll have Max rent one for the weekend," Doss wrote herself a note. "We use it to pick up some of our elderly people for services."

"I'll bet Max has it taken care of already," Cora Mae smiled, not looking at the intercom. "Is there any news of Lucas, Susan?"

"He surfaced at Esther's Follies the other night at a Pace rally, and lots of people call in reports claiming they've spotted him— sort of like Nessy or Elvis. But so far, no Rev." Granger stood to go, adding that the ventilator had been removed from Kristen, since she was so much better.

"They'll need it for the condom victims," Doss added, walking her to the door. "But, even though it's politically incorrect, don't you think it some way it serves them right? I mean, if they're going to fornicate and do all manner of unnatural things with people of the same sex, and stick drugs in their arms to purposely defile the temple of the spirit, then don't you think it could possibly be God's judgement on them, harvesting the fruits of their own immoral behavior?"

"The wages of sin is death, huh?" Susan said. Though she saw the logic, there was something particularly unforgiving, even merciless about the attitude. Not to mention self-righteous. "It's clear that a lot of people believe that."

"I'm not saying I really *do* believe it," Doss hastened to add, "I'm just sort of wondering out loud what people are saying behind closed doors."

"I wonder what Lucas would say?" Granger replied.

Cora Mae walked out with them. "Lucas would say: 'Keep chunkin' those stones, O Guiltless One. But keep your helmet on, just in case.'"

Rhondalynn shook hands and vanished behind the office door, claiming work to be done for Sunday. Susan and Cora Mae whispered as Max saw the phone light up and punched the intercom, turning the speaker to low so all three could listen. The line rang several times.

"Yes?" the familiar deep voice intoned officiously.

"Ryan?" the priest said with a hopeful lilt in her voice.

"You're not supposed to call me at this number," he growled.

"I know it, but I've got some great news."

Granger punched the off button. "We can't listen to that."

"What's the matter with you?" Max asked, disappointed and a touch of anger showing. "This is hot poop!"

"It's illegal, inadmissable, and private," Granger said, pulling on her jacket.

"Susan's right, Maxine," Cora Mae agreed. "Now as Senior Warden I want you to fix that intercom light in her office—with all deliberate speed."

Maxine smiled. "As soon as the Rev comes back."

"Which we all hope will be very soon," Cora Mae said, escorting Susan down the hall and out of the church.

The voice of Ryan Pace through the microphone was clear. "This had better be good, Rhon," he said. "And make it fast."

"I will," Doss said, lowering her voice. "The police think Donna Dillon or Revive Austin is responsible for those condom deaths today."

"Maybe they were," Pace said, his voice flat, hurried.

"Uh-huh," Doss replied.

"Don't call me here again. Meet me tonight. I'll pick you up at the usual place."

The phone clicked. Doss cursed and hung up.

In the basement of the church, Lucas Holt turned off the recorder and put the tape in his pocket.

* * *

Frankie Colovas called Dorati once a day, but not from his room. His room was a small efficiency apartment over the garage housing the car he had driven full time for the last few days. Though he was hired as a bodyguard, the driver had been sick and Doors had volunteered to fill in, save a salary, do double time, and further insinuate himself closer to Ryan Pace, if possible.

Though he had learned nothing of interest so far, his orders from both Nikky and the Rev were to keep listening without doing anything dangerous—like his specialty of snooping through locked doors. It cramped his style, he thought, as he stretched out on the twin bed in the well furnished room. He'd like to wander through the Pace mansion at his leisure. Maybe he could find something about "Dead Ed" in a drawer or safe. Hell, at least he could find some hockable jewelry. From what Dorati hinted at, the Rev might need extra cash for lawyer's fees, even with Mr. Layton. As he contemplated how he might access the house, his pager erupted. Pace was ready to go out.

The candidate's standard procedure was to get in the car and tell Colovas the destination, then close the glass partition in the limo and make calls or work. But today he just gave directions, which made Doors wonder if he thought somehow Frankie would alert someone to be there ahead of them. Furthermore, Pace announced the streets and turns piecemeal, in five minute segments, and left the window up to converse with him. If Doors had been wired or attempted to contact anyone, Pace would have subverted it this time. But none of that was true, and Frankie's feelings were a little hurt about it.

"Times like this I think you don't trust me, Mr. Pace," Doors said.

"Don't take it personally, Frankie. Until I get elected, I trust no one. When I take the oath of office as the Senator from Texas, I'll trust even fewer people than that." He poured himself a glass of Driskill Springs water and propped up his feet. Frankie watched him in the rear view.

"Why do you drink that water instead of tap water?" Colovas asked. Maybe a change of conversation would draw him out, give Doors something to tell Dorati and the Rev.

"You mean why would I pay a dollar a bottle for something that I can get out of the tap? Especially when I'm frugal about everything else?"

"Sort of," Colovas said.

"Turn left on to MoPac and get off at Bee Caves," Pace ordered. "Because this water comes straight from the spring that connects to the aquifer under all of Central Texas, six counties from Kinney to Hays." Doors saw him smile. "Drinking this keeps me humble. Any time I think I'm important all I have to do is imagine what it's like to be one glass of water in a system that supports two million people a day. It puts my minuscule life back in perspective."

Colovas thought that sounded reasonable, like pissing in the ocean, but he did not say it. "Yes sir, I guess it does." Remembering his place on earth had never been a problem to Frankie. All his life people reminded him how low and incompetent he was; except the Rev of course. It was in prison when Holt explained to him in common sense street terms just what the hell Jesus really meant, that Colovas had suddenly and incomprehensively turned around. Jesus had been one more authority figure giving him shit for not being good enough, not being religious, reading his Bible, going to church, loving his drunk abusive parents. But Holt told him Jesus was a bigger rebel than Frankie ever thought about being, got into more trouble and ended up executed by the State. If he was around today we'd be singing The Old Wooden Electric Chair. Jesus was in the acceptance business, not the condemnation business, like watering a dry plant, Holt told him. Maybe that Driskill water was like that for Pace. Maybe he wasn't such a bad guy after all. Maybe Kristen was wrong and Pace wasn't her evil enemy, just her political one. But then what did 'Dead Ed' mean? And what about those geography maps?

Pace spoke. "Back under MoPac to Barton Springs Road and left at the soccer fields."

Doors knew where they were going. The Zilker Park Clubhouse was often rented for weddings and parties. They passed the soccer fields and turned off the paved road to a dirt one leading up into the woods. Frankie stopped at the Clubhouse. It was closed and he asked if Pace had had a reservation.

"Don't need a reservation if I've got you, do I?" He nodded toward the building. "Open the back door and return to the car."

Frankie did as he was told, though he didn't like being used this way. The door was a piece of cake; he didn't even have to break the lock. He did manage a quick look inside before he walked back to the driver's seat. Pace ordered—that was how Frankie felt—*ordered* him to stay in the car like a dog. But Colovas had already been to prison obedience school, and failed.

When someone came up the opposite path, Doors rolled down the electric window and climbed out silently. No door noise. He crept to the opposite side of the one room building and peeked in the shutters. Pace had his back to him, but the other man Colovas vaguely recognized as someone from St. Margaret's; someone the Rev would know. He strained to listen but only caught a few words echoing off the cement floor in the cinder block room. But the gestures were enough.

Pace was clearly threatening the man who cowered in front of him. He held out pictures from a brown envelope and raised his voice. Doors knew it was blackmail but wondered what the payoff could be. Certainly it wasn't money. Pace had plenty of that. So it must be information. He had to get closer to find out.

Moving slowly around to the door he had opened before, Frankie knelt down and stuck his head inside the room. It was hard to do with the stupid hand cast. He was covered from view by a stack of drink bottles, but if either of the two men turned to leave, he was busted. And he would have to leave time to rush back to the car.

"Damn it, Atkinson. Either you find out or I release these to the Statesman and you'll never get another architect job as long as you live."

Case Atkinson, Colovas thought. That was it. He remembered the name from some meeting at church, and he'd heard 'Dez talk about him. He was on the Vestry, a friend of the Rev's, and gay. Doors wondered if Holt knew what was in the pictures. Probably did, he thought as he pulled a little closer into the room. He knew as much about everyone else.

"I don't *know* where he is," Atkinson pleaded. "I've tried anyone who might be in contact with him and they're all tight lipped about it. The man's got protection around him like Jesus in the tomb guarded by angels."

"Then you'd better come up with a way to bust him out— and soon. The election is day after tomorrow and I won't win unless people are distracted by him, see him as a symbol of liberal thinking, want to punish him by voting down what he stands for—thinking he can get away with murder—by voting for me. He's the only thing between me and the Senate seat, Atkinson. As a fugitive he's old news. He's got to be visible to hate." Doors saw him put the photos back in the envelope. It was time to get the hell out of Dodge. He backed away and did not notice a beer can on the floor by his foot until he heard the metallic crunch.

"What was that?" Pace turned in the direction of the scraping sound and pulled a gun. He walked in Frankie's direction as the ex-con broke out in sweat.

"No, wait a minute," Atkinson pleaded again. "The place has field mice who hide here in the winter. Come back just a second."

Colovas held his breath, praying Pace would listen to the wise man. He heard the hammer click closed on the gun and carefully backed out the door. But he heard the final words.

"I don't know where he is, but I know how to find him. And I promise I'll lead you to him by tomorrow."

Colovas hurried around the building as he heard the two close the door and Pace coming fast behind him. There was no way in hell he would be able to get into the car in time and close the door noiselessly. He would have to try the one trick he had learned at the pen from a guy who made it look easy. With five steps left, Doors *dove* through the open driver's window.

Pace rounded the corner of the Clubhouse and saw no one behind the wheel until, slowly, the figure of Frankie Colovas rose in the seat like a balloon at a fun house.

"Dropped my cigarette on the floor," he said when Pace got in the back. Dorati would have an earful for the Rev today, assuming Pace let Colovas anywhere near a telephone.

* * *

Holt put his finger to his lips, indicating for Brickhouse to be absolutely quiet. He removed a stone plug at eye level and watched Susan step down from the ladder. She had removed a ceiling tile in this sub-basement room and hung paper clips on what the wiring plans had indicated were the computer lines in the ceiling.

An incredible woman, he thought as she descended the steps. She had guts and brains—and she seldom got the two confused. He had enjoyed this year off and on together while Kristen was charming the Legislature and gearing up for this election. Susan had seen him off at the Austin Motorola Marathon and met him at the finish line, just as she promised. In fact, this year had felt like a marathon for the two of them. They ran from one topic to the next when they were together, not unlike twenty years ago at U.T., though they both had mellowed since then and were far less viciously argumentative now. Not that they didn't have problems or disagreements. Those abounded, but there was a steadiness about her, a confidence and certainty that Kristen not only didn't have, but never would care to acquire.

Kristen and he had met once early on during this time just to check in. But their reconnecting turned out to be a function of alcohol and sleep deprivation. In the morning Kristen was gone when he awoke, and they hadn't met again until the threatening letters began.

The Rev watched Granger look around the room, then slip quietly out the door and lock it from the outside. He had strong feelings for her, but she seemed not to have the same for him. Or she did but she didn't. He couldn't tell if it was something he was communicating about his hesitance to take the next step of deepening their relationship and commitment, or if it was the wall he lately felt from her.

Then too, working closely with Kristen these months had rekindled his emotions about her, just as he was unsure about Susan. He heard Brickhouse mumble behind him. Lucas would have to sort out where he stood with both women, but that sorting would have to wait until the election was over. If Kristen won, he may not have to sort at all; unless he liked commuting to Washington.

He told Brick to follow him through the hole he was about to create by pulling cement blocks out of place. In fact, the builders of the new APD building barely missed discovering the underground tunnel a few years ago. This sub-basement wall was only a foot away from the tunnel and had been easy for Holt and Dorati to cut through for access to APD itself, should they need to get in—or out—in a hurry.

Once inside the tiny store room filled with boxes, files and dusty cabinets, Brick quickly connected clips to the computer wires, booted his notebook, and they were in business.

"Can you access the Humble, Texas police computer?" Holt questioned.

"Only because of the great job training program I was in at the pen."

Holt knew he was not talking about anything sponsored by the state. The prison system had a computer class, figuring it would equip the inmates with good job skills on the outside, enabling them to find employment. But they forgot they were dealing with sociopaths, some of them very smart; so while the other men played at Microsoft Word and WordPerfect, Jimmy Brickhouse learned "Hacking For Dummies" from Petey McGaskill, a two time lifer who accessed the world through his palmtop.

Brick pushed a button. "Bingo! Next stop, Ryan Pace's criminal history as a rich little shit before he got right with Gawd." Jimmy raised his hand and threw back his head. "Thank ya, Je-sus."

Lucas Holt shook his head. He loved the imitation of the "fundies"—Fundamentalists who took credit for "finding" the Lord, like He was lost. For Holt, religion was not about man's search for God, but about God's search for man—which was something to be unpretentious about, not self-righteously proclaiming that they're better or more saved than other people because *they* found the Lord. Piety made him puke. He could handle hypocrisy; it was religious presumptuousness at any point on the theological spectrum that sent him ballistic, and the liberals were often more flagrant about it in their own way than the fundamentalists. But Pace was the current incarnation of the conservative end of the pious presumptions, demanding that everyone come *up* to his particular religious standard of moral behavior—now that he had gotten his wild oats out of his own system, of course, and repented mightily, of course.

"I hope he's got a rap sheet a mile long," Holt said, "and that some of it is *after* his profession of new found faith."

Brickhouse frowned. "I don't believe this shit, Rev. Look here." He pointed to the screen; the *blank* screen. "Check the label, man."

Lucas Holt read the word "EXPUNGED" at the top of the file. Another sentence included the explanation: "Charges dropped upon satisfactory mediation and restitution."

"The boy worked his program, just like AA," Brickhouse said. "Went back and asked forgiveness from anyone he'd hurt and made amends." He looked up at Holt. "Guess you gonna have to call him *Saint* Ryan now."

Lucas knelt down and stared at the screen. "There's a devil in there somewhere, Brickhouse. It's just not in the obvious place." Holt thought a second. "Can you access the campaign fund?"

Jimmy indicated that was public knowledge since it had to be reported to the Federal Campaign Commission, and pulled it up with a few keystrokes. They scanned the list and found nothing.

"The boy's gettin' bucks from some high rollers," Brickhouse commented as the list scrolled by.

Holt tried to connect the dollars with the companies and individuals. Most were from Texas, though the out-of-state list was surprisingly long. "Hold it," he said at last. "Scroll back a page, slowly." The names dropped onto the screen one at a time. "There it is."

He pointed to the name of Rhondalynn Doss.

Brickhouse looked at him. "Now ain't that just a kick in the head?"

"Not necessarily. It makes sense that she supports him, given her theological positions."

"Those must be *some* positions if she's givin' the boy ten grand a pop." Jimmy's face grimaced. "Either she's independently wealthy—"

"She's from Scarsdale, so that's possible. Or it's also possible she's channeling for somebody who supports him but doesn't want to be named."

"Oh shit," Brickhouse said when the screen went blank. "They spotted us."

"What?"

"Lines are a two way street. Somebody nearly as smart as I am figured out they were being observed." He pulled the clips off the wires and shut the notebook. "We're outta here."

"How long does it take before—?" Holt began until he heard voices in the hallway. "Shit, Brick. Get through that wall."

"Not without you, man." Brickhouse pulled the ceiling tile closed as the voices came closer.

"Do it *now*!" Lucas ordered and Brickhouse scurried through the opening at the bottom of the wall. The Rev moved three boxes from their dusty positions on the floor, stood on them and moved a ceiling tile not concealing computer wires up and off its track. As the people outside tried keys in the door, Holt poured himself through the hole in the wall.

He and Brickhouse moved the cinder blocks back into place just as the door opened and three cops with drawn guns stormed into the room. One was Lieutenant Granger.

"Don't breathe," Holt whispered.

"Not a problem," the man on the tunnel floor replied.

Lucas put one eye to the tiny peep hole and watched.

"The tracer said the intercept came from this room," a large cop growled. "So where the hell are they?"

"Somebody was here—look at these boxes," the shorter cop said.

"Must have crawled in through the ceiling, don't you think?" Susan said, pointing to the tile Lucas had removed. "They couldn't have gotten in this room any other way now, could they? I mean, what the hell did they do? Come through that wall?" She laughed.

"Lieutenant's right," the growler said. "These false ceilings are all connected. They must've broke in somewhere else and dropped down here to get at the wires better. Wonder what the hell they wanted?"

Granger ushered them out the door and inserted the key to lock it. "Police files make interesting reading," she said, then whispered into the darkened room, "I hope."

Brickhouse thought it was a bad idea but the Rev insisted. There were a couple of things from the house he needed and it would only take a couple minutes to run in and out. Even if it was being watched, which he agreed with Brick it was, they could park in the alley behind the house and be in the back door before anyone saw them. The police would have started out the surveillance of the house from front and back, but as the days went by, manpower being what it was, they would cut back the watch to one car, unmarked and parked down the street in front of the house, where they could see any activity and eat doughnuts at the same time.

"Still think it's a bad idea, Rev," Jimmy said as he stopped his restored white Corvette two houses down in the alley.

"Where'd you get this car, anyway? That Dell computer store think you're related to Michael himself?"

Brickhouse grinned from ear to ear. "Let's just say I do a little extra on the side. Campaign funds like the ones we called up back at the police station? They're kinda hard to keep track of sometimes. Keep findin' their way into other people's accounts, you know."

"Confession is tomorrow at ten." You could take the man out of the prison, but it was harder than hell to get the prison out of the man, a fact for which he was more often grateful than not. As they approached the rear of the house Brickhouse crouched with his gun drawn, though Lucas had thought that unnecessary. Holt pointed to the unlatched door and slowly swung it open. "Unless the cops forgot to lock it, we've got company."

Brickhouse whispered back. "And unless you park your car in the kitchen, somebody's spilled gasoline all over the place. There's a torch in here, Rev. Careful."

Holt motioned for them to take opposite directions from the kitchen. Knowing where furniture was in the dark, Lucas went into the dining room that led to the living room. Brickhouse slunk down the hall. The sweet smell of gasoline permeated the air. "Boom Perfume," they called it at the prison.

The Rev heard footsteps on the staircase and went to the base, where a man was backing down. "Need some help, asshole?"

The figure fell a step, dropping the red can of gasoline, before he righted himself and held a gun on Lucas Holt. "You must be unarmed in addition to stupid, Chaplain, or you would have shot me already."

"Maybe I hate brains on my carpet, not that that's a problem in your case, or maybe I didn't want the house to go up just yet," Holt said, drawing the man down the stairs to the area by the front door. "Even in the dark your ugly face looks familiar."

"Shut up, Chaplain." The man held the silenced gun barrel directly to Holt's chest. "I can shoot you point blank and the only flame will be in your heart, preacher man."

"Bad idea, mofo," Brickhouse said, with his gun to the intruder's skull.

Lucas slowly took the gun from the cursing man's hand. "Brick, you remember 'Terrance the Terrible' Thompson? Biggest snitch this side of the Red River? Had private quarters in the pen to keep him away from the rest of the men, 'cause he'd informed on most of them?"

"I never snitched on you, Brickhouse," the man protested.

"Damn right you didn't, Thompson. Because I never talked to you, never told you nothin', never got close enough so you could overhear my conversation and go report it to the man to jack up your commissary." Brickhouse turned him around. "I heard that private room where you humped everything the guards got for you didn't keep you very safe, though, did it?" Jimmy snickered. "After the inmate party got done your new nickname is 'No Balls' Thompson. If my information is correct you be snitchin' soprano now."

The man cursed and swung on Brickhouse but Holt grabbed his arm. Lucas despised the man not for snitching but for the lying, cheating, and manipulating he did specifically to hurt other people for big money. He didn't deserve having his balls cut off but he didn't deserve living in the prison penthouse either. The question was who he worked for now and why? Ironically, for someone who made his living snitching, Thompson wasn't talking. He seemed to fear his employer more than the two men who had captured him.

"That's fine," Holt said. "Don't talk." He gave Brickhouse the man's gun. "Shoot the bastard with this if he moves." He picked up the gasoline can and doused the intruder with what was left.

"Damn, Rev," Brickhouse frowned. "If I have to shoot him, the whole house *could* blow up."

"Life is full of risks, Jimmy. He looked down at Thompson. "Let's see how risky you feel, Thomas." He disappeared to the kitchen and returned with a lighter.

"We got a bunch of people sick and dead due to some bad condoms and needles, not to mention a lot of other crazy shit going down. I'm wondering if you don't work for the guy that's doing it." Holt knew he had nothing to go on with the man, but this was the closest they'd come to capturing the opposition red handed.

"I don't know nothin' about all that mess," Thompson cried.

"Okay. Then let's find out what you *do* know," Holt said, motioning to Brickhouse. "Out the back door. If I'm going to burn you, it's not while sending my house to remodeling heaven."

They led the writhing man to the back yard, where Holt held the lighter to Thompson's face. "I ask the question, I count to three and flick this baby. Just think, you can avoid Purgatory by going up in flames."

"Fry now. Pray later," Brickhouse smirked.

Holt scowled at him. Brick was enjoying this entirely too much. "Who sent you here? Was it Pace? Commissioner Dillon? *WHO*, damn it!" Holt shook the man, held the lighter under his nose, hoping he would answer before he passed out from fear.

"One," Holt began.

"Light him up, Rev," Brickhouse said. "It's as bright as he'll ever get."

Before Holt could say the second number a red dot appeared on the kneeling man's chest. By the time Lucas knew what it was the man had jerked back, then lurched forward with blood spewing from his neck.

"*DAMN*," said Brickhouse. "That dude's wasted."

"It came from somewhere in the alley. Run see if you can find anything."

They heard a car screech away and knew any chase was futile.

"Leave the sucker, Rev. We got to get out of here. If the cops didn't hear that shot, they're either deaf or working for the shooter."

Holt laid the man down on the grass and ran off to the car with Brickhouse. He would spend the night back in the tunnel alone, wondering what the hell they had gotten themselves into.

And how they were going to get out.

• Seven •

Rather House perched on the crest of a hill at the corner of Duval and 32nd Street, regally overlooking the Episcopal Theological Seminary of Texas. The prominent Rather family had donated the land for the seminary fifty years ago on the condition that the house be kept intact in perpetuity. Used as guest rooms for visiting dignitaries, including famous cousin Dan, the first floor of the three story Texas Victorian was a favorite place for student and faculty luncheons, such as the one presided over by The Very Reverend J. Everett Bergen.

The Dean of the seminary smiled politely at the big haired blonde with superfluous make-up who had droned on for twenty minutes already. When her husband got an urgent call to a strip joint in South Austin, Donna Dillon had been kind enough to fill in for him at the last minute. She was supposed to talk about "Cops and Clergy—How To Tell The Difference." It was a obviously something she thought up on the way over and was definitely too cutesy to play this audience where people ducked out in record numbers.

Seminary students were among the most critical audiences in the country, Bergen thought, checking his watch again. They expected the speaker either to *be* God or personally *know* God, and to exercise the proper respect and admiration before a group who had been *individually called by God* and so had special knowledge that allowed them to debunk whatever the speaker touted in favor of their own personal view of the Gospel. And everything else. Infallibly.

Bergen wrote a note and slipped it in front of her, indicating the students' need to get back to classes. The seminarians would say they needed to get back to Earth. She wound it down and stopped to the nearly riotous applause traditionally reserved for either very good or very bad speakers. The Dean could tell by the look in her eye that she thought she was one of the former.

He stood and presented her a sweatshirt with the seminary insignia on the front and a coffee mug for her husband, who he fervently hoped would come regale them with what had happened at the strip joint. Including a field trip. God knew this group could use it.

When all the phony greeting had finished, Donna Dillon and the Dean were together at the table. "We are just delighted that you could be here today, Mrs. Dillon," Bergen said with his most polite and toothy smile. He always felt like he looked like The Kingfish when he did that, conning white folks.

"Cut the bullshit, Dean," the Commissioner's wife said. She pulled a pack of unfiltered cigarettes from her purse. "Can I smoke in here?"

"I'm afraid not, perhaps we could walk outside?"

She closed her purse and followed him out the back door to the garden. "What I really wanted to talk about is the leftward leaning of the church and how that should be addressed in seminaries such as this one. The church used to be one of the most stabilizing elements in our society, don't you think? And now it serves only to further confuse people by not taking serious stands on anything, like abortion and poverty and queers." She puffed furiously on the cigarette. "That's what I really wanted to say, in place of my husband you know."

Bergen wondered if anyone was listening. They hadn't had a lynching on campus yet, but this woman might begin a tradition. For somebody that looked like a ditsy blonde, she could be hard and opinionated. "I'm sure many on the Board of Trustees would agree with you, Mrs. Dillon. But I must say I am not one of them.

In fact my charge as Dean here has been to balance the theological message by encouraging dialogue between the different stances." Too bad there was no one else around for that speech, he thought. Where was the Board of Trustees when he wanted to impress them? "The Episcopal church has, in fact, taken strong stands on each of the issues you mention, and others. You may disagree with those stands, but we have taken them."

Donna Dillon crushed out her cigarette on a flagstone. "Like the stands you have taken with Rhondalynn Doss, Dean Bergen?" she said without looking at him.

J. Everett Bergen was speechless. She might as well have called him "Jawanda" in public. How the hell did she know? He and Rhondalynn had been incredibly discreet. Could Rhon have told her? Why? If she knew about the affair, what else did she know?

"Oh, don't look so sheepish or surprised. I'm the Police Commissioner's wife, you idiot. He talks to me. The Commissioner commiserates, if you will. And he runs BCI checks on license plates on cars parked at other people's houses." She glared at him. "Careless people. You're being very careless in your old age, Everett," she chided, walking slightly in front of him.

Maybe smugness would deter her, buy time for a better answer. "I don't know what you're talking about." She'd have to be more specific before he asked what she wanted, and certainly she wanted something.

"Sure you do," she took his arm in hers and strolled back toward the house. "Don't you know that some people would find your little arrangement with Reverend Rhon just a bit inappropriate? Take the Board of Trustees of the seminary and the Bishop for instance."

"They don't bitch about Lucas Holt," he defended. Nothing better came to mind.

"Aside from the current matter of attempted murder, Holt's not screwing anyone who reports to him like you are. Haven't you heard of sexual harassment?"

"Harassment isn't exactly what's going on here."

She continued, unrelenting. "And he's not screwing outside his race like you are. This is still the South, you know. And Holt's not the Dean of the damned seminary." Donna Dillon quieted her voice. "If the Trustees find out, you'll be like the grocery store manager who got his finger caught in the meat grinder. They fired them both."

Thankfully they had been out of earshot of classrooms since she had first confronted him. Now that they were approaching the house, Bergen stopped and asked, "Are we talking blackmail here, Mrs. Dillon?" She didn't bat an eye in response, and he hated it.

"I believe we could be, Dean, but not regarding you unless somebody other than me knows about it." She lowered her voice. "You see, Rhondalynn has a penchant for passion with the prominent, to coin a phrase."

Bergen frowned at her. "If you mean she's having interactions with others in town, I don't believe it."

"'Interactions?' That's an academic way to put it." The blonde smirked at him. "Do Deans do it academically?" She pointed to the house. "Proof of the pudding, so to speak, is in my purse in on the table, if you care to look. Bring the purse out with you. I want another cigarette."

Bergen hated this woman. He hoped she'd die a prolonged, painful and suffocating death from lung cancer—in the next ten minutes. It wasn't so much that he didn't believe Rhondalynn was screwing other people, or care for that matter. He had few feelings for her; she was a convenience, as well as a means to an end. What bothered him was that somebody other than he knew she was with someone else. And, of all other people, it had to be Donna Dillon.

Nodding at students still sipping coffee in the Rather House dining room, Bergen responded to their taunts about the purse. When he got to the foyer he opened the brown leather bag and saw the envelope of pictures right next to three glass vials, like the little containers in which single flowers were sold but smaller and sealed top and bottom. Glancing behind him, Bergen slipped the three tubes into his pants pocket, then glanced quickly through the photographs.

Nice shots, he thought. Must be a hell of a camera to get that detail through bedroom miniblinds. He stuffed one photo into his coat pocket, put the rest back into the purse and closed it, walking down the front steps to the waiting Commissioner's wife.

"Blackmail material if I ever saw it, Mrs. Dillon." He smiled and handed her the purse. He would speak with Rhondalynn this afternoon and find out where they had been discovered. It would not, could not happen again.

"I'll stay in touch, Dean," the woman said, lighting up as she walked to her white Cadillac parked in the Rather House visitor's space. "It's always nice doing business together."

"Yes, isn't it," he said softly. He watched her back out of the lot and turn down Thirty-Second street. Perhaps she would have a fatal accident on the dangerous downtown stretch of expressway on IH35, or be hit by a low flying plane from Mueller Airport. The sky was clouding up with predicted severe storms; maybe she'd be struck by lightning, or skid off the road into Town Lake. Or, he fantasized, maybe he'd just have to kill her himself.

On the other hand, he thought as he walked down the hill from Rather House to his office, she was good for some things. He listened to the gentle tinkle of the glass vials in his pocket and took out the picture one more time.

She had taken the time to warn him that others might become aware of his 'interaction' with Doss and that it could be the end of them both. For the time being, his secret was safe with her. For the time being, that was a comfort. He smiled at the photo. At least it wasn't *his* face clearly visible beneath the upright Rhondalynn Doss on the waterbed.

It was the face attached to phone poles and billboards all over the state of Texas. Only here it was attached to the naked body of Ryan Pace.

* * *

The Lamplight Tavern was a local bar on the Post Road in Scarsdale, New York. Despite its location in the wealthiest village in America, it mainly catered to the people who cooked, cleaned, drove and coddled the inhabitants of that village. The place had barely survived the cutesy renovations of the downtown district and, despite its capitulation to the commercial desires of the city aldermen, it stubbornly retained one small booth in the back that remained as smokey, beer stained, and greasy as the original working class Tavern had always been.

Nikky Dorati sat in the booth next to Albert Scottino, the kid across the street in the Little Italy section of Manhattan where they had grown up. Scotty had met him at LaGuardia in the limousine usually reserved only for Mr. and Mrs. Karl Kamm, who were, at present, pleasantly drinking their way to Europe on the QEII and assuming that their chauffeur was detailing their car.

"I *am* detailing it," the grey headed man with the large moustache said, punching Dorati. "I just have more details to take care of than they thought. Like *you*, for instance."

Dorati had taken the red-eye flight from Austin and arrived at 9:05 a.m. Since he had no luggage they had driven directly to The Lamplighter in time to catch the morning break crowd before some had to get back to serve "luncheon" which was somehow different from "lunch"—or "groceries" as they called them in Texas.

"Thanks for pulling this bunch together," Nikky said, looking at the three men and two women sitting around the booth table chomping doughnuts and slurping coffee. Scotty had done his best on short notice, as he had explained in the car. Each of the servants had at one time worked in the Doss mansion, and knew others who had also worked there, switching employers as they often do. And each of the servants had the same opinion of Rhondalynn Doss.

"She was incredibly kind to us," the cook said. "Always going out of her way, being polite."

"It was no surprise she went into the ministry," the maid and butler agreed. She was hard on her parents because she never rebelled, that we knew of. She was a stickler for responsibility, though. Made her parents look like slobs in that department. Room was always neat as a pin."

"And loved growing things," the old gardener added. "Always bringing things home from some nursery or other for me to plant."

Twenty minutes later, Dorati thought he would die of a sugar overdose. Rhondalynn was so saccharine and perfect as to preclude any wrongdoing ever, according to these people. Well, most of them. When the coffee and doughnuts ran out all five filed out of the booth and left, but Scotty rose and asked the chauffeur to stay for another cup.

Nikky thought the man looked older than Scotty by about ten years. While Scottino's hair was grey, Harold Givens had a shock of white hair loose as a haystack under his black brimmed cap, with a two day growth of stubble poking through his flushed cheeks. He had been noticeably silent in front of the others, occasionally nodding, looking tired, eating more than his share of doughnuts.

"What do you want from me?" Givens asked, a suspicious tone in his voice. "I ain't done nothin'."

"Of course you ain't, Harry," Scottino said. "But I thought maybe there was something you might've forgot with all those people around. You were her personal driver for years, weren't you?"

Givens looked at them, and licked his lips.

"Forgive my manners, Mr. Givens," Dorati said, waving at the Lamplighter bar tender. "What's your pleasure? I'm buying."

After three shots of Wild Turkey, Harold Givens still proclaimed that Rhondalynn Doss was, in every way, the Blessed Virgin Mary. The fourth and fifth shots caused him to remember that she wasn't so Blessed on those frequent forays from Scarsdale into Harlem in the middle of the night. By the sixth Turkey Shot she had lost her Virgin nature, dogging it in the back seat of his limo at three in the morning."

"There was this one time," Givens slurred, "Planned Parenthood or somebody was testing out those female condoms and she tried one. Didn't tell the guy." The chauffeur could hardly contain himself. "When they finished, the thing slid out. The guy freaked. He thought he'd gutted her! I about peed my pants."

The next drink Dorati poured a half a shot at a time, not wanting to lose Givens before all the truth poured out of the bottle. In Turkey Veritas.

Rhondalynn paid the man well to keep her secrets, even supplied him with the alcohol he wanted. But when she left so did the dole, with an implied threat that, if he talked to anyone about her, or her proclivity for black men, she would fix it so he never drove a car again. Harold Givens wasn't sure if that comment referred to his license or his anatomy. She had indicated it would not be pleasant to find out either way.

The old chauffeur tapped the shot glass on the table and spoke very slowly. "Then there was the thing about the money—"

"What money?" Dorati said, paying close attention to the words as Givens leaned closer to the table and his eyelids looked hard to keep open.

"Wasn't even—her money. Lots of it too." The man's arms now cradled his shaggy white head and the cap dropped onto the table.

"Whose money was it?" Dorati spoke loud into his ear.

"He—brought it. She—she sent it."

Scottino looked at Nikky. "Did he say *spent* it?"

Dorati looked at his watch. "Ask him when he wakes up. I'll call you later for the rest of the story." He stood and hugged his old friend. "Right now I gotta go someplace your limo wouldn't last five minutes."

When Nikky stepped out of the cab at 125th and Lenox he was aware that the only other white thing in the vicinity was the crosswalk, and he hoped he would not soon be an outline in one. He had done some of his "work" in Harlem in his active years and he was surprised how his comfort level had dropped with his distance from the area, and the work.

He went into the restaurant whose name had been given to him by a former family contact he had phoned from Texas. "Moteesuh's" was owned by a retired Baptist preacher with a bad sense of humor. The name of the restaurant supposedly came from a racist joke the preacher had been told about the African tribe producing butlers for white folks. They held the pitcher and said: "Mo-tee-suh?" Dorati snickered as he went in and took a seat. If he told that joke in this place with fifteen African-American faces unsmiling in his direction, he'd be the punch line. But here he was sitting in a restaurant making fun of prejudice.

The Rev was right—laughter was the one thing that cut through it all and showed up even the most evil intent to be stupidly inept. Dorati wished Holt was sitting next to him right now. The collar might preclude him having to use the .38 holstered in the small of his back. Or the small .22 strapped to his ankle.

A waitress arrived but did not take his order. Instead, she gave him the bill and left. Dorati read it.

"Follow."

He pushed back the chair and, with thirty eyes watching him like he was an alien, which he was, Dorati followed the waitress into the kitchen, past workers with various implements of death in their hands, and out to the back alley where she left him and locked the door.

Been here, done this, Dorati thought, ready to take a hit from the shadows of the alley or the dumpster. Instead two black men appeared, one with a large .45.

The one in the Brooks Brothers suit without the gun spoke first. "You the honky we suppose to meet here?"

"I don't see no other honkey in the 'hood, do you?"

The other one in jeans and a leather jacket patted down Dorati, finding the .22 at his ankle. "Woosie gun for somebody tough as you supposed to be," he chuckled, stuffing the gun in his waist. "Maybe all those years in the joint softened you up. Especially since we hear you got religion."

Big mistake, Dorati thought. He wasn't going to get what he wanted from these guys, and they were looking to score status points off of him. Like the man who shot Liberty Valence.

"As I see it," Dorati said calmly, "you mofo's have two choices." He edged closer to the man with the gun.

They both laughed and asked what those might be, considering he was an old white dude in the center of Harlem without his piece.

"You can tell me what you know about J. Everett Bergen, a preacher who ran a church and a thrift store and a day school around here somewhere."

"What's the other choice?" the man with the gun asked.

"I hurt you." Nikky did not hesitate. Before he got the sentence out, he knocked the gun from the man's hand, whipped out his own .38 and held it to the head of the man in jeans, while the suit stepped back.

"You choose," Dorati continued. With his free hand he reached down to the man's waist and cocked the trigger of the .22 that pointed down his pants. "But first a word from our sponsor." He pulled the trigger.

The bullet scorched the man's crotch and blew off some toes. He collapsed to the pavement, screaming. The suit looked on, unmoved. "Why should we trust you, honky?" he said. "How we know you not the man?"

"The phone call that connected us told you that. And he's already not going to be pleased with your lack of trust and cooperation. You want me to square it with him, you talk now. If not, we walk away and you deal with him yourself."

The suit stood rigid, his eyes considering Dorati. The man on the ground shouted. "Tell him, Shibaq! Dammit! Tell him! I'm bleedin' to death down here, man!"

"There ain't much to tell about the preacher dude. Bergen done a lot of good for the 'hood, raised a lot of dollars from that church of his, ran day care, helped addicts, pregnant girls, welfare mothers, gangs. He grew up here, knew everybody. Sucker could have run for Congress. Been another Adam Clayton Powell. But he was too dedicated to do it."

"That it?" Dorati asked, sure that it was not. The suit was clearly covering Bergen, protecting one of his own, keeping him safe from whitey.

"Screw this shit, man!" the voice from the pavement shouted. "Shibaq won't tell you nothin' man. Neither will I. We don't rat on brothers. You done time, you know that." He dragged himself up to one foot by hanging on the dumpster door. "But you want to find something, you look at his newspaper column."

"Shut up!" Shibaq shouted, moving closer.

Dorati shot him in the knee.

"Shit!" Shibaq yelled, dropping to the ground.

"Next one takes off an eyelash."

"Third shot they call the cops," the other man said. "You look at that column the preacher wrote under that other name."

"What other name?"

The man told him, and Dorati's eyes widened. "Are you shittin' me?"

"Look here, man. You shot my foot, you crippled my main man over there, and you got connections that could put us both in the East River by midnight. Why the hell would I shit you now?"

Dorati restrapped his .22 and to his ankle. Out of the corner of his eye he saw the suit on the ground reach in his jacket.

Nikky fired and knocked the gun away. As the man on the dumpster lurched for him, Dorati broke his nose with the butt of the .38. "If the name you gave me don't work, you'll get swimmin' lessons in the East River. In the meantime," he said to the suit writhing on the ground, "if anyone asks you who did this, you tell them some dude with a woose .22, mofo."

Certain that someone had called 911 by now, Dorati quickly left the alley and nailed a taxi driven by a guy who thought he'd make double the fare for getting this paleface out of Harlem, which he did.

An hour and several phone calls later—one of them to an informative Albert Scottino—Nikky had everything he had come to get for the Rev on Doss and Bergen. But since he was in the neighborhood—New York City—and since he had some time to waste until his plane left for Austin, he decided to make one more stop on his way to LaGuardia. What could it hurt?

The cab dropped him at 815 Second Avenue, national headquarters of the Episcopal Church. Dorati gave the driver instructions and, like a salmon swimming upstream, pushed against the flow of bodies gushing out the front revolving doors. He squirted into the lobby and checked the building directory for the area he wanted, then took the elevator to the fifteenth floor. The last employee was locking up the Human Resources office and Nikky smiled as he passed her in the hallway.

Waiting until she was on the elevator, he returned to the door, fiddled with the picks Doors had loaned him, and entered the office. The computer surely had a password, so he ignored it and found his way to the file cabinet room two doors deeper within.

Thank God the church still didn't rely on computer backup and kept handwritten duplicate files, much like the ancient scribes in the monasteries. Knowing the church through the Rev, Nikky figured the file he wanted was in a separate cabinet from the rest of the peon clergy, and he was right. It was in the front of the room by a window and some smart-ass secretary had cut out a little pointed hat to decorate the top. A bishop's hat.

Dorati opened the lock and pulled out the "A-K" drawer. He had just removed the file on Emilio Casas when he heard voices in the outer office. He knew he had three options. Hide in the bathroom. Try to make them believe he worked there. Or shoot them. He would try them in descending order of physical damage.

From the bathroom he remembered he had not closed the drawer.

"Either somebody left this open or we got us a burglar in here, Frank," Dorati heard the one guard say.

"Guess we better check the whole place, just in case. Though I don't know what anybody'd want these files on a bunch of sissy-pants preachers for."

Option two, Nikky thought, required drastic action as the two men approached the glassed-in john.

Non-Frank opened the door to find Dorati sitting on the toilet reading a magazine.

"Who the hell are you?" the guard said, holding his breath at the odor in the room.

"Bert Adams," Nikky said, having read the name on the magazine mailing label. He explained that he was checking a reference in one of the files and probably forgot to close the cabinet. "You want my address too? So you can check I work here? I got the shits so I waited till everybody left to come back here and take a dump before I went home—that's home at 4435 Larchmont Drive, Mamaroneck. Go ahead. Call it in." Dorati loudly broke wind. "You'll excuse me if I don't stand up."

Frank joined non-Frank and quickly backed away from the room.

"We'll leave you be, buddy," Frank said over non-Frank's shoulder. "Just make sure the doors lock behind you on your way out."

"Sure thing, fellas. Thanks for checkin' on me," Dorati said as the two guards fled the area.

When he heard the outer door slam shut, Nikky pulled the folder out of the magazine and read the file on Bishop Emilio Casas of the Diocese of Austin. Ten minutes later he closed and locked the door to the Human Resources Office of the Episcopal Church with a smile on his face and photocopies in his pocket.

As the plane took off from LaGuardia, Dorati sat back in the first class upgrade he had conned out of the SkyLounge agent and smiled at the flight attendant.

"Something to drink, Mr. Dorati?" she asked with a plaster smile.

"Rye. And keep it comin'," he said as he ran a credit card through the seat phone. The tone rang five times before the voice answered.

"Yo! Rev! Nikky here, man! I'm on my way home with the goods." He paused to let Holt speak. "No kidding, Rev. Don't go to sleep. This shit is worth waitin' for. And while I was in town I also got you a little ace in the hole you can use with another one of your buddies next time he gets nasty with you." Dorati frowned as the attendant handed him his rye. "No! Don't go tonight. At least wait till I get there and clear it with security." He listened to the protest, knowing he couldn't win. "Okay, Rev. Have it your way. But be back to the place by midnight. And bring an open mind."

✳ ✳ ✳

At nine p.m. Marion Josey parked her car in the nested part of the San Jacinto Hospital parking garage reserved for employees. She got out, hit the electronic lock, then stopped a second to pull her long brown hair back into a pony tail and wrap it with a rubber band. It would be a long night in ICU attending Kristen Wade, or pretending to attend her. Maybe they could get in another few hands of cards or, now that the patient was supposed to be feeling better, they could call up a movie on the cable and watch some buildings blow up or bad guys get clobbered. If things got real quiet, she could sit Omar with Kristen and slip out to turn a few tricks before the sun rose and the hospital awoke from its nightly coma. She had agreed to do this stint as a favor to Jill, but the truth was it was getting old and so was she. There was money to be made and she was missing out on her regular job.

It wouldn't be much longer, anyway, she thought as she picked up her purse and trudged toward the stairwell. The election was day after tomorrow and there wouldn't be any further need to keep Wade under wraps. Hell, she was already giving phone interviews, keeping her name before the public, playing the fallen heroine.

Josey opened the door and stepped inside before she realized the stairwell was dark. The light was probably just out, but she still put her hand on the small spray canister of mace slung on her purse.

"Evening, Marion," a female voice echoed around her.

"Who's there?" she said, stopping on the stairs and aiming the mace straight ahead. A strong medicinal odor filled the blackness as one rigid hand held her arm while another clamped a cloth to her nose and mouth. She inhaled once and dropped into deeper blackness.

"I'm your replacement, honey," the voice said, as a woman in blue scrubs dragged her backwards under the stairs, taped her mouth and wrists and ankles.

Ten minutes later, the husky woman strode into the San Jacinto Hospital ICU, spoke briefly with the charge nurse, and went straight to Bed 16.

"Who are you?" Omar Kandu frowned at the stranger.

"Marion's sick, honey," the woman said, introducing herself as Paula Roberts, tossing her heavy purse onto the wooden cabinet holding the blue patient chart. She winked at him and claimed Marion said he was good for springing for pizza for the patient late at night.

"Guess I'd better check on the patient," Paula Roberts announced, her hand on the room door.

Kandu gently removed her hand. "Bad idea," he shook his head, "if you know what I mean."

"I've seen people on the pot before," the woman snickered. "And I *am* a woman."

"Visitor," he whispered, not letting go of her hand.

"Ohhhhh," the nurse replied, backing off. "Got it." She sat on the high stool by the chart. "You mind getting us something to drink while I catch up on charting here? Got to enter nurses notes that I examined her and found her vitals fine—just for the record."

Kandu grinned. "Right about now her vitals are more than fine." He turned to go to the nurse's lounge for a couple of soft drinks. "Don't let *nobody* near that door," he ordered. "I don't care *who* they are."

"Got it." Nurse Roberts turned from him and opened the chart. She began writing numbers in various boxes, seeming to ignore the big man's absence.

As soon as he was out of sight she bent further over, removed a small, silenced .38 from her purse, and held it under the loose scrub top. She slipped off her perch and, glancing quickly around to assure no one was paying attention, she put her huge hand on the door to Bed Sixteen.

Lucas had been in the room five minutes when Kristen stood from the bed and untied the strings of her backless hospital gown. Holt pulled her to him, felt her warm flesh and pressed her lips to his as the door suddenly opened.

"What the—?" Kristen started, as she turned around.

Holt saw the woman's gun and pushed Kristen aside toward the bed. He heard two spits from the nurse's hand and saw Kristen's belly turn crimson. From his own waist he yanked the Smith & Wesson and was about to fire when a cursing Omar Kandu yanked her by the neck from behind.

The woman raised her gun to Omar's head as he grabbed her hand and pulled the trigger at her own temple. Kandu slammed and locked the door against the pounding of other staff. He dropped the dead woman to the floor as Lucas ran to Kristen.

"Get somebody to help her!" Holt yelled, watching the blood gush from her belly.

"You get out of here first!" Omar yelled back. "Go on! Go, Rev! It's no use you gettin' caught now, man!" He pulled Holt away and pushed him toward the rear door. "Quick now! I'll get her taken care of." He forced the shaking Holt through the door toward the service elevator.

As he made his way down the stairwell to the loading dock, the Rev felt stunned, racked between his desire to be beside Kristen and his guilt for having let her get hurt. He should have thought faster, moved quicker, known what was happening. He was furious at the sons of bitches who did this and at himself for thinking he could play in this league without injury to someone he cared about, and loved. And, he thought as he hurried through the parking lot into the night, he was damned sick and tired of hiding.

He felt like the enemy had won again, knowing that the headlines on election day would read that the candidate for U.S. Senate had been shot again, and that the Reverend Lucas Holt had been spotted running from the scene. Again.

The image of Kristen lying limp and bleeding fueled his determination to make it safely to the tunnel, to lure them there after him, where he would even the score.

Vengeance may belong to God, but Holt would provide the opportunity—and maybe the means.

• Eight •

Susan Granger faced Marion Josey and Max over the patient in ICU Bed 16.

"I am *so* sorry," Josey said. "When that stairwell light was out I thought about going back to the car. It was so stupid. I feel like I'm responsible for this."

Susan shook her head as Max walked around the bed and hugged Josey. She knew it would all fall apart, that she never should have gone along with this. Now Kristen really was shot and this prostitute felt responsible. What would they do now? Where the hell was Lucas?

"Honey," Max said, "you're lucky she didn't bag you in the car and kill you. You didn't do this. Besides, right before you got here, the doctor gave us an update."

"She's right," Granger reluctantly admitted. "Prints say this woman's for hire, not in the same sense you are, of course." She turned to Max. "Fill her in."

Granger listened to Max explain that the doctor had just been by with a real nurse, accompanied by real cops and the real Omar, who had been thoroughly exonerated by the ICU staff as having acted in self defense, not to mention saving the Rev's life.

The doctor indicated that Wade was also a lucky woman. Holt had turned her at such an angle that the bullets went right through her abdomen, missing bone and major arteries. One had severed her appendix and they had removed that along with about two feet of intestine torn by the shots. That was the good news.

The bad news was that her assailant had used "dirty bullets" from a small caliber .22 which were coated with some kind of bacteria that was causing serious infection. The Centers for Disease Control in Atlanta recognized the scenario when they were called. Militias around the country were dipping their bullets in everything from dog feces to AIDS infected blood. Fortunately for the victims, most of the harmful bacteria or viruses had long since dried out and died, but occasionally, like now, it had been done recently enough to implant the material in the body as the bullet tore through flesh and blood. In Kristen's case it was probably fresh pigeon droppings from the parking garage.

Her tissue wounds would heal. The question was whether she could fight off the sepsis—the infected blood that was causing her extremely high temperature.

Susan took Kristen's limp wet hand and spoke to Marion. "They've got a plastic mat under her with cold water circulating through it and a high dose antibiotic pumping directly into this tube in her neck." She looked at Kristen and wondered what was going through her morphine sedated mind. Was she thinking of the election? Dreaming of Washington? Or of Lucas Holt? Susan wondered what the hell Kristen wanted with him? Stupid question; she wanted the same thing Susan wanted. But she could have anybody and she kept coming back to Lucas. Susan felt so different from her—dowdy, unattractive, with a job at the opposite end of the food chain. Maybe she should give up trying. "She'll pull through this," she said, finally. "She has to."

They sent Marion Josey home with a promise to keep her informed. Max wiped Kristen's face with a cold cloth as Susan did the same with her hands and feet, until the nurse opened the door and announced they'd have to let her rest for the evening.

They passed by the other ICU beds on their way out of the Unit and Granger, knowing the nurses wouldn't give out confidential information even to her, asked Omar what he knew about the conditions of the patients in beds One through Five.

"Big time dyin'," he said. "Look at those nurses takin' care of 'em. Suited up cap to shoe covers, double gloved, breathin' through special face masks."

Max stopped between Beds 3 and 4. "I know these two. They worked for me for a short time, then left to do exotic dancing at a new club south of the river." She looked through the glass at their staring eyes and open mouths. "What is it?"

"Yo, Colette," Omar said to the nurse outside the door. "What'd you tell me that was?" He nodded at the two women. "It's okay, they're family."

"Botulism," she replied, continuing to chart. "It's not contagious, but we're suited up in case there's some other bacteria attached to it. The toxin attacks the central nervous system and causes immediate neuromuscular dysfunction. You lose control of all your muscles, have total body seizures, get a fever that burns your brain out, and die." The long haired nurse looked up. "If you're lucky. If you're not, we pretend we can do something for you, like with these five, and we prolong the agony. Or at least we did." She pointed to Bed 1. "Until that doctor showed up."

Max, Susan and Omar looked at the totally gowned and masked figure in the room leaning over the patient.

"He walked in from Recovery and talked with the attending for these five women. Next thing I knew we d/c'd all aggressive treatment but comfort care and upped the morphine—like we should have done when they came in."

"What's he doing in there?" Max asked the nurse, but stared at Susan.

"Just checking them. He's been in each room. That's the last one." She pointed to the opening door. "Looks like he's leaving now."

Susan strode over to him.

"Don't touch me, Lieutenant," the voice behind the mask said, as the other two joined her. "You wouldn't want to take any nasty little bugs back to your nice cozy police department, would you?"

"Can't get bugs from botulism, mister," Granger said. "You're just gowned up so nobody can recognize those gorgeous eyes."

Maxine smiled. "You're in there anointing them, aren't you, Rev?"

The muffled voice responded. "Couldn't send 'em Home without a proper finish. Had to grease the way for them. You never know. Can't hurt. Might help." He dropped the small oil stock into a sealed plastic cup and handed it to her. "Take this back to Maggie Mae's and sterilize it in boiling water for twenty minutes."

Susan shook her head and smiled at him. "You take some weird risks, Lucas." This was why she loved him. He went where few people would ever go and did what few would do. Just like her Dad. Just like herself.

"So do you, Lieutenant." He winked at her.

"My main man!" Omar said. "Anything else you need, Rev?"

"Yes there is," Holt said, pretending he was gathering the family of a patient around the room for a conference. "I want you to detail Lieutenant Granger for the rest of the day."

Susan looked puzzled. "I don't need this guy shadowing me, Lucas. I'm not being followed."

"It's an unmarked Commissioner's car, Susan. I saw it when Dorati dropped me here." He turned to Kandu. "She can't lose him, but you can."

"Anything goes?"

"Anything but hurting the tails."

Susan knew that ranged from a potato up the exhaust to shooting out tires. More laws broken. More hell to pay. More problems when it doesn't work out.

"Listen, Lucas," she said. "I'm not so sure I can go along with this any more."

"Do it, Omar," Holt replied.

"Shit." Kandu frowned as he left. "Okay."

"Just one more day, Susan," he said.

"I don't know."

Maxine winked at him. "Hurry back. We need you bad." She blew him a kiss and started to go. "Let me put it another way. If you don't get your skinny butt back in that office soon, I *will* take the bitch off the count."

Lucas smiled behind the mask. "Give me twenty four, darlin'," he said.

"I'll fix the program so you preachin' Sunday, then," she replied, leaving the unit.

Susan looked into the familiar eyes that showed above the mask. "I'm having trouble here, Lucas," she shook her head. "We need to talk when this is over." Hopefully she would have her feelings straight by then. Hopefully he'd still be around.

"I know it." He looked back at her, clearly showing his deep feelings, yet pulled to the woman across the room fighting to live. "I am too. Things are moving too fast. We'll talk. I promise." He glanced across to Bed 16. "Walk down the hall with me as if you're discussing the patients. We have to figure out how to take care of Dillon."

Granger felt Holt's frustration as he punched the wall plate that swung open the ICU doors. She wanted to put her arm around him but couldn't. He would have to shed more than the protective mask and gloves for them to touch each other. But that would have to wait. For now, they needed all the protection they could get.

※ ※ ※

Cora Mae Hartwig peeked around the corner of the Sacristy into the church. Individual mourners sparsely dotted the pews in the sanctuary, like widely separated grains of a newsprint photograph. These people didn't know the ten-year-old kid dubbed the 'Dumpster Boy' by the local media. They came because they didn't know him and should have. Some were from St. Margaret's, some from other congregations, others from the street. If you put the picture together, she thought, Lucas would say it spelled community.

"People can be so compassionate, and yet so mean," she said to Travis Layton, who pulled on a cassock and surplice with the help of Case Atkinson.

"You talkin' about the congregation out there or the Reverend Doss?" Layton asked. "Would you hand me that pectoral cross, Case?"

Atkinson took a large Celtic cross with a yellow ribbon from a cabinet hook. "She really left?"

"Yes, she did," Cora Mae replied. She thumbed through the Prayer Book for the Order for Burial and handed it to Travis. "Said she had to do home visits on people who needed her and weren't drunk in a dumpster no matter how old they were." She poured coffee from a thermos and gave it to the old lawyer.

Layton took a long drink. "So as Senior Warden this task falls to me. I just hope I can get through it." He took another drink and looked at Cora Mae.

"That's why I'm here to help you, Travis, dear. I'll be right back to light the candles and do the readings." She took Case by the arm. "And I asked you to come down to answer a question for Max about the Treasury area." Cora Mae led Atkinson into the hallway. "If you'll take the elevator down there, Max will show you the problem with one of the old pilings."

"No problem." Case nodded and got on the elevator. "I'll try to get back up for the service." He heard Cora Mae mumble something unintelligible as the doors closed.

The elevator descended three floors to the sub-basement of the foundation, where the collection of religious relics was housed. Nearly all of the priceless works of liturgical art had been returned after the "Saints of God Murders" were brought to an end. The doors opened onto the glass case highlighting the Spanish chalice encrusted with jewels. Case never ceased being awed by its design, and the dramatic display on black velvet with high intensity light shining on it.

But outside the light there was a shadow. And the shadow spoke.

"You wanted to see me," Holt said. "Here I am."

For a moment Case Atkinson looked stunned. "But—I thought they'd *take* me to you."

"So your blackmailer could follow you to me?"

Case drew a deep breath and stepped back. "What? How?" He hung his head. "Lucas, I'm sorry," his voice cracked. "I didn't know what else to do."

Holt went to him, hugged him while he cried. Strains of organ music sounded vaguely in the background, resonating down deep into the earth, reminding him of the scene of mourning being played out above.

"I can't believe you came to me," Atkinson whispered.

"You were right, Case. I'm still your priest. This is what I'm *supposed* to do. It's what Jesus did on the lake when the disciples were in the storm. It's what all those people are doing upstairs right now, coming to each other in the midst of the storm to try to calm the waters stirred up by the tragedy of that dead kid, or maybe just hold on to each other as it rolls over them." He led him to a seat and sat opposite. "What's your storm, Case?"

The architect quit sobbing and took a deep breath. "It's really bad, Lucas. Happened when I was a kid," Atkinson began. "And I assume this is of a confessional nature, unrepeatable."

Holt nodded and wondered how hard it would be, how bad it would seem. Doors had told him all that happened at the Clubhouse, that Pace thought Atkinson's career could be ruined by it. Lucas took a deep breath and relaxed. In all the years he had listened to confessions at the prison, the story was never as unforgivable as the confessor thought. People were always much harder on themselves than God was.

Case began, looking at the floor. "As a teenager, I became really confused about my sexual orientation. I felt caught between what my parents and society said, and what my hormones were telling my brain." He looked up at Holt, then back down. "I tried dating girls, even tried some petting, but I always ended up having more fun with boys."

Lucas nodded. "Okay."

"Well, once when my parents were out of town, another kid and I got drunk and took Polaroid pictures of each other, stupidly posing with his two dogs in suggestive positions."

Holt could see him blush. "Is this the bad part yet?"

Case looked up. "Sort of." He kept his head raised now. "At the time we thought it was uproariously funny. But then we continued to look at the photos from time to time together as a prelude to exploring our homosexual feelings for each other. When we went our separate ways after graduation, the other kid swore he had burned the photos."

"And now they're back?" Lucas asked.

Case nodded. "It seems the guy joined a fundamentalist religious group and 'reformed' into an anti-gay spokesman for them. As a part of his repentance, he produced the photos as evidence of his sinful past and of the sins of homosexuality against God and nature." Atkinson hung his head. "I'm sorry Lucas. Really sorry."

Holt laid a hand on his shoulder. "Keep talking."

"It wasn't long before the network got the photos to Pace to use as he saw fit—and he saw fit to use them to get me to lead him to you." Case shook his head. "I feel so bad about this."

"And you've never told anyone about the pictures?" Holt said, struck once again by the depth of what people hold inside, let fester, hold secret as though they could never be acceptable if the truth about them were known.

"Never. I thought they didn't exist. Then when I knew they did, I felt they were a part of my sordid past—and now I'm not even worried about my career." He began to cry.

"It's the adoption, isn't it?"

Case nodded and tried to stop. "It's one thing to be a gay architect in a liberal community, but one look at those photos and we would *never* get that kid, no matter how hard Travis tries."

Lucas handed him a paper towel and tried to keep his temper in check. He hated it when people used power unfairly, were rigid and judgmental against those more vulnerable. Fortunately, the God Squad could fix this.

"I need your forgiveness, Lucas. And God's."

"I'd absolve you of your sin if I could find one," Holt smiled at him. "Other than being a teenager. God knows we all need forgiveness for that."

Atkinson looked up. "The sin is letting myself be used to get to you. Being so afraid of losing that kid that I was willing to risk you for the adoption. I feel like Judas."

"Who, just for the record, was forgiven. But let's get this straight. You're not Judas and I'm not J.C." Holt took his hand. "Go back to Pace and tell him you found out where I am."

Case pulled away. "No! I can't do that, Lucas."

"Sure you can." Holt did his best to sound convincing. "Tell him to bring the pictures to Mother's at midnight tonight. I'll make sure his operatives see me going in, but when he walks in he'll find Omar and Travis waiting for him." Holt had learned the art of sociopathic lying from the God Squad, and he was good at it. Prison education was always a two way street. Right now he had to distract both Atkinson and Pace in order to do what needed done.

"And you will be where?"

"I'll be back in church with you Sunday morning if all goes as expected." Lucas patted him on the back. "But I need to ask you something else. You've spent time around Pace. Has he mentioned the phrase 'Dead Ed' or anything like that? We think it may be a code name for an assassination."

Case's eyes widened. "My God! What's this man up to?"

"Maybe nothing. That's what we're trying to find out. Ring any bells?"

"Only thing comes immediately to mind is Deep Eddy Pool on the Colorado."

"That's what everybody says. Maybe we should just accept it as the obvious and go from there. Maybe it's somebody who goes there a lot, or lives near there."

Case narrowed his eyes. "Or lives in Westlake on the opposite shore of the river from Deep Eddy? You know there are some pretty fabulous homes visible from there. You could shoot from Deep Eddy and hit the kitchens of about a dozen mansions in the hills up there. I know because I built the views."

The deep base of the organ continued again and the elevator light dinged. Cora Mae, dressed in an acolyte's red cassock, scurried toward them.

"I slipped out of the service to tell you that Ryan Pace and the police are outside and threatening to search the church when the funeral is over."

"Shit!" Case said. "I told him to follow me to find you. I guess he figured since I disappeared in here I was with you."

Holt shook his head. "No problem. You two go back up to the sanctuary."

"But how will you get out of here?" Case said, worried.

Cora Mae Hartwig winked at Holt and led Atkinson onto the elevator. "He'll be fine, dear. He passed Ascension 101 in seminary with flying colors."

The doors were nearly closed when Case pushed them back open with his hands. "Wait a second," he said. "What if 'Dead Ed' was a person's name? Like Eddie Wilson who owns some restaurants?"

Holt nodded at him. "Good suggestion. Now get out of here." He watched the door shut, then turned to the Treasury. His eyes studied the small calligraphied placard describing a silver pyx to hold communion wafers.

"1823 A.D.," he said aloud. "A.D." He said it again. "A.D." What if that was it? What if they were *initials*? Not A.D. but *E.D.* What if 'Dead Ed' was really 'Dead E.D.'?

His excitement was drowned by the sound of the descending elevator. He quickly moved to the tunnel entrance and vanished behind the stone.

∗ ∗ ∗

The figure bundled in rain gear walked with an umbrella down West 29th Street past St. Andrew's Episcopal School to the sign proclaiming that this was the nation's first Hike and Bike Trail. Calf length rubber boots, green rain pants and coat all matched the fisherman's cap pulled down around the obscured face of the walker. The rain had increased from drizzle to steady drops, and no other people were walking or biking.

A hundred yards south of the entrance to the school the trail veered off into side trails, most leading back to the main route beside Shoal Creek to the river. The rubber boots slipped on the wet rock trail that led off from the rest into dense tangles of bushes and vines, ending under a dark cliff overhang that seemed to be a huge rock wall.

Folding up the umbrella, the figure moved aside a few well placed rocks, according to the instructions given by the operatives who had found the place. Two minutes later, the boots were inside where a flashlight led them through the initial entrance to the tunnel, until the series of timed lights made it unnecessary.

It was not long before the limestone bridge came into view, along with the obviously inhabited area around it. A stream of water about a foot wide flowed slowly under the bridge, filling the tunnel with the fresh smell of rain from outside.

A small hand placed a rain gloved finger on each object. Everything must be touched but not moved; the cot with its papers and magazines, the cooler, the porta-john, the chair, now marked by an unnoticeable energy, anointed, cleansed, claimed for God's purposes, for their purposes, which were one and the same.

Why else would God have led them here? To this of all places?

Smiling, heart pounding, the figure removed a map, placed it on the bridge beside an architect's hand-held compass to check the calculations. Eyes widened, looked again at the rocky bottom of the tunnel, marked the map one last time, incredulous at the ironic good fortune, thanking God it was more than that. Then, with the map to plot the exact location, a penny was slipped under a rock to mark it.

This was even better than the spots that had been planned above ground—less visible, better access. And, with Lucas Holt here, more perfect.

As if it had been planned by God.

Hurrying to leave, the figure stepped over the fast flowing stream, vaguely aware that it had doubled in width.

• Nine •

Holt watched her repeat her statement.

"Yes, Commissioner, that's what I said." Granger sat on a wooden crate of bullets and spoke into the phone. "I want you to come to the munitions storeroom right now. Alone. It is extremely important." She paused and looked at Lucas. "Right. Good." Granger closed the flip phone and pulled out her .44. She checked the cylinder, shoved two rounds into the empty slots and held the gun in her lap with the safety off.

Lucas sat silent, trying to control his nervousness.

"This better work," she said aloud, then sat back to wait the eternity until the door opened. She pictured Dillon slamming down the phone, timed him striding from his office to the back stairs instead of wasting time on the elevator, opening the fire door at the end of the hall, putting his hand on the doorknob. Which now turned.

The towering Christopher Dillon pushed open the door to face an armed Susan Granger.

"What the hell is this?"

And an unarmed Lucas Holt.

"Shit!" he said, watching Holt lock the door behind him. "I should have known you two love birds were in this together."

"Sit down and shut up," Holt ordered, watching the big man's hands. Along with the eyes, they were precursors of movement.

"What the hell do you think you're doing Lieutenant?"

"Do as he says, Commissioner," Granger said, holding the gun on him. "Just listen to reason for a minute."

"Reason at the end of a gun?" Dillon clenched his hands and Holt grabbed a nightstick from an open box. "I don't think so." He started to move and Lucas crashed the stick down on a crate, smashing the lid.

"Sit down or the next thing to break is you," Holt warned.

Susan kicked a chair over to Lucas, who pulled the angry man into it and secured his wrists behind with her handcuffs. Holt calculated that, if this whole thing went South, all Susan had done here was hold a gun that nobody had yet proved was loaded, and a court might believe she did that under duress from him.

"DAMMIT, YOU TWO! LET ME OUT OF HERE!" Dillon yelled. "I'LL HAVE YOUR BADGE FOR THIS, LIEUTEN-ANT!"

Lucas slammed a roll of duct tape onto the crate next to them. "You can shut up or I can shut you up," he said. "Your choice."

"SHUT YOURSELF UP, YOU SHIT EXCUSE FOR A PREACHER," Dillon continued to bellow. "WHEN I GET OUT OF HERE I'LL—"

Holt ripped off a length of the silver tape and slapped it over the Commissioner's mouth, then wrapped two more long strips under his chin and around behind his neck. Dorati had taught him always to secure legs to the chair as well, since they were the most powerful and lethal muscles in the body.

Granger lowered her gun and stood by Holt. "You said you didn't want to see me again until Lucas Holt was beside me, in handcuffs." She holstered her gun. "You got what you asked for."

Holt glanced at his watch. They would have to hurry to keep the schedule. "Here's the deal, Commissioner," he said. The Rev walked as he talked, glancing from Dillon to the now seated Granger. "First off, I made her do this."

"Lucas," Susan began.

"No, we have to tell him the truth. I did. I apologize for the inconvenience, but I couldn't exactly drop in to your office to chat. She was afraid if the God Squad captured you, someone would get hurt." It was probably a good enough lie to work for Travis Layton, if it came to that. He knew from the look in Dillon's eyes that the Commissioner didn't believe a word of it, but that didn't matter. What mattered was what he would have to say under oath that he was told.

Holt continued. "Now I'm going to make some assumptions. You can nod or shake your head, or you don't have to answer at all, just listen and take this all in."

Dillon's eyes followed him, and Lucas knew he was thinking of two things: escape and revenge. Holt whacked the baton on a pole. "Quit trying to kill me and listen up."

The Commissioner's eyes squinted.

"Better," Holt said. "Here we go." He perched on a box of tear gas grenades. "I assume you're as right wing as they come, that you have militia connections from New Mexico to Louisiana, and that, if the time was right, you would muster them in defense of what you believe to be the right course for the nation."

Dillon's eyes did not disagree.

"Because of this, it goes without saying that you are a strong financial and political supporter of Ryan Pace and his cronies."

The Commissioner made no response.

"Furthermore I assume," Lucas said, "that you controlled your background checks so that Governor Doggett has no knowledge of your private associations and, quite frankly, has no need to know because—and this is a major assumption that I hope to hell is correct—you are at your core a law abiding man. I'm counting on that."

Dillon glanced at Granger and Holt knew he was pleading with her, ordering her to do something as a cop, to stop this kidnapping, this embarrassment, this humiliation.

"I can't help you out here, Commissioner. I am in fear of my life," she said for the record. "Except to say that I think he's right about you, so far."

The Commissioner rolled his eyes back to Holt, who stood and looked directly at him.

"I also assume you don't know shit about your wife."

Dillon's face colored.

"Like the fact that she's contacted militias on both sides of the border, and that she's fluent in Spanish."

The Commissioner grimaced.

"That's right. I imagine she openly struggles with the language to cover her fluency, enabling her to use your Mexican house servants in El Paso to make contacts with dealers across the border."

Dillon shook his head vigorously.

"I can give you names of the contacts if you wish so you can talk to them yourself. They'll tell you how they helped her bring in illegal weapons shipments for her militia friends." Holt looked around the munitions room. "Stuff that makes these toys pale by comparison." Holt knew Christopher Dillon was on the point of exploding. There was one more card, however, that needed to be played.

He tossed the barf bag with Donna Dillon's name scribbled on it in the lap of the struggling man. "The weird thing is that she recently had been getting stolen lab animals from Mexico. Animals used in laboratory experiments over there, still alive. God only knows what she did with them." He bent over and looked directly at Dillon. "Or what *you* did with them?"

The Commissioner shook his head violently, kicked at the tape restraints on his legs and broke through one of them, knocking Holt against the boxes and tipping the chair over backwards.

Granger helped Holt to his feet and watched him tightly secure the leg against the chair.

"What goes around comes around, Commissioner," Holt said, leaving the man on his back on the floor still bound to the chair. "Instead of worrying about my relationship with Lieutenant Granger, you should go home and have a little chat with your own wife. My guess is that she took you at your right-wing word in your home harangues and now is out-righting you at your own game, using your office as a cover for her own activities, at one level thinking you'd be pleased, at another knowing you'd be furious at making a complete travesty of the law."

Christopher Dillon was flushed and breathing hard.

"Do it now, Lucas," Susan said. "Before he has a heart attack."

Holt held up a small object. "When you wake up, this handcuff key will be taped to your hand." He doused a sweet smelling chemical on a washcloth and Dillon's eyes squinted with hate. "I expect we'll round up the 'Dead Ed' assassin tonight—to be delivered to you in time to make the morning press run of the Statesman. If we don't, you two are out of jobs, so instead of being pissed off, you should wish us luck."

Dillon jerked at the restraints, showing his defiance.

"Sweet dreams," Lucas said, holding the chloroformed cloth over the Commissioner's nose long enough to assure that he had actually inhaled it and had not just held his breath.

"You're right, Susan." Holt took her hand as they were about to leave the munitions room in separate directions.

"What about?"

He held her face and kissed her. "This better work."

* * *

Jimmy Brickhouse nervously shifted from one foot to the other under the portico outside classrooms at the Episcopal Theological Seminary of Texas. The rain had picked up during the afternoon and flash flood warnings were being issued for low lying areas around town—standard procedure for any significant rainfall in Austin. The usually shallow creeks suddenly had more water than they could handle and overflowed into low water crossings, blocking roads temporarily. But it wasn't the rain that made Brickhouse nervous. It was the place.

On Friday afternoons faculty and students usually left before four and hit the local watering holes to relax and swap sermon ideas for their Sunday placements. Brickhouse knew this because a friend of his tended bar at the British Pub around the corner. But as the students left today, they paid particular attention to the black man loitering in the classroom area.

Did he need a lift to a homeless shelter? Would he like to see a social worker? Was there someone on the staff he needed to see? Could they assist him in some way? All polite ways of asking who the hell he was and why the hell was he standing there? At least the last one asked if he wanted to join them for a beer.

He told them he was just waiting for the rain to stop so he could walk back to his car which had stalled a couple of blocks away and no, he didn't really want a ride there. What he wanted to tell them was that he had trailed their Dean all afternoon and now was waiting for the Rev and Dorati to take over. But the dudes and chicks in the black shirts and white collars made him nervous. They dressed like the Rev but they weren't like the Rev. Though he knew it was probably his own paranoia, he felt like they judged him, or would if they knew him. He wanted a cigarette worse than he had in the three years since he quit. And the rain reminded him he had to pee.

Brickhouse breathed a sigh of relief when the black Beemer rounded the corner of Rathervue Place and parked in a slot marked "Faculty Only." Holt and Dorati hurried through the rain to the shelter of the portico.

"Yo, Rev," Brickhouse said. "Here's what's happenin'. I been on him all afternoon except for about an hour when I figured he was teachin' a class here and I grabbed a burger around the corner at Trudy's."

Brickhouse further explained that the seminary had cleared out for the weekend and that he had seen the lady preacher from Maggie Mae's walk up the hill to Rather House about an hour ago. Last he checked they were not on the first or second floors, so they had to be up in the Bishop's Quarters, where visiting faculty stayed.

"Good job, Brick," Dorati said.

"Lay low and keep your cell phone on," Holt added. "The next twelve hours are crucial."

"You got it, Rev," Brickhouse replied and held a newspaper over his head to run to his car, also parked in the faculty lot.

Lucas and Nikky climbed the wet stone steps in the rain, entering Rather House by the screened porch. Just as Brickhouse had said, the first two floors were vacant. As they approached the stairs to the third floor, Dorati whispered to Holt.

"Step on the far left or right side and they won't creak."

Holt nodded and followed him. About halfway up they heard noises from the Bishop's Quarters. Gasping. Moaning. Calling the Deity.

"That's why it's bad to be an atheist," Holt whispered.

Dorati turned and looked puzzled.

"You've got nobody to call on when you're having an orgasm."

Nikky stifled a laugh. "Sounds like he's doin' to her what she's doin' to Maggie Mae's."

They stood in front of the door and shrugged their shoulders. Dorati mouthed the word "Locked?" and made a turning key sign with his fingers. Holt shook his head no and pointed his nose in the air to signal arrogance. An overly confident Dean would assume all the students were gone and that they had the whole house to themselves. He took firm hold of the knob and quickly thrust open the door.

"Hi Rhon! Hi Ev! Don't get up!" Holt said to the naked bodies astride each other on the bed. "This gives new meaning to 'anticlimactic.'"

The woman screamed and the man shoved a hand under the pillow.

"Down, Rev!" Dorati yelled, pushing Holt aside and holding a gun on the man on the bottom. "Just keep all your hands where I can see them and take that one slowly out from there." Nikky cocked the hammer. "And don't do nothin' we'll all regret." He stuck the gun in Bergen's mouth and carefully removed the .38 as his hand came out from the pillow.

"Let me put something on!" Rhondalynn pleaded, tears running down her face.

Holt tossed her the pillow from under Bergen's head. "Just relax—if that's possible in that position—and shut up," he said. "We won't take long." He picked up the bottle of chilled champagne next to the bed as Doss crawled next to Bergen and pulled the sheet up around her.

"Help yourself," the Dean said with an insipid tone. "And you'll probably want her to go along with it."

Holt shook his head and showed the bottle to Dorati. "Bad year for both, wouldn't you say?"

"Anything without a screw top is okay with me, Rev," Nikky replied, holding out a glass from the tray of food.

"Here's to old friends," the Rev said, clicking glasses with Dorati. "Like the one in New York who likes his Turkey Wild, Rhondalynn."

She glared at him. "Harry Givens doesn't know shit from Shinola," Doss replied with a sullen tone. "That old alky can hardly drive, much less think straight. Whatever he told you was drunken fantasy."

"Yeah, that's the words he used exactly," Dorati snickered. "'Drunken fantasy.' But it was you and your partner here doggin' it in the back seat."

Holt saw Bergen react. "Keep those palms visible, Ev," he said, "if you want to be able to walk down the stairs." He picked up a piece of shrimp and swallowed the champagne. "So Nikky and I are guessing that the three of you—Rhon, Pace and Everett—met at a fundy fund raiser in New York. Is that correct?"

"You're the smart ass, Holt," Rhondalynn said, furiously angry. "You keep talking."

Holt glanced at Nikky who knew the signal to keep an extra eye on her. They had done this before in prison. When someone got angry they got stupid, acted impulsively and often got dead.

"Okay." Lucas moved beside the bed and punched in some numbers on the phone, then hit the speaker button. "But let's do it with the proper company." This call was in honor of Max and Cora Mae and Travis Layton and everyone else at St. Margaret's.

"What the hell do you think you're doing?" Bergen growled.

"Diocesan Office," the secretary's voice came across the box.

"Bishop Casas, please. This is Lucas Holt."

The line froze, then dialed, then a voice hurled out.

"Where the hell are you, Lucas? Stay right there and I'll have the police pick you up. Don't worry, I'll come along if you wish."

"You'd love that, wouldn't you Emil?" Holt shook his head. "No, this time the call isn't about me. It's about your two fair haired favorites, Everett Bergen and Rhondalynn Doss." He motioned to them. "Say hello, kids."

The two mumbled greetings as Lucas explained they were in the guest quarters of Rather House, drinking champagne and porking their brains out. A long silence followed from the stationary box by the bed. Finally the bishop spoke.

"And your problem with that would be what, Father Holt?"

Lucas looked at Nikky. Either The Right Reverend Emilio Casas, Bishop of the Diocese of Austin, had had a personality-altering stroke or God spoke to him in the night and made him a Democrat. Of course, Holt thought, catching Bergen's self assured smile, there was always one more possibility.

"Ding. Ding. Ding." Holt nodded to Dorati. "Third lemon just dropped into place. And hot damn," he said, pouring more champagne for himself and Nikky, "I never even considered it before now."

"If you were smart, you'd let Dean Bergen hang up the phone now, Father Holt," the speaker pronounced calmly.

"Hell, you know I'm not smart, Bishop. That's why you dumped me on St. Margaret's in the first place, isn't it?" He walked around the bed, closer to the speaker. "Let's see if I've got this straight, Emil. Correct me if I'm wrong any place here, just butt right in and stop me."

The speaker was silent.

"You know about their affair and condone it, though you have loose bowels in public whenever my name is mentioned with Kristen Wade or Susan Granger." Lucas frowned, thinking. He had to get this right before he pulled the classic con—bait and switch—on the titular head of the church in this state. "So you must in some way not only condone them going to Oink City here, but you must support what they're supporting politically—the agenda of the religious right—something you can't publicly do in this liberal diocese."

"As you have said to me so many times, Father Holt," Bishop Casas replied, 'What else is new in Fantasy Land?'"

Lucas put the champagne down and caught Dorati's sign to check his watch. If the diocesan office was wired, or if Casas had slipped a note to his secretary, APD could be rolling up momentarily. "Let's ask Dean Bergen that question, shall we?"

"Screw you and the horse you came in on, Holt," Bergen sneered.

"Fine." The Rev ignored him and spoke to the Bishop. "Ever hear of Dierdre Edmunds?"

The voice acknowledged that he and everyone else knew the famous ultra-conservative columnist for the Concord Register in New Hampshire. "So what?"

"So she's in bed here with Rhondalynn Doss."

The box was silent. Either Casas was hoping the police would arrive and was stalling for time, or he was trying to put together in his head what Lucas had just implied.

"Time's up!" Holt said. "Everett Bergen *is* Dierdre Edmunds."

"That's bullshit!" Doss exclaimed, holding the sheet to her chest and glowering at Lucas. "Edmunds is farther right than I am!"

"That's ridiculous, Father Holt," the Bishop demanded. "Why would Bergen do such a thing?"

"I'll tell you why, Bishop." Everett Bergen sat up in the bed. "I did it for the money. That column paid more than double my stipend as a full time and a half priest in that parish in Harlem. And it was money that I could use for the people in my parish." Bergen smiled proudly. "It gave me great satisfaction to feed the homeless, run drug programs and pay for abortions with money from people who despised everything I spent it on." He looked at Holt. "You don't think I really believe that crap, do you?"

"Don't you, Bergen?" Holt replied. "Or did that money in fact go through Rhon to support your favorite candidate?"

The Bishop intruded. "That's the most outrageous—"

"No, Bishop," Holt responded. "The most outrageous thing is that you're fine with them porking in the Bishop's Quarters but what really upsets you is the Dean sleeping with the enemy and writing under a pseudonym—and writing right wing diatribe that even you can't condone—no matter what he says is the reason."

"He's just pissed he got suckered," Nikky said.

"Who is that?" the Bishop yelled, clearly unnerved. "Is that one of your hoodlum friends?"

"Gotta ring off now, Emil," Holt said. "We'll chat later."

Nikky unloaded the Dean's pistol and dropped the bullets into the champagne bottle. The gun he tossed into the bathroom commode. "We're outta here, Rev."

The two stood in the doorway and Holt turned around. "One more thing, you two. We know about the 'Dead Ed' assassination and we've got it stopped."

"What are you talking about?" Rhondalynn asked in a serious tone.

Lucas thought for a second maybe she didn't know about it. Though it could have been an act. She seemed to be acting pretty good with Bergen when they entered the room.

"I'm surprised you don't know, Rhon," Holt said. "You seem to be on top of everything else."

They closed the door in time to hear the champagne bottle break against it.

Once outside and in the car, Nikky spoke first. "Think he can find you tonight, Rev?"

Holt wiped the rain off his forehead with his shirt sleeve as he looked out the foggy window. "Only the assassin will find me tonight."

＊ ＊ ＊

Frankie Colovas should have turned left off of Lamar onto Seventh Street toward downtown. He hoped his boss in the back of the limo was so buried in the newspaper that he wouldn't notice they had gone on to Sixth and turned right—toward the lake. It was mid-afternoon and raining and Ryan Pace was supposed to hold a campaign meeting at One American Center in fifteen minutes. But Frankie had other plans, if he could hold him off a few more seconds.

"Where you going?" came the voice from behind the paper.

"Last chance to get gas before I go downtown, Mr. Pace," Doors lied.

"Wish you'd have taken care of that before now, Frankie. You know how I hate being late."

"Just be a minute, sir. You'll get where you're going on time." Though it wasn't where Pace planned, Colovas thought as he pressed the gas pedal and raced under MoPac toward Lake Austin Boulevard.

By this time, Pace had put down the paper and was checking his watch. "There's the gas station on your right," he said. "Why are you in the left lane?"

Ignoring him, Frankie turned the stretch limo down the short road to Deep Eddy Pool. At the same time he flipped the switches to put up the glass partition between them and to lock the security latches on the car doors.

"What the hell are you doing?" Pace said, drawing his gun.

"Bulletproof both directions, Mr. Pace," Colovas said, smiling into the rear view. He had also disabled the electrical controls from the back, so that the candidate was trapped in a steel and glass box.

"You'll never get away with this, Colovas. I'll have your ass so deep in solitary you'll go blind if you ever see daylight."

Frankie parked in the far corner of the vacant lot above the spring fed swimming pool. Even at this time of year, with this weather, intrepid exercisers would venture out after work to do laps in the marked lanes. But they would think little of a stretch limo parked here with people talking in it, especially if one was a jogger—like the figure now finishing his run on the trail.

"Here comes your appointment, Mr. Pace," Colovas said, opening the passenger door for Holt to get out of the rain.

"Sorry I'm dripping on your leather," Holt said to the infuriated man in the back seat. "Maybe the rain will dilute the sweat from running. Felt good, you know. First time I've been able to run all week, you've kept us so busy."

"Damn you, Holt! I'll have you in the hole next to this idiot before I'm done. This is kidnapping. And that's a federal offense."

"No, Pace," Lucas replied. "*You're* the only federal offense around here. But that's just as a candidate. I intend to make sure you don't get inflicted on the entire country tomorrow."

"You are pathetic, Father Holt." Pace leaned back in the seat, and Lucas knew he was resigned to the conversation. Like a horse with a new saddle, he'd stopped bucking. For the moment.

"I don't like extremists of any ilk; right wing, liberal, libertarian, socialist, whatever. You have no sense of balance. For you to be right, someone else always has to be wrong. For you to win, someone has to lose. For you to have power means that someone has to be powerless." Lucas knew the lecture wouldn't do any good, but he had to say it while he had the man captive, if only to get it off his chest. He was surprised it didn't make him feel any better. Maybe it was because he knew it was futile, wasted breath. "It's not you personally I don't like—though I'm sure I would if I knew you better—it's your extremist position that hurts others by definition."

"Jesus was an extremist," Pace shot back. "He pissed people off all the time."

Lucas glowered through the partition. "Don't give me that messiah shit, Pace. A lot of things you may be, Jesus isn't one of them." Time to drop the bombs. "I don't recall Jesus plotting an assassination like 'Dead Ed.'" He caught the shocked look on the trapped man's face; but was the candidate surprised to hear of the idea itself, or surprised to hear he'd been discovered as a part of it? "And I must have forgotten that passage where Jesus extorts information from an architect by threatening to publish foolish pictures from youth." Holt looked at Doors. "You remember anything like that, Frankie?"

"Not in *your* Bible classes, Rev."

"You don't know anything, Holt," Pace said, shaking his head with a smile. "You're bluffing as usual. You know shit."

Trump card. "We know about your little arrangement with the Very Reverend Everett Bergen alias Dierdre Edmunds, amassing large contributions to your campaign through Rhondalynn Doss. Jesus did say something about that—'look for your money to find your heart.'" Holt frowned. "But was it her money, his money, or the church's money?" He nudged Colovas. "Remind me to ask Lieutenant Granger that, will you?"

Pace quit smiling. "I believe this interview is over."

"Not quite," Holt said, looking at Doors. "You got the pics?"

Colovas handed him a manilla envelope from under the driver's seat. "Kept them in a stack of magazines in the living room."

Ryan Pace sat forward and banged on the glass. "How the hell did you get those?"

"Looks like that adoption is back in the works," Holt said to Doors. He tore up the envelope without looking at the pictures. "Negatives?"

Doors took a small packet from the visor. "Found them in the medicine cabinet, behind the razor blades."

Pace was beside himself, cursing them both, banging on the glass with his gun. "I should have kept an even closer eye on you than I had planned, Colovas. You're fired, you no good thieving son of a bitch. FIRED!"

"Fine with me," he said, tossing Holt the car keys as they both stepped out into the rain. "You were an asshole to work for, anyway. A pompous asshole."

"Want to know what prison's like," Holt said, "in case you end up there instead of the Senate?" He held the keys up to the back seat window, then hauled back and tossed them out into the rapid flow of the Colorado.

Pace furiously banged the gun on the side window, causing a slight crack, then hammered at it repeatedly, like a rat clawing his way out of a sinking sack.

"Kristen Wade will kick your butt tomorrow," Holt shouted above the shattering glass.

Pace bellowed back. "If she's *alive*!"

The Rev nodded to the tires and Colovas punctured all four with a stiletto. Holt pulled off the carphone aerial and bent it till it broke. It was not as good as shooting out his knees.

* * *

Kristen was awakened by the loud voices of two orderlies who approached ICU Bed 16. She opened her groggy eyes to see the unit clerk hand her nurse an order sheet.

"Yo, Cindy, here's the deal," the clerk said. "We got a c.v.a. comin' up in ten minutes and 16 is stable enough to move out to make room for him. These dudes from transport will take her to Room 299."

Wade tried to force her eyes further open but didn't seem to be able to do it. She had felt okay yesterday talking to the press, even had sat up in bed for the interview. But now she felt heavy, lethargic, like her limbs were cement.

The unit clerk spoke: "Where's Omar?"

"Taking a leak," the short haired nurse replied, pulling the chart together. "And the cops are changing shift like we are, flirting with 3-11 in the break room. Should I wait till they get back?"

Yes, wait. Kristen tried to mouth the words. Something was wrong. Please.

"I don't think so," the clerk replied. "Two-ninety-nine's just outside the door to the Unit and ER's already sent the stroke this direction, so we need to get her movin' and fast. You know what Dr. Sjonsby will do if we don't get the patient in here STAT."

"You got it."

Suddenly aware that she somehow might have gotten too much medication, but too weak to protest, Wade had no choice but to passively watch the orderlies and her nurse quickly pack her up to move to a room. They assured her she'd be as medically and physically secure there as here and that they desperately needed the bed for a seriously ill patient.

"We'll get her moving," one orderly told the nurse. "You can send the chart and her stuff over with a volunteer." He and the other man pushed the bed with Kristen in it through the door and down the narrow corridor leading out of the Unit.

She saw the blurred room numbers as they passed them.

295. 297. 299.

Shit. They *passed* 299.

She felt a needle stick as a waiting elevator swallowed the three and closed behind them.

Two minutes later Omar raced through the hall to room 299 and found it empty. He looked out the window and saw a hearse leaving the front entrance, followed by a large rental van with New York plates. As he squinted through the rain at the van's license, he noticed something hanging out the back. The dark blue sheet was the kind used only in ICU.

• Ten •

The Rev sat in the back seat of the '84 Corvette driven by Jimmy Brickhouse. All the appropriate people were unnerved and hopefully agitated into some foolish action that would lead them directly to him—and to the Squad and Susan. Brick had picked up Doors and himself at Deep Eddy and told the Rev that Case Atkinson had to see him immediately. But before that Lucas Holt had something for them to do.

"As soon as it's dark I want you two to break into the Seminary office and pilfer the Dean's computer. Doors can get you in and you can get to the files. Somewhere on that thing he may have a list of all the organizations he and Pace are connected with."

"Pace?" Colovas asked. "With the Dean?"

"Apparently Bergen funnelled money into Pace's coffers through Rhondalynn so, if we're lucky, you'll find a connection in those files, and a cross reference, no pun intended, with their affiliations."

He told them to copy all the files onto a separate disk and erase the hard disk. That way they'd have information to hand over to Granger as well as doing their part to foul up whatever network had been developed.

"Then find Rhondalynn's office there and do the same. He may be slick enough to have stored the stuff on her computer without her knowledge, especially if the two systems are connected." Considering the two systems had been connected in the Bishop's Quarter's earlier that afternoon.

"No prob, Rev," Doors said, slapping hands with Brickhouse.

"Here's your stop." Brick halted the car in the alley behind Las Zapatas. "Have an enchilada for me," he grinned. "Mes'can soul food, man."

Holt waved them off and entered the kitchen. The smells of such places always made him relax. They reminded him of the local place with the unlikely name of "Papa Moe's" in Smithville where he grew up. The refried beans, cheese and tortillas were comfort food, and his mother or father often carried him home from there half asleep when he was small. The memory put him in touch with how tired he was now of all that had happened, of all he had put Kristen through. He imagined her in the Intensive Care bed and he felt for her. He would call and check in with Omar when he finished here. She only had to hang in there one more night and the worst would be over. With the election tomorrow, she would likely be launched to Washington. He wondered what that would mean for him. For them. If there was a them. If he wanted there to be.

The Rev picked up a coffee mug from a counter, and filled it at the huge stainless urn. In a small room by the rear door he could see two men sitting at a table with plates of food. Travis Layton and Carl Atkinson.

Layton stood and hugged him. The old lawyer smelled of Bugler and Black Jack, just like Lucas' father had his whole life. "Miss the hell out of you at Maggie Mae's, son. You okay? You look like you been rode hard and put up wet. As your probable attorney of reference, I cain't ask you if you shot Kristen either time, but I'm assuming that you did neither."

Lucas quickly explained the sting to them both, leaving out details that he tell Travis later if he had to.

My God, son, trade coffees with me." Travis swapped out their mugs. "I ain't touched this one yet, and it'll warm your innards better than yours will. And you need it."

"I'm fine, Travis." He pointed to the map spread out over the table. "What's that?" He sipped the booze laced coffee and made a face at Layton. "And why did you two want to see me?"

"I got to thinking about what you told me yesterday about 'Dead Ed,'" Case began. "I know it could still be a person, somebody with the initials 'D.E.' or whatever, but I couldn't get Deep Eddy out of my head. So I checked out how you could foul the Deep Eddy spring if you wanted to, and here it is." Atkinson pointed to one spot on the map.

"I first thought you could drill down or explode a device upstream to get the poison into the system. But look here." He moved his finger along a line leading to the river. "It would quickly wash into the Colorado and dissipate and not really do any damage—like the coliform in Barton Springs. They close the pool a couple of days and the natural washing out of the system cleanses it, especially if it rains, and we're back to normal again. Mother Nature takes care of herself pretty well."

Lucas Holt followed the line further toward the city. "What about down here?"

"Those are the old storm tunnels the city built at the end of the last century to control Little Shoal Creek," Layton added. "They stopped building them because they were too close to the Balcones Fault Line. Couldn't trust their stability since those tectonic plates slip around down there all the time."

"I know that, Travis. It's where I've been hiding since I vanished from the scene of the alleged crime."

Layton shook his head. "Bad idea, son," he said. "Damn things flood at a moment's notice."

"And you see how they're all connected—beneath them I mean?" Case drew a line from the tunnels. "The streams from the tunnels, thanks to the excavation necessary to create them, lead directly underground to both Deep Eddy and to the Colorado River."

Layton took a drink of coffee, frowned and said, "Of course they're all connected under that to the Edwards Aquifer. This whole damned part of the state practically floats on it from here to San Antone."

Lucas looked at the lines. Lines. Were these the kind of lines Doors saw when he was hiding in the closet of Pace's campaign office? "What would the parts per million of a substance have to be to do any damage to the streams or the river?"

Atkinson shook his head. "I'm an architect, not a chemist. My point was that no matter what you did, the system seems to self cleanse. It would take one hell of a pollutant to completely foul either Deep Eddy *or* the Colorado. So I'm back to thinking the assassination is about a person with the initials 'ED.'"

Lucas stared at the map. "But we've been over the list of nearly everyone in town who would count. Who the hell have we left out?"

Travis accepted a mug of coffee from Rosie with a wink. "What about Donna Dillon?" he mumbled.

Holt turned to him. "Huh?" It didn't make sense.

Layton took a long slug of the coffee. "I was at a reception at the courthouse when the Commissioner first came to town. I got to talkin' to this gorgeous Barbie Blonde and it turned out it was his wife. Hell, I'd had too much to drink as usual and noticed her initials embroidered on her dress right next to that great cleavage. It was EDD, and when she caught me staring at her boobs I told her I was fascinated by her initials. A good save even for an old drunk cowboy."

Holt shook his head and asked what it meant.

"Meant I got to stare at those melons and point to the stitching on the dress, of course."

"The *initials*!"

"Oh, they stood for Esther Donna Dillon. EDD."

Lucas Holt had no time to process what Travis had just told him. He was about to ask another question when Nikky Dorati flew into the room, soaked in sweat and rain. The look on his face said something was terribly wrong.

"Shit, Rev, they got Kristen!"

Before Holt could respond, Dorati's cell phone rang. He answered it and looked at Holt. "It's Cora Mae. Max just got a package at the church addressed to you. There's blood all over it."

Ricardo Valdez held a stethoscope to the side of the package. He had made enough bombs in his lifetime to know one when he saw one. When the Rev asked him to take a look, he brought his equipment with him. He shook his head and opened it, as Max, Nikky and Lucas ducked and looked away, just in case.

Valdez unfolded a bloody hospital gown and handed the Rev a plastic bag with a Polaroid photo and a piece of paper in it.

Lucas held the close up photo of Kristen Wade with a gun to her head. He read the scribbling on the paper. "'Meet in the tunnel at midnight. Alone. No cons. No cops. She's dead meat if you cross us.'"

"Holy shit!" Holt said out loud. "The tunnel! Of course!" Case was right and hadn't even known it. He turned to Dorati. "You've got to *find* her!" he said, quieting down. "Max, get Susan on the phone." He strode into his office. It wasn't Deep Eddy or the Colorado that was at risk here. Both of those things washed themselves clean quickly. "She can pull her officers off of guarding the celebrities in this town. I know what they want to do."

"What is it, Rev?" Max asked, as Dorati picked up the phone. "Is it you they want to kill? Kristen? The Governor?"

"Hell no," Holt replied. "It's much bigger than that." He opened his coat and slammed the gun on his desk. "They're going to assassinate the Edwards Aquifer!"

＊ ＊ ＊

At 10:00 p.m. Granger, Holt and Dorati sat around the table in the "upper room" of the Buffalo Barn Grille. Holt was furious about the abduction of Wade, and made no attempt to hide his feelings.

"Why the hell weren't they *watching* her? Of all the damned stupid things."

"I'm sorry, Lucas," Susan touched his hand. "I feel like I'm responsible. My men were lax on the job, jerking off with the nurses, taking for granted nobody would come to the unit at this late date. I severely chewed butt and gave them reprimands, but that won't help us tonight."

"Omar feels like shit, too, Rev," Dorati said.

Lucas Holt took a deep breath and a shot of Dorati's rye. There was no time now for the luxury of blame and guilt. They had to find Kristen and he had to get to the tunnel by midnight. He looked at the old Regulator clock on the mantelpiece. They had two hours.

"All right," he said finally with a deep sigh. "All right. We can't change what happened, however it happened. We need to stop feeling sorry and angry and get our asses in gear."

Granger poured her beer into a small glass. "I'm running the plate number Omar got on the van through national DMV files. It'll take a while because they not only have to trace it to the owner of the leasing company but they have to have that company track down the rental—and hope it's not under an assumed name with false i.d.'s."

"Omar said there was a hearse in front of the truck," Dorati reminded them.

"I know," Holt replied. "I've been thinking about that, wondering if that isn't better than a van for transporting a body?"

"But the blue ICU sheet was in the van," Dorati said. "Of course that could have been to throw us off, waste time checking on plates and rentals."

Susan put her glass down and suggested having her officers do unannounced inspections of the local funeral homes. If Kristen was in any of them, they'd find her with a search of every room.

"And you'd find her dead," Lucas responded. "The first one you entered would call the rest and warn them unless you did them all at once—and you're going to need a lot of officers to handle something else I have in mind." He turned to Dorati. The Squad could do more than the police, as usual, even though Susan would hate it. "Listen, Nikky. There are nine funeral homes in Austin. I can rule out five of them because I know the owners and their politics. But the other four are run by national chains and seem to turn over funeral directors like they roll dead bodies."

Dorati downed the rye. "Way ahead of you, Rev. I can get Omar, Dez, Brick and Doors ready to roll."

Holt explained that they couldn't do it themselves. They would have to take Cora Mae, Max, Jill and Marion with them to front the search, to distract whoever met them at the front door while one of the Squad was slipping through the back.

"If you find her, hit 911," Granger said to Dorati. "I'll alert EMS to the call and you'll have APD backup in seconds."

Dorati grinned at her. "This'll be a first. The only time these guys ever called the cops was to set them up."

"Don't worry, Dorati," Granger replied. "I don't like it any more than you do. When this is over, we go back to our corners and you stay the hell out of police business. I'm only doing this for Kristen." She looked at Holt.

Lucas looked back at her and wondered why he felt so protective of Kristen. Was it because Susan could take care of herself in ways Kristen couldn't? Maybe he thought Kristen needed him more. But that didn't make any sense. She was running for the U.S. Senate, for God's sake. Her skin had to be thicker than elephant hide. But right now that hide was on the line. A very thin line.

As Nikky made calls, Holt explained his plan. "You're people have to stop this thing, Susan, if it takes every person in APD and the Sheriff's Office searching the aquifer recharge zone in the pouring rain tonight." He laid out the map that Case had provided him. "A friend plotted out the major sites of introduction to the aquifer or to a stream or fault leading directly to it. The problem is that they need direct access that will not be washed out before it reaches the aquifer. To do that they'd have to set off some kind of blast to get down deep enough."

Granger agreed to have members of the APD bomb team posted at each of the ten locations marked on the map, with backup vehicles ready to go to each location. She would try the dogs but didn't know how much scent they could pick up in the wet greenbelt.

Holt continued. "I doubt if they'll use these places. They may be so arrogant about dealing with me tonight that they think a backup device is unnecessary. Whoever shows up will try to introduce the substance directly into the Aquifer from the tunnel, so I can watch."

He gave her the name of the chair of the organic chemistry department at the University of Texas. "He's a layreader at Maggie Mae's. Call him and tell him what's going on. Then have him come up with the ten toxic agents most likely to foul the Aquifer—and their reversibles. Have a car ready to transport the reversibles to the tunnel."

Granger insisted she and APD wait with him.

"Not unless we find Kristen first," Lucas replied. "Besides I need you above ground coordinating the cops. You need to get a wire for me so you and the professor can hear the conversation."

But he knew what she was thinking. What if this was a suicide mission by some fanatic? They had already killed the people in the skin flick, the kid in the dumpster, and five nude dancers. They knew Holt would do his damndest not to let them get away with the assassination of the Edwards Aquifer and that the chances of getting out of the tunnel unscathed either by Holt or his God Squad—not to mention the police—were small. So what would be one more death on their hands? His death. Hell, they'd probably get extra points for it, killing off the progressive priest from St. Margaret's.

"We'll have him covered," Dorati added, putting down the phone.

Lucas shook his head. "You'll be out chasing funeral homes and finding Kristen, Nikky. There's too much at stake here to mess with these people. The sons of bitches want to foul the water mass that supplies two million people, for God's sake."

"So—to be crass—" Dorati replied, "why don't they just kill Kristen and do it?

Holt shook his head. "This isn't just about a terrorist act. It's about power, control, intimidation. That's where the general population is most vulnerable. It's not enough to destroy the water supply for the entire area of Central Texas for the next couple of years. They have to have people know who *did* it. Of course it won't be the right, it will be blamed on the liberal, environmentalist, homosexual, leftist radicals devoid of respect for law and order who need to be put in their collective place. Blame and fear give these people control, sway voters toward their beliefs, and their representatives." He stood to leave. "We've got work to do."

Granger finished her beer. "It just occurred to me that they'll have to kill all of us here to pull this off."

Holt wondered how long it would take for her to get to that. "Very good, Susan. Kristen is down. They may get me tonight. They'll need to bag you because you're the backup." Of course they could just discredit her for failing to bring him in—after he's blamed for poisoning the Aquifer. But they probably wouldn't take the chance that her story might be believed. He handed her an envelope from his jacket. "Here's a ticket under an assumed name in case you need to get out of Dodge in a hurry. There's also a photo i.d. to get you through airport security, and the home fax number of the editor of the Statesman so you can go anyplace in the world and fax him the story."

Susan looked in the envelope. "Canada?"

"For old time's sake," Holt replied, knowing she'd remember the hundreds of hours they'd spent as students debating the Vietnam war and threatening to leave.

Granger nodded to the table. "What about him?"

"Shit, Lieutenant," Dorati answered for himself. "Nobody'd listen to a bunch of ex-cons." He stood and walked over to them. "They think we're the problem."

＊＊＊

Donna Dillon slipped off her pink silk robe and hung it on the hook by the towel. She leaned over to turn off the bath faucet and the frothy bubbles tickled her dark brown nipples. She stood and smiled as she stepped into the oversized antique tub she had acquired on one of her many trips to Mexico. Her reflection in the mirrored walls around the room was picture perfect, from her firmly rounded breasts to her tight butt and flawless face, all courtesy of Dr. Martinez of Monterrey. The flat belly was all her own, the result of thousands of weekly crunches, and she was proud of it, too.

Still standing, she reached to the ledge by the tub and dried her hands on the thick pink towel, then carefully sealed the plastic ziplock bag next to it. Checking the airtight bag for leaks, she bent over and let the hot water slowly engulf her, suck her down into its luxurious soapy perfume. She laid her head back against the velvet bath pillow, closed her eyes and breathed in the heavy scent of honeysuckle oil. She imagined herself a modern day Cleopatra and looked forward to the power and influence she and her husband would have when the election was over tomorrow.

Or that she alone would have, she grinned, imagining herself entirely without him in the house. She could do that, she mused, and find someone else to satisfy her other desires. That would certainly be no problem. It hadn't been so far, anyway, either in this country or across the border. Christopher was so busy with this new position he hardly noticed they spent less and less time in the missionary one. So she had developed her own cadre of lovers, all of them good for something besides sex, something she or the movement needed.

She heard the faint sound of the electric garage door opening and closing. Speak of the devil, she thought, moving her hand slowly down her belly. Maybe she would take him right here, when he came in to greet her. They hadn't done that in years. She would keep her eyes closed until he opened the door, imagining herself coupled on the pink rug beside the tub, her strong legs wrapped around him. She and 'Matt' Dillon would give new meaning to "Gunsmoke."

The kitchen door closed and she heard his boots click on the Saltillo tile in the den, then lost the sound and knew he was climbing the stairs.

The knock was always the same. It had been that way since their first night together in El Paso.

"Enter," she said in her most sultry tone. "Please, please, enter." She opened her eyes to see her sweating husband with a .45 Magnum in his hand. "What's going on? What happened?" she said, sitting up in the tub.

She hardly heard the specifics of his anger. As he raged at her, shouted and cursed, waving the gun, her mind flew in two directions at once . She could defend herself against the things he said, the trips to Mexico, using the help and speaking to them in Spanish, procuring items for militias. She already had rehearsed the scene in her mind in case she needed to play it out. Or she could defend herself against a crazed intruder who barged into her bathroom with a loaded gun and threatened her with ridiculous accusations, jealous insinuations of a man so obsessed with work that he saw criminals even when he came home at night.

With tears in his eyes, he yelled at her to answer him. She worried about the decision those tears conveyed. Her one option was clear. The way would be clear for her after it was done. Her contacts in the local militia would see to that.

Donna Dillon arched her back in the water so that her milky white breasts floated in front of her, and hoped he was watching them. "I knew it would come to this, Christopher. That sooner or later we would have to part company because you are, underneath it all, a weak man, with neither the guts nor the vision to push our movement forward in this country." Concealed by the voluminous suds, she moved her hand to the bottom of the tub and found the plastic bag, grasped the object inside it and lifted it slowly toward the surface.

Wet lines streamed down his cheeks as he cocked the .45. "There's only one way out of this, Donna."

"You're right, darlin'," she replied. "And I'm real sorry about it."

Soap, water and plastic exploded from her hand as she pulled the trigger of the bagged .38.

'Matt' Dillon shot last.

• Eleven •

"Let me see if I've got the story straight now, Francis," Cora Mae Hartwig said as she pulled her red Celica GT into the alley behind the Laurens-Hohman Funeral Home.

"Don't call me Francis," Colovas replied. "Not even my mother called me that. It makes me feel like a talking mule."

Cora Mae apologized, then repeated the scenario they had all memorized over beer and nachos at Mother's an hour before. Max, Jill, Marion and Cora Mae all would approach their respective funeral homes with the same story. They each had a dying relative in the hospital and needed to make extensive funeral plans, with lots of high dollar items from clothes to brass caskets. They had to make the arrangements this late at night while they could still legally sign for them as power of attorney. Once dead, there was nothing they could do.

"That'll bring 'em out to help you in droves," Frankie said. "Meanwhile I'll be in the basement checking for Kristen."

"We agreed on twenty minutes, correct?"

"That should do it," Colovas said, getting out of the car. "I'll meet you back here unless I find Kristen and call 911 from my cell phone."

"Happy hunting, dear." Cora Mae sped off to go casket shopping.

Doors hated funeral homes. It wasn't so much the thought of being dead as the thought of having somebody mess with you when you were. Dorati would be better at this. Where the hell was he? Some flimsy excuse about having to watch over the Rev.

As he opened the back door he hoped like crazy Wade was in there so he could call 911 and get some lights and people with guns on the scene. Other people with guns, he thought as he patted the piece in his waist holster.

The small flashlight enabled him to see his way through the flower room to a door leading to the basement. He heard Cora Mae loudly talking to the funeral director in the front of the building, then heard footsteps on the stairs behind the basement door. He ducked beside the flower cooler just as a large man in a white coat hurried by, tossing off the coat and straightening his tie. He must have been called up front to assist the sale.

Doors wasted no time in getting down the stairs to the darkened basement. The first room he checked was the casket storage area. Crates of caskets were stacked like loaves of bread from floor to ceiling; there was no room for a hospital bed unless it was inside one of those boxes. Bad idea.

The next was a closet of corpse clothes. Racks of suits and dresses looked fine in the front, but were slit up the back, assuming that part would never—ever—be seen. Nothing in here either.

The sleep rooms for the night staff stunk of cigar smoke and contained the standard twin beds with girlie pictures on the walls. A completely stocked liquor cabinet lined one corner, so the job had some perks.

The formaldehyde stench when he opened the next door took his breath away. It also distracted his attention so that he ignored the creak on the wooden stair as his imagination. He entered the room and flashed the light around the bottles and flasks of multicolored liquids and pastes. He heard the beep of a machine that sounded just like the one he had heard in Kristen's ICU room, the little blue box with the tubes coming out of it.

Shining his light in the direction of the sound, Doors saw a blue box with blinking lights and plastic tubing running from it. With the flashlight, he followed the course of tubing from the machine to the arm of the body lying on the slab not three feet away from him. The sheet was pulled up over the face, but the auburn hair spread out over the ceramic slab looked like it belonged to Kristen Wade.

Frankie heard his heart pound in his ears. It muffled the sound of the door opening behind him. He moved closer to the body on the slab and reached for the sheet on the woman's face. Just as he was about to pull it back a hand grabbed him by the shoulder and stuck a gun to his neck.

"Don't make a sound."

That was no problem. Colovas was too scared to yell, though he might need to change his underwear. At least the voice was familiar. He was about to be murdered by a friend.

"It's me. Nikky."

"Shiiit, Dorati! What the hell are you doin'?"

"Be quiet. I came to get you and Cora Mae out of here. You're wasting your time. That's an embalming machine, and this isn't Kristen. Check the toe tag."

Doors shined the light on the large tag around the corpse's big toe. It gave her name and time of death; thirty minutes before Wade was abducted. Colovas looked at Dorati.

"That's right," Nikky said. "The hearse was legit." They moved in silence up the stairs and out the back door. "Lieutenant Granger called us all off when she got the DMV report on the truck license," he said as they walked to the front of the funeral home. "It was rented to Donna Dillon."

                              ✳ ✳ ✳

Lucas Holt stood near the limestone carriage bridge thirty five feet beneath Sixth Street. He took off his raincoat and shook it out, opened his umbrella and propped it up to dry beside the cot. He opened the cooler, took out a bottle of Driskill Springs Water, and walked to the center of the bridge. The water rushing under it had risen an inch in the fifteen minutes he'd been down there, as the storm up above increased in intensity.

The Rev had left Dorati and Granger streetside taking care of the business they discussed earlier. Two tiny microphones were pinned in Holt's clothing—one connected to APD, the other to a laboratory in the Biology building at the university—to provide the information they needed to counter the terrorist attack. Nikky and Susan would hear the name of the substance at the same time as the professor. As soon as they had it identified they could move in and rescue Lucas—and the Edwards Aquifer along with him.

If it worked the way it was supposed to.

They had been so pressed for time that they hadn't tested the radio system. Though the APD tech assured them it would work, APD had been wrong before. He'd have been much happier if Brickhouse had set it up. Cons he could trust. Cops were too confident.

The rising water made him wonder if the whole plan would work. He had lived in Austin long enough to know the meaning of "flash flood watch" and he was watching it now. Alone.

He had been adamant about not having backup down here with him, complying with the demand of the slimeballs who had abducted Kristen, knowing that they had far more operatives watching him now than he could fool or evade. Not even the God Squad could help him with this one. It was one he had to do alone and trust that the back-up would be there if he needed it. *When* he needed it.

Susan had tried to talk him out of it, tried to convince him to let a cop dressed as him be the bait instead, but as usual she lost to Holt and Dorati and as usual she was pissed about it. He couldn't tell if her anger was a way of saying how much she cared for him, or how annoyed she was that he was risking his life for Kristen. Or both. Hopefully they'd be able to talk about it later. Assuming there *was* a later.

He watched as the water increased its force and its depth.

And what about Kristen? Would the God Squad find her in one of the funeral homes? Would she be alright? Would she need him—or want him—to take care of her when she got home? And what if she wasn't alright? My God! What if she wasn't?

He took a drink from the plastic bottle and wondered why, with all this water around, he felt parched? Maybe it was the realization, not in his head but in his gut, that he was totally alone—whether up on the street or down here in a tunnel. Without Susan, without Kristen, without Nikky and the Squad, without the parishioners of Maggie Mae's, it was just him and God. He put the bottle down on the bridge wall and touched the bulge in the middle of his back. Him, God, and the .38.

A cold wave of doubt splashed over him. What the hell was he doing here? Who did he think he was? Why had he gone along with Kristen and dragged Susan and the others into this damned mess in the first place? Why didn't he take Travis Layton's advice and stick to church?

The sound of rushing waters drowned his doubts. He knew why he was here. He was here because they were, all of them, ultimately all in this alone, together. He was here because church was more than a building, more than Lucas Holt, more even than St. Margaret's. That edifice only symbolized the community they had formed around and outside it. And there was a cancer in that community that had to be excised.

But first they had to find it; and tonight they would. Or, he reminded himself, it would find them. More specifically, him.

It was only a matter of time.

"Turn around very slowly, Reverend Holt," a voice back by the entrance commanded. "No sudden moves, please."

Lucas recognized it even above the water sounds and turned to confirm that it was Ryan Pace. "Nice rifle." With the red-eye site it looked like the same one used on the guy who broke into his house.

"Shut up." Pace fired and the plastic bottle of water flew from the bridge wall beside Holt. "The next one takes you with it."

"Why would you do that?" Holt asked as he leaned against the bridge, pressing the .38 reassuringly into his back. He would have to play this carefully, not duck and shoot until Pace had talked. The purpose of the pistol was to hold him off and buy time for Susan and Nikky to get there. Pace had the more accurate weapon, and it was already aimed with the red dot on Holt's chest. "In fact, why have you wanted to get to me all this time?"

"You're a symbolic death," Pace said, stepping closer. "Blaming you for Kristen's shooting, and then finding you dead eliminates you as one more symbol of flushing out what's wrong with this liberal cesspool. With both of you history, we can restore the kind of order that you and your kind have disrupted for forty years."

"Don't you mean *fifty*, you neo-Nazi fascist?" Holt moved to one side to let the bullet whiz past him. He'd have to incite without pissing him off totally, if he was to get the information he needed—they needed. But stalling was one thing, taking a bullet was another—at least before they knew the substance.

"You are out of touch with America, Reverend," Pace said, stepping carefully in the rocky tunnel to maintain his balance. "What this country needs and wants is a return to order, to civility, to punishment for lawbreakers, and to rewarding those who work for a living and take care of their family obligations. They want the bums off the streets and the criminals locked up in prisons so responsible people can go back to assuming their kids can go to school and be safe and educated, not mugged and drugged."

"Nice speech, Adolph, but I want all those things too. I just don't want to kill the First Amendment and Bill of Rights to get them." Holt moved across the bridge, hoping to shield himself behind the thick stone abutment. He hoped Susan was getting all this conversation above the noise of the rising water. And he wondered what Pace had done with Kristen.

"We're not going to kill either one of those things, Holt. We're much too big an organization to need to do that. It'll all be done within the limits of the law. Or we'll just make new law."

Lucas saw Pace step closer to the rushing water, close enough to lose his footing. "What's your email? 'ASSHOLES.COM'?" A bullet ricocheted off the limestone in front of him. "Either you're a lousy shot or you're not going to kill me," he taunted.

"Wrong twice, Holt," Pace replied, stepping back from the water and moving toward the end of the bridge. "I'm just taking my time. And I want to make sure you're really dead when they find your body."

"Like the Aquifer?" Lucas said. "That's the third thing you planned to assassinate, isn't it. Wade, me and the Edwards Aquifer." He leaned on the abutment and casually moved his hand to his back.

Pace stopped. "You damned fool, Holt. We sent those threatening letters to you and her, and to that idiot Lieutenant to keep you occupied while we won he election." He laughed derisively. "We had no intention of actually going through with it."

"The hell we're not!" a voice shouted from the darkness of the entrance. "Drop the gun, Pace."

Ryan Pace spun his rifle toward the shadow. "What are *you* doing here?" His voice was panicked; clearly this was not part of the plan. Holt used the distraction to move his .38 to a front pocket.

Pace shouted above the gushing water. "I never said I'd *do* it! I agreed to the plan, but that was all. The terrorist acts and the threat of assassination was meant to scare votes into my column, to reinforce the people's instinct to move to the right, the far right, because it's the safest place to be." He squinted and squeezed. "But I'm not poisoning the land and you're not either."

Holt ducked behind the bridge as shots pinged in each direction. "Great!" he yelled. "Why don't you two kill each other so the Aquifer and I can go home?"

"Shut up," Pace shouted. Lucas heard a shot and watched him spin and fall face down beside the deepening stream that nearly covered the tunnel floor. Blood seeped through the rocks and puddled on the gravel till lapping water dissipated it in the torrent.

"Come out and show your ugly face, Bergen!" Holt yelled, then looked up over the bridge as the Dean emerged from the shadow with a .9MM held at arm's length. Bergen fired, but the recoil made him slip on the rocks and fall.

"Don't mess with Mother Nature, you Oreo son of a bitch!" Holt shouted, then ducked again as bullets whizzed by.

"What the hell you talking about?"

"I'm talking about you being about as black as that chalk in the wall over there. You're black on the outside with creamy white values inside." Holt edged closer to the top of the bridge wall. If he could distract the man, he could pop up unexpectedly and fire in his general direction. "No true African would do what you're about to do—poison the *land*, for God's sake! That's how I knew it had to be you behind all this."

"Keep talking, Holt," the voice was closer to the bridge. "You're talking yourself right into a watery grave."

Lucas backed up a few feet. "You're the only non-Texan, Bergen. And regardless of color or which side of the Alamo we fought on, no Texan would poison the land. We learned from the Indians and the Mexicans that we're all a piece of it. It would be like poisoning our souls."

"Well, yippie damn kiyay," Bergen mocked, as Lucas stuck his head over the stone railing to fire.

But the rising water had reached Ryan Pace, and its cold shock suddenly revived him. Holt caught the movement and looked as Pace rolled over, rifle in hand, and aimed at Bergen. But the Dean saw Holt's eyes move and turned just in time to pump four quick shots into the now lifeless form.

"Thanks for the head's up, Holt!" Bergen yelled, backing away as the waters spread beyond the narrow creekbed and up to the base of the limestone bridge. "I never would have caught that move." He kicked the lifeless body of Ryan Pace into the water. "Looks like it's just you and me now."

You, me, Susan, and U.T., Holt thought, putting the gun back in his pocket. He didn't think the Dean was going to fire at him right then, not without humiliating him some more to get back for the incident with Rhondalynn Doss. "So I guess the Aquifer and I now are at *your* mercy, Bergen." Time to pop the question. "Just how are you going to do it?"

"You mean you don't know?" the Dean mocked. "There is something the great Lucas Holt and his infamous God Squad failed to figure out?" He retrieved two small vials, about an inch and a half long, from his pocket. Each had a red rubber stopper and contained a clear liquid. "You would be talking about these, Father Holt. I had three of them, but one was used in that obscene flesh farm south of the river."

Holt recoiled like a shot with the realization. "So it was you who killed those five girls from the club?" Listen carefully, Susan; get this, professor. We know what it is now. "The ones who died with *botulism*?"

"No," Bergen laughed. "I do claim the movie theatre and the dumpster dummy, but I'm afraid I can't take credit for the topless whores. They belong to my cohort."

Holt lobbed the name like a grenade. "You mean Donna Dillon?" He watched the grin turn to a smile, and knew he was right. "The one who got you the *botulism* from that lab in Mexico? Speaking of whores."

The Dean shook his head. "Very good, Father Holt. You do live up to your reputation. Of course it will only be for a short while longer." He knelt down and put the gun on the floor of the tunnel. He was far enough away that Lucas couldn't rush him, and Holt hesitated to shoot for fear of the man dropping the glass vials.

"How long have you been in league with her?" Holt stalled for time, time he thought was probably worthless. There was no antidote, no reversal for botulism as far as he knew. It was the most virulent and potent toxin of its kind, if he remembered his college biology right. He hoped he was wrong, that the professor would access a reversible through some computer magic. That's what it would take now. Magic. Or an act of God. If there was any difference.

"You can stall all you want, Holt," Bergen said calmly. "I'm still going to do this, so you might as well know we met at a small social occasion with very select attendees when I first got to town. We immediately saw we could use each other—and Pace—to further our efforts." He looked disdainfully at the candidate's body drifting downstream in the rising water.

"Too bad that didn't work out for you and your boy there," Lucas said. "Hard to win with a dead candidate."

"You might say the same for yourself, Father Holt. Or rather for that insipid bitch Wade." He seemed to be searching for something on the ground. "At least we have someone in the wings— the right wings—ready to stand in now that you and Pace have had it out with each other as he tried to stop you from poisoning the water supply for two million people."

Lucas cursed to himself. He couldn't let himself believe Kristen was dead. It would send him over the bridge firing point blank at Bergen and ruin everything. He took a deep breath. "Donna Dillon again? Is she your stand in?"

Bergen smirked. "No, she had the Mexican connections we needed to get explosives, biological agents, whatever we wanted. That country is a virtual supermarket of terror—for a price. Hell, we put in an order for nuclear waste from their power plants and will have that in a few weeks. Wait till you see what it does to the water supply of a big city like Chicago or Philadelphia. And more importantly, what it does to our ratings in the polls."

"But Pace knew nothing about her?" Lucas edged closer and kept his pocket side hidden by the thick stone railing. He'd thought through the possibilities and there was no other choice if he was to attempt to stop the botulism poisoning. He would have to take the chance of shooting Bergen and retrieving the vials before they were opened—or broken. "He was a pawn?"

Bergen fumbled with the vials, twisting the stopper in one of them, but not opening it. "We organized the Religious Right to get Pace on the ballot when the sins of Bailley Graham were uncovered, so to speak. Pace wanted it so bad he'd do damned near anything to get it. He knew his money and our power could make him President, in time. We could finance and he could produce a right backlash so strong he'd be carried into office on an anti-terrorist, anti-liberal, anti-gay, anti-feminist, anti-everything wave that would splash over this country and put people in charge who will do something about the moral decay of our culture that is leading us down the same road Rome took to oblivion."

"'Extremism in the cause of liberty is no vice.'" Lucas quoted the famous Goldwater speech from 1964, as he cocked the trigger and removed the gun behind the cover of the balustrade. Bergen could not know Holt was using the conservative battle cry to justify his *own* use of violence to save the Aquifer.

"'And moderation in the face of tyranny is no virtue,'" the Dean finished the quote. "I spent years in the tyranny of Harlem watching my parishioners die in front or me because of a system of liberal excess that kept them on the bottom. I wrote that column as Diedre Edmunds because I believed every sentence of it. Only a conservative revolution can save the people in the inner city by killing off drug supplies and clamping down on the violence that ruins generations of families. You and your liberal buddies haven't got the balls to fight the tyranny that is afoot in this country, bringing it down in ways our Cold War enemies never could." He suddenly grabbed the rifle and fired at Lucas.

Holt jumped back, dropping his own weapon, and Bergen fired again, grazing the Rev's right arm.

"Bad luck, Father Holt. But you've got more guts than Pace had, I must admit."

Buy time, Lucas thought, grimacing at the pain in his bleeding arm. It looked and felt like he had ripped it against barbed wire. If a flesh wound hurt this much, what would a bullet to the body feel like? Maybe if he stalled he wouldn't have to find out. "Just because he balked at destroying the Aquifer?"

"He was only willing to talk about it, but that was it. He had no *real* commitment to the movement. He would have exposed us all if we hadn't stopped him."

"With pictures of him and Doss?" Lucas edged very slowly, one step at a time, closer to his gun. If he could get within five feet he could dive for it and hope Bergen would miss the shot.

"A little insurance like that never hurts." The Dean held up the second vial. "That's why I have double the amount of toxin needed—in case our people have somehow miscalculated." He put the rifle down and started to uncap one vial.

"What about the rising water in here? Won't it wash out the botulism?" One step, then another.

"Even if the Aquifer tries to cleanse itself, which it naturally will, the amount from *both* of these vials is more than enough to contaminate it for months, maybe years. More importantly, the scare factor will keep people away longer than that. Nobody will want to live where there's a chance of dying from botulism in the water. The area will become a deserted wasteland with no water."

"The Three Mile Island of the South?"

"Or Love Canal. Or Chernobyl. Vacant buildings. Empty roads. Burned and looted stores. And people will be so outraged they will vote for anything that will prevent it in the future. This place will be a monument to liberal excess for years."

"About the length of time you'll need to be in therapy, you warped bastard." Three more steps and he'd be in flailing range.

"Not very charitable to your enemies, Father Holt." Bergen backed away from the rising water and scanned the floor of the tunnel. As he did, Holt slid closer to his downed weapon.

"Don't you need an explosive device to force the toxin down into the Aquifer?" Lucas calculated the move. He would have to dive for the gun, roll to his right and fire through the balustrade of the bridge. He knew the chance of actually doing that, even without a wounded right arm, was somewhere between zero and minus ten. But there was no other choice. What the hell, he was going to be killed by this maniac anyway. He desperately wished either God or Nikky Dorati would show up about now, and he didn't care which one.

"I'd only need explosives if, as originally planned, I did it right above Barton Springs, where your APD friends are dismantling some useless devices. But once our operatives followed you—you and that infernal God Squad of yours—and I learned where you were, it turned out that there is a fissure here that leads directly to the Aquifer, and this wonderful setting provides the double pleasure of taking you out along with it." Bergen smiled and found the spot he had marked earlier. "Almost like it was ordained by God."

One more step. "What makes you think I'm not talking to God right now to stop you from defiling Creation? Or to somebody else who is working on a reversible?"

"There are no so-called 'reversibles' for botulism, Father Holt. Nothing to reverse the effect of the powerful toxin. And we're below the depth radio signals can penetrate. So if you are wired, go ahead and talk. Nobody's listening to you."

If Bergen was right and APD was wrong, there was no chance of backup now. Lucas started the final step but was stopped cold by the sight of a .45 Magnum emerging from the entrance. He hoped it was Nikky. If it was God they were all in trouble.

"*I've* listened to him, asshole." A deep voice shouted. "Lift 'em."

Christopher Dillon stepped from the shadow. Bergen cursed and raised the rifle at Holt, placing the vial in his pocket. He was taking no chances missing the spot to dump the toxin, which might give Lucas the time he—or Dillon—needed.

"I had Pace followed all afternoon," the Police Commissioner called above the gushing water. "And once I woke up from the nap you gave me, Holt, I learned he was here. I admit I was surprised when you arrived, Bergen. I didn't suspect you at all."

"That's because your wife kept you uninformed, you stupid hick."

Dillon nodded. "I *was* stupid. Or too much in love to tell the difference. But I can assure you that little detail has been taken care of." He spoke to Holt. "You were right about her, Reverend. Everything you and Lieutenant Granger said. She kidnapped Wade and she tried to kill me."

Lucas looked at him expectantly. "Kristen?"

"She's fine. But the Dean here will be disappointed to learn that his compadre and next in line for the throne is not. EMS is at my house now transporting Wade to San Jacinto Hospital and my wife to the morgue."

Holt felt for the Commissioner's betrayal by the woman he had obviously adored. He found himself relaxing at the news that Kristen was safe. Or maybe he was just losing blood. If the latter, either he or Dillon would have to act soon. It would be hard to shoot when he was blacked out.

The huge cop moved forward. "So you're the last scum bag left to clean out, Bergen. The only safe way out of here is surrounded by uniforms, so give it up and drop the rifle."

"You go to hell, Dillon," the Dean snarled. "I'm the one with the trump hand here. I've got Holt in my cross hairs and the toxin in my pocket. This bastard is the personal cause of screwing up a perfect plan and I'm going to make sure he dies for it, right here in this stone tomb. Then we'll see if God resurrects him from it."

Lucas looked at the gun on the floor of the bridge. Again he was about to leap for it when Dillon spoke.

"You're wrong about the trump, Bergen," the Commissioner yelled. "That belongs to the weather. This storm just dropped six inches in the hill country with more to come here in Austin. The creeks are flooding and low lying areas are being evacuated. And in case you forgot, this tunnel is a storm channel for Little Shoal Creek—which overflowed its banks two hours ago. If we don't get the hell out of here we'll all be *part* of the Edwards Aquifer." He waved the .45. "Now *move*, damn it!"

Holt moved first. He dove for the gun as two shots were fired from separate weapons. One hit the bridge where he had stood. It would have entered his abdomen, punctured his diaphragm and killed him. As he was about to fire, left handed, through the balustrade, he saw where the other bullet had gone.

Bergen lay three yards from the rifle, but right next to the fissure leading to the Aquifer. His left hand was a bloody stub, but his right hand dug into his pocket and retrieved both vials. Holt splashed through rushing, knee deep water toward him and saw Dillon racing to join him. They saw Bergen try to remove the stoppers with his teeth.

Lucas reached him first and grabbed for the vials just as Dillon yanked the man's head back, pulling the stoppers off both of the small glass tubes. Bergen struggled with Holt's weak left handed grasp and tried to overturn them into the fissure. The terrifying sound of rushing water increased as the level quickly rose to their hips.

"I can't hold him!" Holt shouted.

Dillon wrenched the Dean's head and Holt heard the neck snap. The vials dropped from a limp hand and Lucas grabbed them just before they hit the water.

"Give them to me!" Dillon shouted.

But Lucas could barely hear him. The sound was like a train in the distance.

Dillon motioned to him again. "GIVE THEM TO ME NOW!"

Not understanding, but responding to the command, Lucas forced his weakening body up over the top of Bergen and reached out to hand the vials to the Commissioner. As he did, he saw the shadow of something coming large and fast.

"WATCH OUT!!" Lucas yelled, pointing.

A twenty foot wall of water barreled through the tunnel toward them.

"I WILL FEAR NO EVIL!" Dillon shouted. He put the two vials in his mouth and turned from Lucas to face the oncoming wave.

The tunnel went black as Holt felt the impact of the water.

* * *

The police launch had put in at Deep Eddy and searched the north bank of Town Lake for over an hour. Granger and Dorati had had to wait until the storm died down to begin their search, and they knew their chances of finding him diminished with each passing minute.

"I don't think we looked far down the bank enough, Lieutenant," Dorati said above the whine of the boat's engine.

"Dammit, Dorati," Granger snapped. "The map says the tunnel empties out here by Shoal Creek." She knew they were both on edge, wanting to find him—and not find him. It was after five o'clock in the morning, they were cold and wet and had survived the night on black coffee. At least the rain had stopped, and the muddy Colorado, while moving quickly, stretched like a smooth brown mat between the flat running trails on either bank. In one way, Susan thought it the most beautiful she'd seen the river. In another the ugliest, most deadly.

"But the force of the water could have washed him further down stream," Dorati argued. "Swam, I mean."

Susan knew what he meant. She had her own visions of what they would find, and none of them were good. Her worries had started when the damned microphone wouldn't work. At first she thought it wasn't turned on or had problems because of the storm. But by the time her APD experts told her—and the UT professor—that there would not be any transmission at all, she was informed that Commissioner Dillon had already ordered the few unoccupied Sheriff and APD officers to the tunnel and had gone inside to make arrests. When she and Dorati got there, the tunnel was flooded.

The boat suddenly swerved and Nikky caught her before she fell. It was the first time she had been touched by him and she was surprised by his strength for being so short of stature.

"What the hell was that?" she hollered to the front, hoping it was the body of Dillon or Bergen. They were supposed to be looking for all three—but right now only one counted to her.

"Object floating in the water ahead, Lieutenant," the officer at the wheel of the launch yelled back. "Looks like a hand. Coming up port."

"Shit, Rev," Dorati mumbled.

Granger cursed and looked over the side. It was a hand, a stiff one, attached to a soggy black shirt.

"Haul it in," the wheel officer ordered the other cop.

The head appeared, bearded and long haired, as Dorati helped drag the stiffened body of the homeless man over the side.

"Go another hundred yards down the north bank," Granger ordered. "Beyond the power plant and the First Street Bridge, towards Congress Avenue." If nothing else, there might be other bodies down there of the homeless who lived under the bridge.

The gliding glass of the river propelled the launch so that they had to use the engine for control, to slow down and shine the searchlight into every crag of the bank.

Half an hour later there was still nothing. The sky began to lighten and wispy clouds followed the black and white blanket in the distant sky. There were even patches of pink and blue. But Susan resented the good weather; she wanted it to match her stormy mood.

"Where the hell is he?" she mumbled to Dorati. "And why haven't we found him?"

Nikky sighed and scanned the bank. "You and I both know this may take days, and divers, and even then we may not—" He stopped and squinted his eyes. He choked, and pointed. "There he is."

"THERE HE IS!" Susan yelled to the cop at the wheel, her heart pounding with hope and dread. She felt as though the wall inside her had suddenly crumbled, been washed away by the stormy waters that cleansed them both. She was ready to tell him how she felt, ready to listen to him. Anything. If only he was all right.

"Where?" the man shouted again.

This time Granger pointed. "There in that little inlet, directly below the Carillon." She aimed the searchlight at the spot, even though it was now visible in the hazy dawn light.

They held on as the boat lurched forward at full speed, then slowed its wake to turn into the inlet. Granger radioed the EMS copter to land behind the building across from the Carillon, and hurry down the bank.

"God, look at this," Dorati pulled on her arm as they approached the scene, pointing further up and down the inlet where the bodies of Christopher Dillon and Everett Bergen lay strewn in the mud. Dillon floated face down and the Dean lay lifeless, caught in the weeds. Snagged under his arm was a crushed bottle of Driskill Springs Water. "Have A Drink of History," Dorati smirked as he jumped from the boat and quickly waded to the Rev.

Granger was right behind him, elated to hear the beating of copter blades from the street above. She hoped the next beat she would hear was Lucas's heart.

As she approached she saw Dorati press his fingers to Holt's throat. "I don't feel nothin'. Where the hell is EMS?"

Susan fell to her knees beside him, hyperextended Holt's neck and swept his mouth for debris. "Don't be dead, damn you," she said. "Don't be!"

She thumped his chest to start compressions. On the first push, putrid vomit spewed from his mouth.

The black and yellow jackets of EMS techs swarmed over them as the Carillon marked the hour, tomb like, beside the still water.

• Twelve •

The huge wall of water smashed into Lucas Holt, knocked him away from the other two men though he lunged for them, futilely grasped at their clothing as it was wrenched away by the powerful deluge. He could not breathe in the blackness, which was silent now. When he gasped to suck in air he inhaled more water, coughed and desperately struggled upward, instinctively thinking that would mean space at the top of the tunnel. But there was only more darkness, no air, no respite space to breathe as the torrent fully consumed the tunnel, engulfed him like a stone and smashed him against the sides containing it as if to polish him, round off his edges, breaking him instead.

Pain seared his shattered body, his lungs filled to bursting; he knew it was finished. He gasped for air one last time, only to be helplessly swirled down again into the overpowering ebony water.

Then nothing.

The water was gone but the darkness stayed, held him prisoner, entombed him.

Holt lay inert, unseeing, unsure whether or not he could breathe; uncertain whether he held his breath or had no breath.

There was only one way to tell. He opened his mouth and forced the blackness into his lungs. He felt as if he was rising to the surface, but too quickly, coming up too fast, wanting to slow his pace, yet wanting desperately to break from the suffocating vault of darkness.

He broke through the surface and the sudden blast of air choked him, gagged him, doubled him over with stabbing pain in his belly, finally forced his eyes open in the bright daylight to see a hazy group of figures surrounding his hospital bed.

"Yo, Rev," Nikky grinned and grasped both his hands. "Welcome back to life, my man."

Cora Mae wept softly and kissed his forehead. "Lucas, dear," was all she could get out as he forced his mouth to bend in half a smile.

He turned his head to the person at eye level, sitting in some kind of chair. A wheelchair. He gave her a puzzled look.

"It's Saturday late afternoon. Polls close in two hours. Exit interviews say we're ahead." Kristen smiled and her auburn halo hair sparkled in the sunlight. He thought it was the most beautiful sight he'd ever seen, partly because he was still alive to see it, partly because it was attached to the rest of her gorgeous perfumed body, which he could smell from this distance. He was broken, but seeing her in that silk bathrobe with the bumps in front right where they were supposed to be ensured him he sure as hell hadn't broken his spinal cord.

"Vote," he whispered to her, his throat burning from the nasogastric tube descending down it. His eyes moved to the prurient green slime being sucked through the clear plastic tube by the robot-looking pump on the bedside table.

"Hi, Houdini. Some water torture trick." Susan touched his foot at the end of the bed. "So are you saying you want to vote or you want to know why they're voting when the other candidate is on a slab in the morgue?"

Lucas slowly nodded.

Granger looked at her watch and, through her hand radio, ordered a ballot and a notary public be brought to the room immediately. Lucas lifted his eyebrows, impressed at her influence.

"Don't be too overwhelmed," Susan said. "It's not my doing. Governor Doggett actually stopped by APD headquarters to congratulate us and announce personally that the National Guard divers had found Pace down by the Tom Miller dam. Thanks to the catfish they had to use dental records to identify him."

Holt grimaced at the thought. He was still groggy and felt overwhelmed by all the information he was getting. He was still adjusting to being alive.

"The Governor told me to get you whatever you wanted. I took the liberty of explaining to him how modest you were and how you wanted nothing in return for what amounted to a free ride down a natural water slide. But he insisted we all show up at his house—the Mansion—when you two are up and running again."

"And they ain't running the dental records on the ticket, Rev," Dorati explained, adding that everything happened too late to hit the morning papers and that the Governor and Susan decided to wait to hold a press conference until after the polls closed. "If Pace wins, the organization will appoint a temporary second."

"An interim, Nicholas," Cora Mae corrected, dabbing her eyes. "They'll appoint an interim to serve out the term of Senator Graham." Holt saw her pat Kristen. "But I don't think that will be necessary, especially after we get your vote in, Lucas."

Holt tried to clear his throat, sending a long plug of green streaming through the tube, and spoke slowly, quietly. "What makes you think I'm voting for—" He nodded toward Kristen. "—the cause of all this?"

"Because she'll also break your left arm if you don't," Dorati replied. "And you'll need to use that one to vote with, since your right one's out of commission."

"What else?" he said, instinctively inhaling deeply, then re-gretting it with a spasm of coughing calmed only by holding his breath, controlling the flow of air spewing forth from the oxygen canula in his nose. He felt pain everywhere, but reasoned his internal assessment was probably dulled by the contents of the bottle dripping through one of the blue humming boxes sur-rounding his head.

Holt listened as they told him what the doctors and nurses had conveyed to them. His right arm felt stiff and heavy, immobile, and he had been told now it was broken in two places in addition to the gunshot wound; his left wrist was severely sprained, but would recover quickly, so at least he could wipe his own ass at the bedside commode.

"I was so hoping Susan could help with that," he said.

"She's helping with the urinal," Dorati said, then shut up at the look she shot him.

Amazingly he had no broken leg bones, though his body was a mass of cracked ribs, skin contusions, hematomas, and a possible skull fracture that they'd be watching over the next couple of months. Rocks and hurling debris had punctured him "like St. Sebastian, Lucas dear," Cora Mae told him. And of course he had swallowed half of Shoal Creek, bugs and all, so that the severe lung infection was the main danger now. It could progress to pneumonia or total sepsis, killing him, "if the industrial strength antibiotic doesn't wipe out everything else first, so eat your yogurt, Lucas," Kristen advised.

"Speaking of bugs," Holt looked at Susan. "Botulism?"

"It looks like Dillon practiced what he preached, Lucas," she said, sitting on the bottom edge of the bed and holding his foot. He liked her hand on him, like a friend, but more. Even that simple weight on his body hurt, but he ignored the pain. Her firm touch felt certain, stable, unlike Kristen's.

Granger continued. "From what you managed to say when we first found you, we figured you were warning us about his body being dangerous. The glass fragments in his mouth told us the rest. He went directly to the Onion Creek crematory before the botulism toxin turned his body into a six foot biological weapon."

"Where his lovely wife, Donna, will soon be joining him." Dorati said, moving to the bedside table behind Kristen. "The Lieutenant's guys found her shot in the bubble bath. Well actually she was shot in—"

"We know what you mean, Nicholas," Cora Mae shook her head as Nikky pulled a bottle of champagne from an ice bucket behind the table.

"You're on a liquid diet for a while, Rev, so the Squad sent you this liquid and I thought we'd kill it—so to speak—before we all get thrown out of here." He popped the cork and passed around paper cups from the bathroom.

Cora Mae watched Dorati and Granger bump cups. "I never thought I'd see the day when the two of you were on the same side," she said.

"We're not on the same side," Granger replied, shaking her head.

"And never will be," Dorati added, pointing his cup toward the bed. "But that don't mean we ain't both glad the Rev is still kickin'."

Cora Mae explained that the historical society was glad too. They had taken a new interest in the underground tunnel system and were exploring the idea of opening it up as a tourist attraction. "Except when it's raining," she smiled.

"We're blocking the entrances to the tunnels for the time being," Susan said, "until somebody decides what to do with them—other than Dorati and his friends who I'm sure would love their access to various businesses at odd hours."

Dorati reminded her that *he* was not the one who had engaged in a total hoax on her own police department and then gagged and drugged the Police Commissioner just to get his attention.

"He did that," Granger said, pointing to Lucas, who was trying to get the paper cup around the nose tube. He knew the bubbly would go to his stomach and be pumped out through the tube, but what the hell. It would look better than that green shit.

Kristen handed him a straw and raised her cup. "Thanks to all of you who came looking for me. Have you found the people Donna Dillon paid to drag me from the hospital to her basement?"

Granger indicated that they could track the house servants from employee records. She had also turned over to the feds the information they have on disk and barf bag about the militia connections to supply sources in Mexico. Reluctantly she acknowledged that Brickhouse and Colovas had "acquired" the disks for her.

"You're looking a little green around the gills, Rev," Dorati said. "Maybe we should all go."

Holt shook his head against the huge white pillow. "One more round," he said, as an APD officer entered with a piece of paper and a notary. Lucas winked at Susan as he marked the ballot and watched them leave with it. "What service. I should get banged up more often."

"Please," Granger replied. "And if you and your God Squad bozos get any more hare brained ideas, keep them to yourselves."

"Look whose talkin', Lieutenant," Dorati countered. "You loved being on the other side of the law and you know it, from faking Kristen's shooting and letting the Rev escape, to trapping the bad guy in the tunnel last night."

"Did not."

"Did too."

"Did not."

"Children!" Cora Mae interrupted, as the phone rang.

Lucas nodded for Kristen to touch the speaker button on his bed, a convenience for people with broken appendages. "Hello," she said for him.

"This is Bishop Casas. Is Father Holt there?"

Assuming he'd need it, Nikky poured the Rev another round of champagne and held it for him while he spoke.

"I'm here," Lucas responded with a stronger tone now that the tube was wetted down with bubbly. He had awaited this call with considerable anger. "Though I don't know why you bothered since you were so eager to see me gone from St. Margaret's."

"Now, now, Father," the voice in the box softened, either hoping for reconciliation, or pulling rank. "We are in the forgiveness business, are we not?"

Holt took a sip and let go of the straw. "We are also in the hold your feet to the fire of responsibility business, Emil." He carefully controlled his urge to cough. "Not only did you not support me or the congregation while I was accused and not yet guilty, but you also installed your puppet priest to change the entire program that Maggie Mae's has worked so hard to establish in the inner city."

The Bishop cleared his throat. "I'm sorry you feel that way, Lucas, because I'm leaving the Reverend Doss there as your assistant until further notice. She's done a good job while you were running around Austin with your outlaw friends, risking your life needlessly when the authorities were well on the case, abandoning your priestly duties at the church."

Holt winked at Dorati. "I don't think she'll be staying on at Maggie Mae's, Bishop."

"By what authority do you speak, Father Holt? Certainly not by moral authority. Her relationships with Dean Bergen and Ryan Pace pale before yours with that flatfoot cop and that leftist politico."

Granger leaned toward the box. "This is the flatfoot, Bishop. We need you to speak a little louder so the microphone can get it all for the leftist politico holding it."

Casas was silent.

"I believe who stays on at the parish is largely up to the Vestry, isn't it Bishop?" Cora Mae asked, pouring herself more champagne and obviously feeling no fear.

"Too bad you all had to be there to hear the plain truth about this priest, but if you can't take it you shouldn't mess with him in the first place." Casas didn't miss a beat. Lucas assumed he had protected himself well from any associations with the religious right that he so vehemently supported. But there was one thing he

Charles Meyer

hadn't protected himself from and, thanks to Dorati, the Rev knew it. "To answer your question, Miss Hartwig, you are correct that the Vestry has some say in who is placed there, but as Bishop I have the canonical authority to override your choice in the best interests of the parish. Rhondalynn Doss has done nothing wrong other than be led astray and used by two men who were plotting around her. In addition to her duties as your assistant, Father Holt, both during and after your convalescence, I have already appointed her interim Dean of the seminary."

Dorati grinned at Holt, who responded after another quick sip. "Oh, I don't think she'll be doing that either, Emil."

"I think this conversation is over, Father Holt," the Bishop said with a hint of threat in his voice. "I hope you get well soon and that the healing of our Lord will—"

"Wallingford." Lucas interrupted him, and waited.

Nothing came from the box. Then: "What did you say?"

"I said 'Wallingford,'" Holt repeated, looking at Nikky while the others frowned, puzzled. "I believe it was a *Mrs.* Wallingford, who said to pass on her regards."

Casas paused. "That would be particularly difficult since she currently resides in Austin Memorial Gardens."

"Yes, Emil," Holt replied, enjoying the hell out of this. "But even from her casket her *memory* lingers on, in the form of one or two of her evidentiary letters—from your file in New York."

The Bishop cleared his throat again, and spoke nervously. "That file was *sealed*, Father Holt, and you have committed a felony in opening it."

"Did I say I opened it?" Holt shot back. "No, I think the originals are right where they were. But what if I have copies here to read for the flatfoot and the leftist and the old lady and the con? And what if they chose to drop a dime to the paper?"

Long silence, then: "That was a very, very long time ago, Father Holt."

"Young and foolish, Emil? Hard to believe. But it may play well enough for you to keep from being deposed. I don't know."

Silence. "Perhaps we should talk about this in person."

"Perhaps we should talk about it in front of all these folks you so condescendingly insulted, Emil. Perhaps an apology is in order, followed by a phone call to Rhondalynn explaining that she will not be making any decisions at Maggie Mae's or the seminary because Cora Mae and Travis will continue to fill in for me, and you will allow the Board to choose its own seminary leader."

That was it. He had shot the wad. It had taken all he could muster to get it out and he now was spent. He hoped the Bishop was through resisting, because Lucas would pass out if he had to push any more.

The sound of a deep breath came through the speaker. "I sincerely apologize to Lieutenant Granger and Miss Wade. I regret any discomfort anyone else in the room has felt with this conversation. And my next phone call is to the Reverend Doss."

Dorati and Cora Mae shook hands. But Lucas knew the Bishop wasn't through. He held up his weak left hand to calm them, as a nurse entered the room with a full syringe on a tray.

The Bishop continued. "But you all need to know that this is not over. I will continue to watch the ongoing ministry of Father Holt at St. Margaret's with great perspicacity."

The nurse edged Holt up in the bed and rolled him onto his side, facing Kristen and Cora Mae.

"One slip, one mistake, one oversight or scandal to harm the reputation of the church in general or parish in particular and I will not only bring him down, but all of you with him."

Inappropriate champagne giggles filled the room as the nurse pulled up the Rev's gown and exposed his butt for the shot. It was right in front of the speaker.

"Exactly which part of that do you find most amusing?" the Bishop said indignantly.

"None of it, Emil," Cora Mae said. "We're just glad to see the moon come up."

Lucas saw Kristen punch off the phone as Dorati and Susan helped the nurse reposition his aching body with new pillows in the bed. As the group had faded in, they now faded out behind his heavy eyelids. He felt what he knew was Kristen's hair touch his face as she kissed him, because he smelled her familiar scent.

As the blackness returned he whispered: "Voted... you."

"Voted you, too," he heard her echo as he floated down into the water once again.

✳ ✳ ✳

The Good Friday sun warmed the late March bluebonnets around Town Lake as Holt, dressed in running shorts, t-shirt and visor, walked the trail with the similarly dressed Susan.

"Doctor said I can't run for another month, yet," he said. "Something about my head splitting open."

"Bad for Kristen's carpet," Susan replied.

"Yeah, I guess," he said, knowing she was not going to help with this. In fact, she was going to be her usual honest self about it, which would make him do the same. He walked slowly, though the pain had all but subsided from the punctures. His scabbed skin looked like he had smallpox or an outbreak of Kaposi's so that people gave him a wide berth on the trail. He had not seen much of Susan in the last three weeks and had invited her here to walk with him after the Good Friday noon service. She had agreed, but it was his nickel so he'd best get on with it. "What'd you think of the sermon?" That was a stupid start.

"Good. Even for you." She took a deep breath. "I like the way you left him dead in the tomb."

Lucas wondered if she was making a theological reference or making a comment about where he himself should have been left. "Good Friday isn't Easter yet. He's dead and everybody's depressed and angry and abandons him. We have to live with that despair a couple of days or Easter's not the surprise it was to the disciples who hadn't read the script."

"Is that what this walk is about, Lucas? Living with despair?"

He waited till a group of walkers passed. "Look, I know you were hurt when I moved in with her, but it's just because we both needed someone around to take care of us. It's temporary, as we're convalescing."

"'Convalescing'? There's a new term for it." She sounded just like he knew she would. At times like this the penitentiary looked great. Or maybe a monastery in west Texas where the only other creatures of the opposite sex were the jackalopes.

"Anyway, I'm going to stay with her till she leaves for D.C. in a couple of weeks."

"Why are you telling me this, Lucas? I don't have time for this shit. I feel like that country western song I heard on the way over here: 'Here's a quarter. Call someone who cares.' I'm incredibly busy pulling together the loose ends from the Aquifer case, not to mention the administrative load from filling in until Governor Doggett appoints another Police Commissioner."

"Why did you turn it down?" When in doubt, change the subject. Maybe some distance from the topic would help.

"Hard to follow a hero," she replied. "And after that tearjerking ceremony honoring his bravery I didn't think I wanted to try." He saw her sigh. "But don't change the subject, Lucas. I was on to you when we were in college taking this same walk down this same trail. And it always ends the same. We end up friends until we're both lonely and then we look good to each other again, but we're not sure if it's nostalgia or good sense."

Holt smiled at her and shook his head. That's what he loved about her. Her good sense. She always nailed things right on. She was honest, straightforward and didn't take any of his shit. "Right, again." But there was still Kristen who needed him, at least temporarily. And, truth be told, he needed her sensuality that he found so restorative, like falling back into a soft feather bed that enveloped and welcomed you, required nothing in return and made no promises or demands, with the possible exception of walking the dog, since Aspen was back from the kennel.

He was aware that Susan had stopped and was holding both his hands to keep his attention.

"So I'm going to jog off into the sunset without you for a change, and spend the next few months pulling my own stuff together, personally and professionally."

Holt looked at those dark brown eyes that evoked a flood of memories and feelings, especially of the last weeks working side by side to plan the Aquifer strategy that had ended only a few yards from where they stood now. Maybe this was yet another ending, a death that had to be entombed with all the accompanying despair before they could know the surprise outcome—whatever it was. Still, they were in the same town and APD and Maggie Mae's were only three blocks away from each other. In separate tombs.

"Dinner occasionally?" he ventured, realizing he was trying to leave a crack of light in the darkness.

"Don't call me. I'll call you." She pecked him on the cheek. "See you in church, Father Holt."

Lucas watched her pick up her pace and vanish around a turn in the trail. He wondered what would happen when Kristen left. That depended on what terms she left on, what their arrangement was when he put her on the plane and what happened once she actually got there, immersed in the distracting whirlwind that was Washington. It remained to be seen if he and the new Senator Wade could continue what they had now, having been brought back together by their wounds.

"Foxy chick," the walker behind him commented. "For a cop."

"Thanks, Dorati," the Rev said without turning around at the familiar voice. "Why were you following us?"

"Not 'us.' You." They walked together across the wooden bridge over Shoal Creek. "Never know who's still out there pissed off about what you did."

"What *we* did."

"Yeah, but you're the one who made the paper. None of the rest of us could take the glory—or the heat if our parole officers found out."

Holt took a deep breath and patted Nikky on the back. "Thanks, in case I didn't say it a thousand times before." He looked down at the stream quietly flowing into Town Lake, joining imperceptibly. "Where were they?"

Dorati pointed to the places where he had spotted Everett Bergen and Christopher Dillon in the morning haze. "And you were over there." He indicated the area on the shoreline. "Not breathing."

The thought caused him to sigh and he coughed, his lungs not fully healed from the infection. "If you don't mind, Nikky, I think I'd like to be alone here a while."

"Sure thing," Dorati nodded and kept walking. "Later, Rev."

Lucas knew what he was thinking, because he was thinking it too. Holt would never be alone as long as the God Squad was in town. He turned too quickly and pulled at a suture in his side. It felt like a knife puncture and he stopped to let the pain pass. He leaned on a metal bench.

He would sit here for a while and watch people, watch the water quietly flow into the lake, watch his thoughts float by as he put the finishing touches on the Easter sermon in his head.

• Epilogue •

The sweet pungence of lilies greeted Holt as he stepped up into the pulpit on the next to last verse of "Christ The Lord Is Ris'n Today" with its ten-syllabled alleluia.

The weather was theologically reversed. Good Friday had been bright and sunny as Jesus entered the tomb. Holy Saturday the clouds from another storm front moved in and kept the day overcast for the contemplation of despair at Jesus' death. But the Easter Sunrise Service had had to move indoors when the rain started at six that morning. As if trying to keep the rock of the tomb stuck in the mud so Jesus couldn't make his exit, the rain had continued unabated.

Holt looked over the congregation as he always did, scanning for particular faces. Travis Layton was in the very back by the baptismal font, organizing the lay chalice bearers to distribute communion in the aisles to accommodate the crowd. He would listen to Holt's sermon and give him feedback about it for a week over lunch and Vestry meetings. Lucas smiled at him, knowing there would be a lot to give feedback about.

Max and Cora Mae sat near the side door, ready to duck out when he started. They had already heard the sermon at the soggy sunrise service and needed to get the coffee hour ready for the "C&E" members. Those were the ones taking up all the regulars' space in the pews, the "Christmas and Easter" Christians who came twice a year whether they needed to or not. They would stay at coffee hour and renew acquaintances and bitch about changes in the church and then thankfully disappear until

December at midnight. Holt called them "Cockroach Christians" because they scurried out to church, chewed a wafer, and scurried back into the woodwork of their homes again.

He glanced at the altar behind him where Case served as lay reader beside Kristen who had filled in at the last minute for an acolyte who overslept.

Nikky and Susan sat at opposite ends of the church, with Brickhouse, Omar, Doors, and Valdez scattered like leaven in the crowd. Holt knew this was more than random seating on their part, and that they were each ready—and placed—in case a religious fundy appeared with a huge grudge and no sense of humor.

He was glad to see Valdez sitting down. The poor Sexton had spent most of the morning placing pots and bowls in the attic to catch water leaking in from the damage from the previous storm, the one that had flushed Lucas and the other three men from the tunnel. Roofers were supposed to have started work last week, but showed up long enough to tear off a section of slate and leave flimsy plastic sheeting in its place.

The last verse began and Lucas smoothed out his notes. He would have to make sense of all that had happened, put it in Biblical perspective, show them that what occurred was the same as what occurred Easter week. That part was easy.

When Jesus died power imploded into the disciples in ways that could not have happened while he was alive. When Lucas went underground the church took over his duties, became him in a way it could not have done in his presence. Now both were empowered in different ways than before.

But he wondered how the people sitting here would take to his understanding of what happened in the tunnel that night? For it seemed to him that the Aquifer, sentient, knew exactly what was going on, felt the threatening tone of hostility in the tunnel, flushed out those who would harm it and, as quickly and gently as it could, deposited him on the shore.

At first he'd thought he was just stretching his theology. He imagined God flushing Jesus out of the tomb because it was harmful for the world to keep him in there, though that is precisely where most people would like him, safe and dead.

But Good Friday afternoon, as he had sat again by the place where he had been lost and found, he felt a visceral connection with the Aquifer, as though they had faced their deaths together and survived. They had both escaped, leaving empty tombs behind for people to gawk at, speculate about, wonder in fear and joy if their own tombs could likewise be vacated.

The hymn ended.

Holt began.

"The right is not right and the left is not wrong," he began. "Extremism in any form is the enemy. My experience in the tunnel taught me this, and more. We are called to sit down beside the still water and reason together. If we do not do this, and if we do not include nature as a part of that conversation, we risk our own peril."

Ten minutes later Lucas had laid out all he had to say to a congregation intent on understanding what he meant, some of them obviously in concert with him. Even the C&E people were paying attention, though he couldn't tell if it was the content or the shortness of the sermon that pleased them more.

He was about to finish when a sudden bolt of lightning crashed through the sky outside and rolling thunder rumbled like a wave through the spacious church.

Lucas looked up at the roof, then down at the water that had dripped on his bandaged hand. He smiled at the congregation and said: "I hope that means She agrees."

He turned and walked to the altar, grateful they had been resurrected again.

PHOTO: BILL KENNEDY

Charles Meyer is currently Vice President
of Operations at St. David's Hospital
in Austin, Texas. *Beside the Still
Waters* is his third novel in the
Reverend Lucas Holt series.